THE BORROWED BOY

DEBORAH KLÉE

Deborah Klée

ISBN: 978-1-8380804-0-2

First Printed, 2020

Published by Sherman House

The Borrowed Boy

by

DEBORAH KLÉE

For David and Irene.

1

I t was the boy's curly blond hair that caught Angie's attention, distracting her from the goblin thoughts that had plagued her since she received that letter from the hospital. The letter that told her the results were through. Angie could guess what those results were: she had cancer. The summons to see the consultant was just so that they could break the news gently. Give her a leaflet, telling her that she wasn't alone – and that was a joke, because Angie had spent a lifetime of being alone. But she did wonder how long she had left to live.

Poor old Aunty Mo had a bleed, her menopause had been and gone by then, and just three months later they were burying her. Loitering by the spider plant, in an attempt to lose her sherry glass before Uncle Jim refilled it, Angie overheard Mum say that Gran had died of the same thing in her fifties and it was a curse on the women in their family. Not on Mum. It was a weak heart that carried her off, and she was well into her seventies. But if anyone was to be cursed it was Angie. It shouldn't have come as a surprise, but it did. How was she to know that time was running out? There should be some kind of official warning.

Angie had lain awake most of last night. Best not borrow another library book, which was a pity as she'd been meaning to read *The Hitchhiker's Guide to the Galaxy*. And it wasn't worth doing anything about that damp patch in the corner of the ceiling. Instead of dwelling on what she couldn't do, maybe she should make the most of what time she had left. Angie caught her breath – *the time that she had left.* Was her life ending because she had wasted it? *I'll make the most of every moment, if only you'll give me more time*, Angie bargained with a God that she had ignored since Sunday school.

Angie had overheard the girls in the factory, where she worked as a machinist, talk about their bucket lists, the things that they wanted to do before they were too old, or died. Brenda wanted to ride an elephant and Sonia talked endlessly about visiting New York. Angie had never given it much thought until now. What did you put on a bucket list when you hadn't done anything? Hadn't moved from the terraced house in Dagenham where she had grown up, hadn't had an interesting job, hadn't fallen in love or married, hadn't had a child, hadn't gone abroad.

Angie buried herself under the duvet. How did you make up for forty wasted years? One fateful day had robbed her of the life she might otherwise have had. So much had been stolen from her and now time was running out. Angie kicked her legs and wailed. She pounded her fists into the mattress. Too late. Too late.

The digital clock clicked to 3.42 am and Angie hoisted the slipped duvet back onto the bed. She may have wasted forty years but she wasn't going to waste another day. Another hour. Another minute. From here on – every moment of every day was going to be *lived.* But how?

4.25 am. She knew what she had to do. She would go back to Jaywick Sands. It wouldn't change what had happened all of those years ago but she didn't want to die without saying goodbye to what was her favourite place in the world. Top of her bucket list: go back to Jaywick Sands. It was a pity that the other things she had missed out on weren't so easy to find.

With a sense of purpose, Angie got up and waited for the world to rouse itself, so that she could start her journey. The hospital appointment was for nine o'clock. She would hear what they had to say, and then take straight off. With a bit of luck, she could be on a train to Clacton by ten-thirty,

The Tube carriage was packed, barely room to breathe. Squashed near the door, Angie spied the pretty child holding his mum's hand. Angie wondered idly whether his mum's hair was that golden colour when she was a girl, instead of the nut brown that swung in a ponytail as she fussed with her bag. Some women dyed their hair. Brenda, at the factory, had been peroxide and then auburn. Mahogany she called it. Why would anyone choose to be that colour? Angie hated her own red hair but could see no point in trying to look like someone else. She was born Angie Winkle and Angie Winkle had frizzy red hair.

The train was coming to a halt, like a roulette wheel picking which passengers would be favoured with the coveted doors. Slowly, slowly. They were going to be lucky. The doors would open right in front of the boy and his mum. Angie tried to imagine being that woman; a swingy ponytail, pert breasts. But, it was having a child that Angie envied most. What was it like being a mum? Holding a tiny warm hand in yours? If only she had done things differently. But it was too late; the crumpled letter in her pocket, a reminder of the years she had wasted. Overhandled, overthought, overread, the letter scorched her thigh. It wasn't fair.

What was the girl doing messing around with her child's backpack when she should have been ready waiting to get on? The zombies were ready – lined up, their eyes fixed on the exact spot where the doors would open, ready for the off. But oblivious to her fortune in standing in exactly the right place to bag a space on the crowded train, his mum was releasing the red and green rucksack from the boy's back.

At first the crowd flowed around the boy and his mum. But then they caught the child up in their wake and swept him like a piece of flotsam into the carriage. Angie kept close to the little blond head, keeping an eye until his mum got on. The boy could only be three or four years old.

Angie craned her neck to keep his mum in sight. People were forcing their way into the carriage, but she was waiting for some kind of invitation. For someone to say, *room for you here.* What was the matter with her? Just get on. Get on! Angie felt the mum's panic, but there was nothing she could do to help. The doors started to close. An ashen face, mouth in an O, eyes wide; the realisation that she had lost her child.

Something or someone must have stopped the doors from closing because they opened again. Just for a few seconds. With a look of relief, the mum smiled thinking they had opened for her. Angie desperately wanted to shout out, *Help that woman. She's been separated from her child.* But she couldn't. Everyone would look at her. *Get on! Get on! You stupid woman, get on the train!*

The doors closed against the bent backs of commuters as they took up the shape of the carriage. His mum had missed her chance. How could she be so careless? The boy was very still. A soft toy masked his face. Angie wondered whether he even knew that his mum was still on the platform watching the train disappear into the tunnel.

Don't worry, angel. I'll keep you safe. Angie rested a hand on the boy's shoulder and a warmth flooded through her, as though her soul was being nourished. The boy glanced up at Angie and smiled. No one else seemed to have noticed what had just happened. If they had, they were pretending to be busy, studying the back pressed up against them.

Don't worry, mate, I'll look after you. The train lurched as it twisted through the tunnel and Angie steadied the boy, holding him close, until it came to a stop.

'Come on, darling.' Angie led the boy off the train. He was far too trusting; his mum should have told him about Stranger Danger.

The letter in her pocket cooled. Directions to the hospital scrawled on the corporate red and blue paper temporarily forgotten, as she focused on the child.

She crouched down. 'It's alright, sweetheart, we'll get you back to your mum.' She wasn't sure how, as there were no guards on the platform. The golden-haired angel offered Angie his raggedy bunny.

'Who's this?' Angie flicked a soggy ear.

The boy yawned.

'Reckon you could do with a little nap. Where was your mum taking you?'

The boy sucked his thumb.

Several trains had come and gone with no sign of the boy's mum. The commuters had thinned to a trickle, just a few stragglers scattered the platform. A gust of air threw up a discarded newspaper and Angie's wraparound skirt flapped open. A fast train was approaching. As Angie cradled the boy to keep him safe, his baby scent of vanilla and soap triggered a memory. Angie squashed it back to a safe place.

Sometime after the train had passed and the air had settled, a blanket of burnt rubber and oil, Angie was still hugging the boy. She imagined them captured in a photograph. A summer garden replacing the dismal grey of the platform – grandma and grandson. A birthday celebration, her fiftieth. There would be an expensive cake with sugar roses and lots of friends and family toasting her with bubbly wine. She would allow her grandson to have the teeniest sip and his face would pucker, making them all laugh.

The boy interrupted her daydream, as he pointed to the rail tracks. 'There.' Angie peered over as a black rat darted into the shadows.

Still no guard. Angie didn't have a plan. She knew that she wouldn't leave the boy until she could hand him back to his mum. The little love wound his fingers in Angie's hair. He had better be careful, her hair was known to harbor all sorts of lost property. Only this morning, she had discovered a pair of tweezers in there, from where she had been coaxing a denim collar right side out.

'What's your name?'

The boy offered Angie his toy. 'Kroliky.' Angie wasn't sure if that was the bunny's name or the boy's.

'Licky?' she asked.

The boy laughed. 'Licky.'

'Okay, Licky, let's go and ask a guard to help us find your mum.'

Angie wasn't one to volunteer to do anything. The thought of being the centre of attention made her stomach flip. But needs must. They couldn't wait on the platform all day.

A black man collecting rubbish in a big cellophane sack directed Angie to an office. It was hard getting him to talk – another one who avoids the limelight. *We're like those rats hiding in the shadows, while everyone else gets on with their life. Funny how we see each other when nobody else does.*

Three uniformed staff milled around the doorway of the office. *So that's where all the guards were hiding.* She tried coughing but remained invisible. For the boy's sake she summoned her courage.

'Excuse me. Could you make an announcement over the speaker?' Blood pumped in angry bursts. It throbbed in her neck, strangling her voice. Everyone was looking at her. Angie clutched the boy tight, drawing strength from a maternal urge to do the right thing.

'Please could you say that his mum should wait at Liverpool Street Station and I'll take him back?' She sounded too loud and brash.

The man in the office whipped round to face her. Angie had become important. 'How did you come to have this child?' He made it sound like she'd kidnapped the boy or something.

A heat rose in Angie's chest, as it always did when she became the focus of attention. 'He got separated from his mum. Can you tell her to wait at Liverpool Street?'

Angie had already turned when he replied. 'I think it's best you leave the child in our care. We'll alert the police and see that he's safely returned.'

She couldn't hand the boy over, not when she had promised to help him find his mum. She squeezed the boy and he wriggled against her. 'No, you don't understand. I'm a friend of his mum. I'll go back and meet her at Liverpool Street Station – by that statue. The one with the kids.'

He smiled, all cheerful, like they were mates. 'Why don't you both stay here with me and I'll make an announcement for Liverpool Street and other stations on this line.'

If she did that, then it would all be over. If she could just cherish his warm weight a little longer, his baby breath on her neck. 'Well, if you can't be bothered to help me,' she blustered. 'I just wanted a simple announcement to be made while I took him back.'

The man got a call on his phone. Behind him a bank of

7

CCTV screens showed commuters getting on and off trains. Another phone rang. The man covered the mouthpiece and turned to Angie. 'Okay, I'll make an announcement that you'll be standing by the statue on Liverpool Street Station at the entrance to the Underground.'

Angie left him before he changed his mind. 'We're going to get another train. Find your mum. I bet she's waiting at Liverpool Street,' Angie chirped to the boy, as they waited on the platform. 'I don't think your name's Licky. What is it?'

The boy gave Angie his bunny. 'Licky.'

'Ah, this is Licky. How do you do, Licky?' She flopped the rabbit's head up and down. The boy laughed and snatched him back.

'My name's Angie.' She pointed to her chest. 'Angie. What's your name?' She tapped the boy's chest.

'Danek.' He spoke clearly, despite his accent.

'Okay, Danny boy, here comes our train. Now, hold my hand tight. You don't want to get lost again.'

A blast of diesel and warm air preceded the train. Angie's cardigan twisted around her and the letter worked loose. It slipped from her pocket and was swept up on a gush of air – a ball of red and blue. It skittered in a zigzag between the feet of commuters until Angie could see it no more. It was a sign; she wasn't meant to go to the hospital – not today. Today, she had been sent a little boy to take care of. Make every second count.

2

Nikoleta crumpled in pain and then howled. The people around her, the ones who'd been waiting three rows deep to squash onto the next train, shifted slightly, as though proximity would taint them or make them responsible in some way.

The dinosaur rucksack dangled from her wrist. Two minutes ago, it had been on Danek's back. They were a unit, the two of them. The next hour or so, their journey to Earl's Court, finding the apartment Kamil had rented, was as certain in her mind as the past – getting on the scheduled flight from Warsaw early that morning, travelling to London on the seven forty-two from Stansted. She had held the directions in her head, every stage of the journey. But now it was unravelling, as though a thread was being pulled with Danek as he disappeared into the tunnel. Leaving Nikoleta bereft, lost, and very, very afraid. What had she done?

'This can't be happening, *Matko Boska.* Kamil will go crazy.'

She searched for someone – anyone – to acknowledge what had just happened but people turned their heads. It was a nightmare. She had only been in England a few hours and she had lost Kamil's only son. Danek was the centre of Kamil's world. From the day they first met, Nikoleta knew that however much Kamil loved her, she would always come second to his beloved son. That was one of the things she loved about Kamil – his love for Danek. Nikoleta adored Danek too; he was a beautiful child. And now she had lost him – in a foreign city, with nobody to turn to for help. She felt sick – paralysed with fear and disbelief. *Please someone help me.*

Nikoleta was still pleading with the faceless commuters when another train pulled in. Just as before, commuters crushed into the full carriages, their places on the platform were taken up by new arrivals until only Nikoleta knew that a few minutes ago she had been holding Danek's hand. As before, the commuters stared ahead. Kamil said that the English were kind and welcoming but to Nikoleta they seemed cold and heartless. She had to find someone in authority.

Nikoleta battled her way through a relentless stream of people. Her mind had gone blank. Years of English classes at school – multiple-choice tests. It was all there, somewhere, but her frantic brain scrambled everything she knew.

'Please, please,' she cried in Polish.

Nobody looked at her. They averted their eyes as though embarrassed by her distress or stared ahead, their eyes wide and glazed like mad dogs. Danek was being carried further and further away. She was losing valuable time.

A man bumped against her and said something. Nikoleta turned to smile; at last someone who cared. But the man tutted and pointed at her wheelie case.

Nikoleta pursed her lips. She had to toughen up. London was nothing like home. All these people from different nationalities none of them stopped to see her and listen. *Matko*

Boska! Please let Danek be safe. Please someone take care of him.
No time to pray. No time to panic or cry. She lifted her case –
thank goodness she'd only brought hand luggage – and
climbed back up the stone stairs and over the bridge. Here
there was more space, as people swarmed like ants from the
ticket office.

Just a few minutes ago, she'd bought a ticket. Danek was
excited about the train journey. He had never travelled on a
train under the ground. Nikoleta hitched his dinky rucksack
back up her shoulder. She had promised Danek a milkshake
when they got to Earl's Court, a proper American-style one,
thick and creamy. She'd tried one as a child in Warsaw when
the first McDonald's arrived, back in the early 1990s. Now
there were bigger, better versions. She had been as excited as
Danek to try everything new. But now all of that faded and
Nikoleta was ashamed of her childish wishes. What kind of
mother was she, to lose Danek within a few hours of arriving
in the capital? How would she ever forgive herself?

Nikoleta had laughed at her parents when they said that
London was a dangerous city. 'It's no more dangerous than
Warsaw or Krakow,' she had scoffed. But when Nikoleta
checked it out on the internet she saw that Poland had a much
lower crime rate than England. And London had more crime
hotspots than anywhere else in the country, not that she
would admit this to her parents. They were anxious enough
about Nikoleta and Kamil's plans.

Someone would stop and help her. A man in a uniform
leant against the ticket barrier.

'Please, please help me.' Nikoleta spoke slowly, self-
conscious because of her accent.

The man pointed to the machine and said something
Nikoleta didn't understand.

'My boy. I've lost my little boy. He got on the train without me.' The words tumbled out, part English and part Polish. She sounded hysterical. She *was* hysterical.

People turned to stare, as they passed through the metal gates. The man in uniform lunged between them. He checked tickets and released the barrier, never losing concentration.

'Push it in there.'

It took Nikoleta a couple of seconds to realise the man in a denim jacket had spoken in Polish. When she tried to find him, he was already merging into the crowd. Nikoleta dragged her case behind her, not caring any more if she ran over people's toes or tripped them up.

'Please, please, wait!' Nikoleta could no longer see his faded blue back. She called louder. 'Please help me!' She stumbled on in her high heels, scanning the sea of people, desperately seeking a blue denim jacket.

'What? What do you want?'

Nikoleta nearly bumped into the man who had stopped in front of her. His body was still, but his eyes flicked with impatience, his gaze on the way ahead, mentally he was still surging forward with the crowd. Never mind the roughness of his words, Polish had never sounded more beautiful.

'I have lost my little boy. He got on the train without me. The doors closed before I could get on.'

Said out loud, Nikoleta was stabbed again with the physical pain – the shock of being separated. She trembled. Her brain, arms, and legs felt numb as though icy water filled her veins. Danek was only four years old. A four-year-old abandoned in a foreign city, prey to any sick person. Nikoleta had handed Danek over. She might as well have sold him to the highest bidder.

The man's eyes widened. There, she had shocked him. It was a truly awful thing to do. Nikoleta hugged her arms. She couldn't fill the void, the empty space. Her breath came in short gasps. For a second or more they shared the horror; their eyes locked. But then he looked away and physically shook himself, as though shedding the burden.

'That's terrible. I am sorry to hear of your troubles but I don't know how I can help you.'

In Poland he may have been an old classmate, the son of her mother's friend. Everyone there was a friend of a friend. People didn't always get along, there was a lot of suspicion, especially amongst the older generation. But, when one of their own was in danger they helped. This man would not turn his back on her if they were in Poland. His mother would be ashamed if he did. Nikoleta relaxed, confident that he would do the right thing. That he would help her find Danek.

'Please, tell me what to do. I've just arrived in England and everything is so confusing. We have to find him before it is too late.'

The man steered Nikoleta to one side, away from the stream of commuters. Nikoleta could tell, from the way he checked his phone and looked everywhere but at her stricken face, that he didn't want to be there. That he regretted ever having opened his mouth.

'Which Tube line were you getting on?'

Nikoleta looked at him blankly.

'Which platform were you on?'

Nikoleta pointed back behind her. *Think, think.* The man shook his head and checked his watch.

'Platform one!' Thank goodness she remembered. They would find Danek.

'Where were you going to?' the man asked.

Why did it matter? They were losing time.

'Earl's Court.' At least she remembered the station. The shock of losing Danek seemed to have wiped her mind.

'You should have got the Central line to Holborn and then changed to the Piccadilly line.'

Now he was looking interested – smug even. What was the matter with him? Danek was on a train heading to God knows where and he was showing off his knowledge of the London Underground.

'How will we find him?'

The man held up his hands. 'No. I'm sorry but I can't help you. I'm already late for work.' He backed away, bumping into a stout woman.

Nikoleta shadowed him as he weaved between bodies. 'What shall I do? Where will I find him? He is so little.'

The man stopped. 'Someone probably got off the train with him at the next station. Go one stop on the same line. I bet he's waiting for you now.'

'Thank you. Thank you.'

It wasn't too late. Of course, some kind soul would have seen what happened. There were more good people in the world than bad. She had read somewhere that most people were kind. You only had to look at how people behaved when there was a disaster. People were basically good. Danek would be safe.

Nikoleta's body wasn't listening. Her legs wobbled, slowing her pace. It was like being in a dream when you desperately needed to get somewhere but your body was too heavy to move.

Why hadn't she thought of taking the Tube one stop at a time to see if Danek was waiting for her? Several trains must have gone by since they got separated. If only she had caught the next one. What was the matter with her? Of course she should have caught the next train. At least she would have been following him.

As the train pulled into Moorgate, Nikoleta was waiting at

the doors. Blurred faces whipped by too fast for her to see if Danek was amongst them. As the train slowed down, she scanned the platform. Mostly adults. There was a woman with a pushchair. The train jarred, then stopped. Nikoleta elbowed her way off the train as others started to board. *Please God let him be here waiting for me.*

The platform was quieter than Liverpool Street. Danek should be easy to find. A black man with grey hair chased a ball of red and blue paper as it blew past her. He picked it up with a long stick. But no Danek.

There was an announcement over the loud speaker. Nikoleta understood the words 'lost', 'boy' and 'wait.' The message must be for her. A young woman was sitting on a bench, listening to music through headphones. Nikoleta touched her sleeve.

'Excuse me, what did that announcement say?'

The girl pulled the plugs from her ears. 'Sorry, what was that?'

Nikoleta tried again. The girl shrugged. A train pulled in and the girl got on.

Nikoleta cursed her rubbish English teacher and her own disinterest in the subject. If she knew then that one day Danek's life would depend on it, she would have studied the language every minute of every day.

'Where are you from?'

Nikoleta spun around to see a middle-aged woman dressed in a smart jacket and trousers. 'Toresnica. You speak Polish!'

The woman shrugged. 'Of course. You were asking about the announcement?'

'Yes, yes. I got separated from my little boy, Danek. I need to get help. I thought maybe –'

The woman interrupted. 'Yes. The announcement, it said

that your child has been taken to Liverpool Street Station. You are to wait by the statue of the refugee children at the entrance to the Tube.'

'Thank you!' Nikoleta forgot herself and hugged the woman, who stiffened and then took a step back.

'I'm sorry. I'm just so happy. Thank goodness he's safe. I can't thank you enough.'

Which way to Liverpool Street Station? In her hurry, Nikoleta had forgotten to ask. There were so many platforms, which one would take her back?

It was hopeless. She was rushing along a tunnel that could be taking her in the wrong direction. Ahead, a busker played 'Johnny B. Good'. Nikoleta turned back, irritating the commuters who had to step to one side. Nobody would hear her over the electric guitar.

When the crowd thinned and it was quieter, she asked an elderly man. 'Liverpool Street?'

He frowned at her.

'It is just one stop.' She held up one finger. 'Liverpool Street?'

'Ah, that way.' The man pointed to a sign: Northern line Southbound.

'Thank you,' she called over her shoulder. Just one stop. Please Mother of God let him be there.

Liverpool Street Station looked different. Maybe she had arrived in another part of the station. Nikoleta followed the signs to the way out. The statue of the children must be near the entrance. But there were so many exits. She tried one and then another. There was no statue. Nikoleta's stomach lurched. The sign said Old Street Station.

3

'The next train leaving from platform twelve is the ten seventeen to Clacton calling at...'

From her waiting place by the statue, Angie heard the announcement. Her rail ticket was good for any train outside of rush hour but if she let the train go she would have to wait another hour. As it was, she wouldn't have much time in Jaywick. Finding Danny was an unexpected joy but she had to give him back and be on her way. She had set her heart on going back to Jaywick and deep down Angie was afraid that if she didn't seize the day, as it were, then her nerves would get the better of her and she would slope back into the shadows. *Come on, Danny's mum, what's keeping you?*

Danny was perched next to a bronze boy on the plinth of the statue as he concentrated on nibbling a Mars bar. Angie folded back the wrapper to make it easier for him. 'Ever had a toffee apple, Danny? It tastes better than that and healthier too. You'd love Jaywick Sands.'

Angie fished in her enormous handbag for a tissue. She couldn't see the point in dainty bags that hardly held anything.

Danny offered up his face like a sunflower searching the sun. His big eyes and chocolate-smeared smile twisted her heart; he was so trusting and innocent. She wouldn't let him down.

It was ten thirty-three. They'd been waiting at the statue for nearly an hour. In that time, they had named the bronze boy *Lost Boy* and made up a story about him and his sister. How they were waiting for some kind person to give them a home in London. You'd think his mum would be frantic. What could be more important than finding her child?

Maybe she had decided to do a bit of shopping to take advantage of the free childcare. It wouldn't surprise her. The girls at the factory were always going on about 'me time' – whatever that was supposed to mean. Selfish, that's what it was. Having a child to love and care for was the most precious gift in the world, especially this little darling. The bronze boy and his sister looked pissed off too; they waited with their suitcase, forlorn and unwanted.

'Where's your mum got to, Danny boy?' Angie wanted the toilet but daren't leave in case she missed his mum.

'You look after me,' Danny said, the emphasis on 'you'.

'I will, love. Angie will look after you until we find your mum.'

It was no good; she had to go to the toilet. Danny would just have to visit the ladies' with her. 'I expect your mum will be there waiting when we get back.'

In the toilets Angie wasn't sure what to do with Danny. She couldn't leave him outside the cubicle, someone might snatch him, but she couldn't bring him in with her, could she? What did mums and grandmas do? There were no other children around or mums who might have given her a clue.

Desperate now, Angie dived into a cubicle taking Danny with her. 'Close your eyes, Danny, and see how far you can count before I shout "ready!"'

18

Angie showed Danny how to cover his eyes and started him off counting, as she hooked down her knickers.

'One, two,' Danny repeated after her.

She was nearly done when the toilet door swung open and Danny darted out of sight. Angie waddled to the door, her knickers around her knees. Danny hadn't gone far. He passed Angie two pieces of toilet paper neatly folded in a square.

'Thank you, love.' Angie took his offering and finished her business with the door open. Everyone had seen everything anyway. But Danny was right. There wasn't any toilet paper in her cubicle. 'Clever boy. Now, you'd better spend a penny too.'

She wasn't bad at this, looking after the boy. She would have been a good mum. How could she have gone fifty-odd years without experiencing this? No nieces and nephews, no friends with kids. No friends – full stop. Who would trust the weird woman with frizzy hair to look after their kid anyway? She knew what they all thought of her at the factory. So, she didn't watch *East Enders* and couldn't give a monkey's whether it was the lottery rollover week or how much Brenda had won at bingo but she saw the way they smirked at each other. Weirdo Winkle. Nobody in their right mind would trust her to look after their kid. But she was doing a better job than Danny's own mum. She hadn't lost him on a crowded Tube.

As Angie balanced Danny on the toilet, her hand brushed the sharp wing of his shoulder blade. He was fragile as a bird, and she was afraid he would break. 'Do a little tinkle for Nana Angie.'

Danny beamed as he obliged. He really was a little angel. His T-shirt rode up when Angie lifted him off the toilet, his skin baby soft beneath her touch, but then her finger detected a scratch. Angie lifted Danny's T-shirt. There was a faint trace of welt marks low on his back. Brushing a finger across the telltale lines, Angie said, 'What's this on your back, Danny? It looks like someone has taken a belt to you.'

Danny wriggled free. Angie tried again. 'Did someone hurt your back, sweetheart?'

'I was a naughty boy.' Danny hung his head.

Angie hugged the little mite. His mum didn't deserve to have him back.

When they emerged from the toilets, the woman with the ponytail was waiting by the statue. She had her back to them, Danny's rucksack slung over one shoulder, as she spoke on her phone. Angie was hit by a wave of disappointment; she would have to say goodbye to Danny. He would never finish the Mars bar tucked away in her bag. She would be forgotten by the morning. Just the old woman in a story about the day Danny got lost. Angie picked Danny up and hugged him tight.

'Look who's over there,' she said, her voice a little hoarse.

Danny twisted around. He should have cried out in joy and struggled to be free of Angie so that he could run to his mum, but he didn't.

'Your mummy,' Angie prompted. Maybe Danny hadn't seen her.

'That's not my mummy.'

Of course it wasn't. An irresponsible au pair who didn't care tuppence about Danny. Maybe she was his stepmum, his dad a great oaf of a man who beat Danny. The boy was undernourished, and whoever that woman was, she wasn't taking very good care of Danny.

'The next train leaving platform nine is the eleven seventeen to Clacton.' Angie dithered, a little toing and froing on the spot. *If the girl turns around and sees us by the time I count to ten, then I will say goodbye to Danny.* Angie hadn't thought through what she would do if the girl didn't turn around.

'You look after me,' Danny said, his chubby hands soft on her cheeks and Angie was torn.

Seven, eight. The girl turned enough for Angie to see her profile. She was smiling. Her charge was missing *and she was smiling* – laughing at something, as she spoke on the phone. The train was leaving in four minutes, what was she to do?

Then Angie made a decision – a huge decision. There was no time to dither; once the girl saw them the decision would be taken out of her hands. Danny was clinging to her and she had promised him that she would look after him. The train to Clacton was about to leave and if she didn't go to Jaywick today then she might never go. So, with Danny jigging on her hip, Angie ran for the train. The guard was about to blow his whistle, as she lumbered through the open barrier. And then they were off, out of the station, on their way to Jaywick.

What had she done? Kidnapped a child? Abducted him? Angie went cold. She had done a terrible thing. But had she? Was it really so bad? In a way she was rescuing the boy. They would have a wonderful day together at Jaywick Sands. When the police came looking for them, she would hand Danny over and point out the marks on his back. 'Thank you for being so vigilant,' the policeman would say. 'If there were more responsible citizens like you, Miss Winkle, the world would be a better place.'

Besides, Danny had been sent to her for a reason. Last night, she vowed that she would make the most of every minute of every day – do the things she had missed out on. She didn't think that being a mum – well, a grandma – was the sort of thing she could include on her bucket list, but someone up there thought otherwise and had sent her this beautiful boy to look after. Who was she to question the whys and wherefores? It was meant to happen.

Angie sank into the seat and cuddled Danny to her. All of

her life she had been hiding in the shadows, ashamed and afraid. She hadn't trusted herself to make the right decisions, not on anything big that mattered. So, without realising it, she *had* made a decision – a decision to let life pass her by. Well, all of that was going to change. She may only have months left to live but she was going to live them in full volume.

'We are going to the seaside, Danny. What do you think of that? We are going to have ourselves a perfect day!'

Danny was already asleep. But Angie's heart thumped reminding her that she was still alive. A lion's roar filled her belly – all of the power she had suppressed the past forty years. It was time to start living without regret.

4

'Please let Danek be there. Please Mother of God.' A flutter in her chest, hope mingled with fear. Nikoleta could see the bronze statue. She must have passed it with Danek as they made their way to the Underground but with her mind on the journey ahead, she hadn't noticed the two bronze children waiting forlornly with their suitcase. Just as Nikoleta must have hurried by, so did other travelers, the last of the commuters intent on their journey and disorientated tourists consulting guidebooks and maps. But there was no curly blond head. No woman and child waiting for Nikoleta. It couldn't be. There must be some explanation. It was the right statue. She was definitely at Liverpool Street Station. Okay, it had taken her a while to get there but surely they would wait? *Keep calm. Keep calm.* But Nikoleta felt sick.

As she approached the statue Nikoleta had been preparing herself for the worst-case scenario that Danek wouldn't be there but really, deep down, she believed everything was going to be okay. She couldn't expect the woman to stand in the same place for over an hour. It was likely that she had taken

Danek for a walk to keep him amused. No child could wait patiently for all that time. Poor Danek, he would think she had abandoned him. That was what had happened. Nikoleta scanned the concourse but there were very few children and none with Danek's distinctive blond curls. Gradually, the reality hit home. The woman wasn't going to come. Nikoleta was too late.

Nikoleta's legs could no longer support her and so she slid down to perch on the plinth of the statue. A bronze boy reproached her, his eyes dead and mouth sullen – *What took you so long? Don't you want me?* How long had Danek waited, wondering if she was ever going to collect him? She had let him down badly – failed at her first job as his new mother. It was time to tell Kamil that she had lost his four-year-old son in London. Nikoleta's hand trembled as she fumbled with her phone.

'*Slonka*, you've arrived? I told you the London Tube was easy to navigate.'

How could she tell him? Kamil always called her *slonka*, his sunshine. It was her optimism but there was nothing she could say that would soften the news she had to impart. Platitudes and words of comfort had no place here. She had done something unforgiveable. 'Kamil, I've lost him. I lost Danek. He got on the train without me.' She was gabbling, hysteria in her voice.

'Slow down, Nikki. Where are you?'

'At Liverpool Street Station. A woman took care of Danek and told me that she would meet me here. I waited but they're not here! What shall I do?'

'Calm down, Nikki, and tell me exactly what happened.'

She owed him that. Later she could collapse with grief and howl, but first they had to find Danek. Nikoleta told Kamil *almost* everything, leaving out how she went to the wrong station. She didn't want him to blame her any more than he did. He had every right to, of course. Losing his son as though he were no more than a package, it was unthinkable – unforgiveable. If they didn't find Danek her relationship with Kamil would be over. Even now, it might be irreparable. But she was being selfish. How could she dare to think of herself at a time like this? Finding Danek was all that mattered.

'I'll phone the police,' Nikoleta said, trying to gain some control over her emotions.

'No, don't do that.' The sharpness in his voice surprised her.

'Why? We have to tell the police, Kamil.' She didn't add that the woman might hurt Danek. It was a thought she had tried to suppress. Being optimistic wasn't always a good thing, not if it meant hiding from the truth.

'No, Nikki. What if they take Danek away from me? I had to fight to get custody. How is it going to look if it comes out that I sent him to England with my girlfriend and she lost him the first day in London?'

'I'm sorry. I'm sorry. I'm sorry.' She was crying now. People turned to look at the girl sitting in a crumpled heap alongside the refugee children sobbing into her phone. 'I'll talk to the police and explain.'

'That's not a good idea. You don't understand how things work in England. We are Polish – outsiders. People will always think the worst of us. Let me handle this. I don't want to lose you as well as Danek. What were you thinking?' He was angry now – furious, understandably. 'He could be anywhere. Anything could happen to him. My boy. My little Danek. God, Nikki – what have you done?'

Nikoleta was shaking. 'What shall I do?'

'Go to the apartment in Earl's Court. I'll get the next flight from Paris and meet you there.'

'I can't. I can't just leave him. What if the woman comes back with Danek and I'm not there?'

'Okay, okay, *slonka*. It's going to be alright. You know that I have contacts everywhere. As soon as I hang up I'll get some of my men onto it. They'll wait by the statue. Trust me, *slonka*, they will do a better job than the police.'

Nikoleta started to correct Kamil. They *had* to tell the police. But Kamil interrupted her. 'Listen to me, *slonka*, you don't know how things are in England. We can trust my contacts here. They'll find Danek. The police will blame us. They always think the worst of immigrants.

'Trust me, *slonka*. Go on as planned. Mrs Lisowski will be waiting for you. I've known her for years; she's a good woman. You know that I will only do what is right for you and Danek?'

Nikoleta calmed a little. It was true, she had seen the way Kamil worked. He was influential, and she believed him when he said that men would be at Liverpool Street Station within minutes of his call. But it still didn't feel right walking away. 'Maybe I could wait here for your men.'

'I need you to go to the apartment. I promise I'll be there in a few hours. Danek may even be home before I get there. Now give me a smile, *slonka*, so I know you are alright.'

'Okay, Kamil.' Nikoleta tried to sound positive but it was hard. She may have ruined everything for Kamil, after months of fighting for custody.

'You are not smiling, I can tell.' Kamil was trying to lift her spirits; she didn't deserve him.

Nikoleta forced a smile as she walked away from the statue. 'I am smiling now.'

'Yes, I can tell. Go straight to the apartment, *slonka*, and I'll join you as soon as possible. I'll make sure Danek is found, they won't get far. There's nothing else you can do right now. Are you going to be okay?'

Kamil shouldn't be worrying about her. Nikoleta was useless, a failure. How would she ever put things right between them?

5

Snuggled against the pillowy folds of Angie's girth, a thumb plugged in his mouth, Danny slept and Angie watched London retreat. Built-up housing gradually became less dense. Tightly packed terraced houses gave way to semi-detached, some with conservatories, others with a trampoline in the garden. Soon there would be green fields, farmland, and footpaths. Angie relaxed with the rhythm of the train and thought back to that first summer in 1972.

It was the best holiday she'd ever had, although there wasn't much to compare it to. Family holidays had been days out to Southend, Colchester Zoo, and a big park with a lake, where they once had a picnic. Memorable outings but they never stayed away for a night.

Angie's and Lorraine's dads worked together at Ford's like most of the families that lived on their estate. There had been a couple of strikes in the past few years – there were no days out those years, they had to 'tighten their belts'. Angie's mum and dad weren't keen on her going to Jaywick with Lorraine.

Dad didn't want to take a 'handout' from a mate. He said he would be beholden and didn't like owing anyone a favour.

'But he owes you a favour, love,' Mum chipped in. 'Didn't you get his niece a job sewing seat covers in the factory?'

Dad thought about this. 'Well, I just told him they was advertising.'

Mum winked at Angie. 'Exactly. If you hadn't told him, his niece might of missed out.'

But despite her support, Mum had some reservations. 'Lorraine's grandparents are getting on a bit. They won't be able to keep an eye on you two. I don't want you getting into any trouble. You're at a funny age.'

Angie harrumphed and sulked. She pleaded and whined. Eventually Mum gave in but she was given a list of dos and don'ts. 'Do everything Lorraine's grandma tells you to. Help around the house. Don't stay up after nine. Don't drink any alcohol. Don't talk to strange men or boys. Always tell Lorraine's grandparents where you're going.'

If Angie was a bit nervous at meeting Lorraine's grandparents she soon relaxed, as they were the sweetest pair. She didn't have grandparents herself. Grammy and Gramps – they said she could call them that – were wonderful. They gave the girls just enough freedom. *Always tell us where you're going and what time you'll be back* was the absolute rule. Apart from that, they were free to run wild. It was like a vast holiday camp full of relaxed and happy people. Four-wheeled cycles with canopies took priority over cars on the wide streets. Couples sat side by side on the bike's bench seat, laughing together. Everyone seemed to be happy all of the time. There was an amusement arcade, a café, and shops selling buckets and spades, honeycomb, and water wings. Angie could remember the smell of sunbaked pavements and the sugar and fat of fried donuts. So different from the drab grey streets of Dagenham.

'Tickets, please.'

Angie woke with a start. Her mouth was dry, her head heavy. She must have been completely out, catching up after her sleepless night. At first, she didn't know where she was and then she remembered with a jolt. Her bravado had withered and was now skulking in the pit of her stomach. What had she done? How could she have been so impulsive?

The guard was waiting. But Danny had gone, leaving a cool patch where his warm body had once been. Angie scanned the seats in front and behind. A few solitary passengers and an older couple had got on since Liverpool Street, but there was no sign of the boy. Panic expanded in her diaphragm like a balloon pressing against her ribcage. Where the hell had he gone? The guard waited whilst Angie rummaged in her bag. He checked her ticket and moved on.

They'd been together for less than three hours and already she'd lost him. What did she expect? Just one child to take care of and she had failed miserably. No better than the boy's hopeless mum. What if someone bad had abducted him? He was such an angelic-looking boy, blond curls and big blue eyes. Far too trusting. *Dear God, please don't let a sicko get hold of him.* Angie's heart hammered, her back sticky with sweat.

As she swayed through the carriage, following signs to the toilet, Angie was light-headed and shaky. She would find the guard; tell him the truth. The boy's safety was more important than anything else. Then she saw Licky spreadeagled on the carriage floor and was overcome by waves of hot and cold nausea. It was a sign. Danny had been kidnapped, carried away by a gang of pedophiles, his toy dropped from an outflung arm as they bundled him out of the carriage. She didn't even know where they were on the journey. Angie buried her face in Licky. He smelt sour, like old bedding – damp and synthetic.

A child cried. Danny?

Two men stood in the gangway at the other end of the carriage. They were blocking access to the toilets on either side. As Angie got closer she heard them talking to one another. They were Eastern Europeans, Polish or something. Then she heard Danny's voice. The younger of the two men turned and opened a toilet door. What the hell were they doing? If Danny was in there – if they'd harmed a hair of his head – she would lay into them.

'Where is he? What have you done with him?' she yelled.

Everyone would be watching but Angie didn't care. The older man muttered something she couldn't understand, before loping off to find his seat. The younger man opened the toilet door to reveal Danny, who reached out his arms. 'Licky.'

Thank God Danny was safe. But what had they been doing with him?

'Ah, this is Licky. He was crying for him,' the younger of the two men said.

'I am sorry if we frightened you. He wanted the toilet. You were asleep, and he didn't want to wake you, so I showed him where it was.'

'You should have woken me,' Angie snapped. She wasn't convinced that they meant no harm. The older of the two looked out of the window ignoring her.

The younger man followed her gaze. 'That is my father. He doesn't speak any English. He is visiting me here in England. Where are you travelling to?'

Angie wanted to say 'none of your business', but she had already attracted more attention than she wanted. A grey-haired couple unwrapped homemade sandwiches from waxed paper. The woman paused, a sandwich wavered midair, her mouth hung open.

Danny said something to the younger man. He looked like a builder, but maybe she was stereotyping him just because he had muscly arms with tattoos and closely cropped hair. He was grinning at Danny – they were having some kind of a joke. Angie laughed with them, as if she knew what was being said.

'Thank you for taking my grandson to the toilet.'

The grey-haired woman bit into her sandwich. Her husband opened a steaming flask.

'So where are you headed?' the man prompted.

Angie didn't want to tell him; it was none of his business. What if Danny's disappearance was on the news and this man reported seeing them? The Transport Police might already be waiting for her in Clacton. But she didn't feel she had much choice. If the man and his dad stayed on the train they would see her get off with Danny.

'Just a day out at the seaside,' Angie said. 'The seaside' could be anywhere along that coastline.

'So are we – me and my dad.'

Angie took another peek at his dad. He had a good head of hair, grey and white, as was the stubble on his chin. The sunglasses that he wore were not really necessary indoors, despite the sun that flashed off the window. *A poser*, Angie surmised. *Thinks he's George Clooney.*

'Off to Clacton for the day?' the younger man asked.

Angie shrugged. 'Thereabouts – you?'

'We are getting off here,' the man said as the train pulled into Thorpe-le-Soken. He spoke rapidly to Danny and then ruffled his hair before leaving. His father didn't even acknowledge them.

Danny seemed happy enough. Angie could only hope that

he hadn't said anything to the men about being taken from his mum. She no longer thought that they had harmed him in any way. It was wrong to take Danny to the toilet while she slept but they meant well. Soon, they would be in Clacton. Angie prayed that the police wouldn't be waiting for them because it would be the end of their adventure. All she wanted was one perfect day with Danny in her favourite place in the world. Who could blame her for grabbing a little happiness? She was just borrowing the boy for one day. One day as Danny's grandma and then she would give him back.

6

Nikoleta walked past the dark green door several times looking for a street sign that would confirm she was in the wrong place. But it *was* Lenham Avenue and the smart four-storey town house with its basement and iron railings was indeed 137.

To leave Liverpool Street Station without Danek had broken Nikoleta's heart. It felt wrong to continue her journey without him. Every fibre of her being ached with longing and regret but Kamil had been very clear in his instructions. How could she have let go of Danek's hand when it was so busy? Nikoleta tried to calm herself before rapping the brass knocker.

The prospect of being greeted by a kindly landlady, an old acquaintance of Kamil's who spoke Polish, was of some comfort to Nikoleta. Right now, she would have loved to have had her own mum there, a constant source of loving kindness no matter what Nikoleta had done. The statuesque woman with auburn hair who opened the door was nothing like her softly rounded mum. Mrs Lisowski was the sort of woman who would arouse her mum's suspicion. Too showy, flaunting her wealth with her sparkly watch and fancy clothes.

Nikoleta steadied her nerves with a deep breath. 'Kamil Król, my partner, booked an apartment with you.'

Expecting a warm greeting, Nikoleta was disappointed again. Mrs Lisowski waved her into a spacious hallway. 'Your rooms are on the top floor. They are modest, but prices in London –' she shrugged '– what can you do?'

Nikoleta followed her landlady upstairs where she unlocked a door revealing a bright room flooded with sunlight from a bay window. The open sash let in a gentle breeze. A double bed, sofa, table, and two chairs were crammed into a room no bigger than a master bedroom.

'I was going to provide a put-up bed for the boy. There's room for it alongside the double.'

She was going to? Had Kamil told her that Danek was missing? Surely not.

'Thank you, that will be fine,' Nikoleta murmured.

'A galley kitchen in here.' Mrs Lisowski opened a door and then another. 'Shower and toilet.'

Nikoleta just wanted her to go, so that she could phone Kamil to find out what the police had said. They had to act fast before it was too late. Nikoleta remembered playing in the furrows ploughed by her dad's tractor, her Sea Wee mermaid doll riding the waves. Mum called her to help with carrying the beets and when she turned back Sea Wee had gone. Her silver-white hair and lurid green tail buried by the churn of soil. Like the commuters folding in on Danek's trail until there was no clue he had once been there, holding her hand, waiting for a train. Mrs Lisowski was talking.

'Kamil can pay the deposit and a month in advance when he arrives this afternoon.'

Nikoleta snapped to attention. She didn't like the way Mrs

Lisowski used Kamil's name; it was too familiar. In the office Kamil was always Mr Król. Kamil did say that he had known Mrs Lisowski for a long time, it was just that he had never used her first name. She was getting like her mum, suspicious and wary of strangers. Hadn't she left Poland to become worldlier?

Nikoleta relaxed her face. 'I am sure that will be fine. Mr Król, Kamil, may not get here until tomorrow but I will let him know as soon as he arrives.' Nikoleta didn't know when to expect Kamil. She didn't even know if he had managed to book a flight.

'He's catching a 15.20 flight from Paris to London City Airport, so should be here by 16.00 UK time or thereabouts.'

Nikoleta was speechless. Why had Kamil told their land-lady his plans and not her? He could have phoned her or sent a message. What else had he told this woman? She had to ask. 'Did Kamil tell you about Danek?' If Mrs Lisowski didn't know, Nikoleta planned to say something of no importance, something about Danek's excitement to visit London. Anything but the truth.

'That you lost his boy on the Tube? Yes, he told me. Poor Kamil, he's devastated. He cannot get here quick enough. I told him I would look after you.'

Nikoleta squirmed, mortified that this woman knew of her stupidity, how she had failed Kamil and Danek. 'It happened so quickly. We were getting on the train together. I don't know how we got separated. I was holding his hand.' *But I wasn't. I was distracted, adjusting the straps on Danek's rucksack.* 'It was terrible. We will find him. I know we will. There must be cameras on all of the platforms. A woman found Danek and tried to return him to me. I was meant to meet her at a statue, but she didn't wait for me.' *I took too long – over an hour. It was my fault.* 'The woman who rescued Danek will make sure he's safe. Someone will be looking after him until Kamil arrives. I'm sure it will be alright.' But she wasn't at all sure.

'Of course.' Mrs Lisowski shrugged. 'If you need anything, you can find me on the ground floor.'

Finally alone, Nikoleta sunk onto the bed. At least Kamil would be arriving that afternoon. Together they would find Danek. It was no good going over and over what happened; she had to move forward, make a plan of what they needed to do. Kamil wouldn't be able to think straight. She needed a pen and paper. Her little wheely case contained bare essentials; Kamil said to pack lightly and they would buy what they needed for their new life once they arrived in London. At the time it had been exciting – so long ago. No pen and paper but she could use the note function on her mobile. Nikoleta pulled out her phone. Two missed calls and a message, all from Kamil. He *had* phoned her. Nikoleta's heart lifted, just a little, for the first time since the train doors slid together, separating her from Danek. Of course, her phone wouldn't have had a signal when she was travelling on the Tube. And yes, he had told her the plane he was catching and when he expected to arrive. 'Stay there, *slonka*, I don't want to lose you too.' It was Kamil's attempt at humour, trying to lighten the mood, but Nikoleta would have liked to meet him at the airport. She wasn't incapable of finding her way around London. It would have been better than sitting in an empty apartment waiting for him. No matter, she would use the time to think through everything that might be useful to the police. There must be things that they could do to help the search for Danek: asking the public. Using social media. She had a selfie of her, Kamil, and Danek taken at Warsaw Chopin Airport that morning. Nikoleta sent it out on Twitter with a message, 'Please help us find our son, Danek. Missing in London' and she added the date. She posted it then worried that Kamil's ex-wife might see it or one of her friends. Nikoleta's finger hovered over delete. Kamil's ex was hardly likely to follow her on Twitter and it was worth the risk if it meant that they found Danek. She imagined her plea reaching out into the ether and prayed that someone, somewhere would help them to find him.

7

Angie alighted the train, unable to relax and breathe in the fresh sea air, whilst her future hung in balance. On one side of the precipice a fall – the police would be waiting, and it would all be over. But on the other side, there was just a chance that they had got away with it and a perfect day would unfold. She squeezed Danny's hand, ready to face whatever the universe decided.

No police, or Gramps with his 'old jalopy', a blue Morris Minor. Gramps's excitement, when they arrived at Clacton for the holiday, made Angie feel like a VIP. It wasn't just for Lorraine, his granddaughter, after that first visit Angie was treated with the same adoration. You'd have thought Grammy and Gramps had spent the entire year waiting for their return.

Angie filled her lungs. Sea air with traces of fried onion and burnt sugar. The scent of magical summers, of anticipation and glorious freedom.

'First we're going to buy you a bucket and spade, Danny boy.' Angie took Danny's hand in hers and led him from the station. It was hard to walk at such a slow pace when inside she was doing a little jig of happiness. 'We'll go to the pier first, because it's close by and you'll love the rides. I wonder if the helter-skelter is still there. It was our favourite. You can sit on my lap and we'll go down together.'

'What is a hellaskella?' Danny had trouble forming the words. A little line of concentration puckered his brow.

'You'll see. There's so much to do and so little time.' Angie meant until she had to take Danny back, but the true meaning stuck in her throat and she had to swallow hard. 'So first the pier and then Jaywick Sands.' Angie hesitated – *the pier*. She froze in the middle of the street. Maybe it was a mistake coming back after all. She couldn't do this. If they turned back now… If they turned back now, she would never see Jaywick Sands or Clacton again. She would not get to paddle in the sea and build sandcastles with this little treasure.

Angie took a deep breath. 'Come on, Danny, we'd better look lively if we are to see everything. First Clacton, then we can pop into Butlins on the way to Jaywick and you can have a go on the paddleboats.

'Perhaps we should go to the beach first. Cool off after our journey – a little dip in the sea. You'd like that, wouldn't you? I'll show you how to make sandcastles.'

Angie swayed Danny on her hip as they made their way towards the pier. She tried to remember a happy day at the pier with Lorraine's grandparents. There was a time. Her first summer in Jaywick. Grammy had packed a flask and sandwiches and Gramps drove them in his old jalopy. Angie tried to grasp hold of that memory, but another more vivid one swallowed it up and she turned her attention to Danny. She would not let the past cast its shadow over their day.

'I'll buy you a candy floss and a toffee apple. A lovely shiny toffee apple. The sand at Jaywick's amazing. Even when the tide comes in, there's always a dry strip of beach to play on, not like Clacton where the waves hit the seawall. We'll have to walk to Jaywick along the beach, it's not far.'

She was talking too fast for Danny to understand, bless him. His screwed-up face as he tried to process the words was comical.

'You'll see,' Angie reassured him. Danny grinned, picking up on her excitement.

When they reached the beach, the tide was on the turn. Plenty of beach for now but it was coming in. 'You can tell because it's bone dry. If the sea were on its way out, it would be damp. Gramps would say perfect conditions for swimming because the sea will carry you back to shore.'

Danny nodded like a wise old sage and replied in Polish. Angie didn't know how much he understood.

The beach was already littered with small children too young for school, mums, and grandparents. Angie wove her way between windbreakers and picnic rugs, trying to find the perfect spot, close to toilets and refreshments. But the dark shadows beneath the pier beckoned, taunting her newly discovered defiance. Angie turned away from the stony boulders and tried to ignore the icy chill that licked her back.

Danny's delight in helping Angie to build sandcastles before trampling them down with his little bare feet melted her heart. It was impossible to feel anything but joy watching Danny giggle as he danced clumsily on heaps of sand before sliding onto his bottom with a look of surprise. This was what she had missed. Angie's heart ached for the children she never had, the grandchildren who would have smothered her in kisses and made presents for her at school from washing up bottles and sticky-backed plastic – pencil holders and the like. She would have oohed and aahed, and kept them until the

43

grandkids were in their twenties and they would have laughed fondly at her for keeping their clumsy creations.

Seagulls wheeled and cried, looking for discarded sandwich crusts or chips. It was really hot now – a fierce heat, like sitting too close to the bars of an electric fire. The tide was creeping in, pushing everyone closer together.

The mum next to them rubbed suntan lotion into her children's shoulders and backs. The girls had long T-shirts to protect them from the sun and the boy wore a baseball cap. A young couple the other side had put their baby in a little tent. Well, you had to be very careful with babies.

'Come here, let's look at your back.' Intent on patting a sandcastle, Danny resisted Angie's attempts to examine his skin. She sandwiched him between her legs. 'You're a slippery eel. Stay still a minute, sweetheart.' Danny's neck and shoulders, once as white as the soft lining of a conker shell, were now flamingo pink, the welts more prominent. Angie felt terrible for not protecting Danny from the sun. Would the marks on his back sting? The poor mite. She was going to have to do better than that. 'Ooh that's going to hurt. Let's put your T-shirt back on.'

In the sunlight, Angie noticed what she had missed in the dim lighting of the station toilet: purple marks across the backs of his legs. Angie hugged him fiercely and he yelped. 'Oh, I'm sorry, darling. We'll find something for that sunburn.'

There was no way that she was going to send Danny back if that was how he was being treated. She didn't care if they were his parents. But, if she was going to take care of the boy then she would have to wake her ideas up.

The woman next to them cleaned her daughter's hands with a wet wipe. She handed the boy a carton of juice, then opened a container and handed out sandwiches.

They would have to go onto the pier for some shade and

something to eat. It was no good Angie being squeamish – this was about Danny boy. They would have a bit of something and then get on their way to Jaywick. Have themselves a little dip in the sea once they got there.

The pier had changed so much since Angie's last visit, she barely recognised it. The huge roller coaster that dominated the pier – the Steel Stella they called it – had gone. As had the Dolphinarium. There, she did have a happy memory of the pier. Just one.

8

1972

It was the first week of their first summer in Jaywick. Everything was new and Angie still felt like a visitor as she got to know Lorraine's grandparents. They must have felt an obligation to entertain the girls in those early days, before Angie and Lorraine claimed Jaywick as their own and filled every day happily doing nothing and everything.

Grammy was in the sun-filled kitchen buttering bread. The radio blared the song, 'In the summertime', and Grammy did a little jig from one foot to another, waving her buttered knife in time to the music. She glanced up, aware of Angie hovering, unsure of what to do with herself. Should she offer to help?

'I'm making us some sandwiches and a flask. Do you drink tea or would you prefer a Coca-Cola?'

'Um, tea's fine.' Angie's palms were sweaty. Through the open back door, she watched Gramps watering his geraniums.

'Lorraine told you about our little outing?' Grammy tilted

her head. 'Cheese or ham? I've got a nice bit of pickle. Let's have both. I like cheese but Gramps prefers ham.'

Lorraine hadn't told Angie anything, she was in the bedroom they shared, painting her toe nails postbox red to match her new diagonally striped red and white bikini. Angie had packed her one and only swimming costume, an all-in-one with a frilly skirt. It looked silly and childish next to Lorraine's but Mum wouldn't hear of buying another – certainly not a bikini.

'We're taking you to Clacton for the day,' Grammy said, as she folded the sandwiches up in the bread's wrapping paper. 'What a pretty dress you're wearing. Green suits you, it matches your eyes. Now go and tell that granddaughter of mine to look sharp. As soon as Gramps has finished in the garden, we'll be off.'

They parked the car along the sea-front and strolled through gardens planted with bright patterns of flowers. Gramps kept stopping to remark on the combinations, asking Angie her opinion. Lorraine waltzed ahead, impatient to reach the pier, but Angie enjoyed discussing what would work well in Gramps's garden and they dawdled behind, drinking in the scent of tobacco plants and stock.

Grammy and Gramps weren't keen on visiting the pier. 'You find an unpleasant sort of character loitering around the pier,' Gramps said.

Lorraine rolled her eyes at Angie.

'Let the girls have a look, Gramps. They're young.'

'That's what worries me,' Gramps said. 'They are young and need to be protected from riffraff.'

But Grammy won as always and the girls were allowed to have three rides each at the pier's funfair. They watched girls scream as they hugged their boyfriends on the Steel Stella roller coaster, but neither of them was brave enough to have a go. They did go on the helter-skelter, even Grammy did. That was a hoot. Grammy's skirt flew up and gave everyone an eyeful of her bloomers.

Gramps sat between Angie and Lorraine on the waltzer. Lorraine winced with embarrassment when he put his arms protectively across their shoulders. But Angie loved it. She felt safe and proud to be part of this wonderful family. A boy with shoulder-length hair swung from car to car collecting fares. Angie noticed Lorraine make eyes at him. Maybe Gramps did too, because he was a bit sharp with the boy when he stopped a while on their car.

Then, there was the Dolphinarium. Angie didn't know that dolphins could dance, and clap as though they had hands. She was enchanted and spent some of her holiday money on a dolphin keyring to remind her of that day.

Following the outing, Angie was completely relaxed in Grammy and Gramps's company. She pretended that they were her grandparents as well as Lorraine's and they behaved as though they were.

That summer Angie had only just got a badge for swimming a width of the school pool. Lorraine could swim a length, dive, and swim underwater. Grammy called her a little mermaid. But it was Angie who Gramps spent hours with, encouraging her, helping to build her confidence swimming in the sea. They swam every day that holiday. Grammy and Gramps's chalet was close enough to the sea for them to run back in wet swimming costumes and flip-flops.

When she went back to school, Angie swum a length. She felt as though she had grown a few inches too.

anny's eyes sparkled when he saw the rides on the pier. Today Pharrell Williams's 'Happy' blasted out. It had been Slade and the Bay City Rollers back then. Angie *did* feel happy, despite everything.

They ate chips on the pier and Mr Whippy ice creams. It must have been Danny's tenth go on the merry-go-round when he fell asleep in the fire engine. It was five-thirty, too late now to get to Jaywick, but Danny had been having such a good time she didn't want to make him get off the ride. They couldn't go back without seeing Jaywick – that was the whole point in coming. Angie remembered her bucket list; she may not get another chance, certainly not with Danny.

Angie lifted Danny from the fire engine. His pants were damp; she'd forgotten to take him to the toilet. Never mind, they could have a little dip in the sea if they went on a bit to Jaywick and she had promised Danny that they would. It wasn't Danny's fault that she was crap at managing her time – leaving everything to the last minute. The last days.

'What do you think, sweetheart? Shall I take you back to

London or shall we go to Jaywick?' Danny wrapped his arms around Angie's neck and rested his head on her shoulder. His hair smelt of the sea and sun. She could still get Danny back to London that evening. Hand him over to the police, with some sort of explanation for the delay. Angie closed her eyes. She would count to five and if the first person that she saw on opening them was wearing red it would be a sign that they should go on to Jaywick. *Four, five.* A teenage boy cycled past wearing an open white shirt and black shorts. No red. Angie searched for another person wearing red; she should have chosen a different colour. Then she caught sight of a red band of colour across a bag on the boy's back. Hoorah, they were going to Jaywick.

Danny nuzzled into Angie. 'It's not far, lamb. I'll carry you a little ways but then you'll have to walk.'

It had only taken Angie and Lorraine about half an hour to get to Clacton Pier from Jaywick – maybe a bit longer, but not much. She'd been fit and young then, a couple of stone lighter, and she didn't have a bunion. Danny fell asleep with the rhythm of her hips. Angie didn't have the heart to wake him – but he was heavy, for such a scrap of a boy. She struggled on, stopping every few steps to get her breath.

'Butlins should be around here somewhere.' Since rounding the corner, Angie had been expecting to see the white buildings and flags. There was a café but no Butlins.

'Wake up, sweetheart, we're going to stop here awhile.' She needed a pee and it was time Danny went again.

There was a café on the seafront in the seventies but it was part of Butlins. It was as though the holiday camp had fallen away, leaving just the café, a fragment of its former glory. The outside tables and chairs, cheerful blackboard messages, and a sunny yellow interior fitted that era as much as today.

'Butlins closed down years ago. Before I was born.' A young woman slid a mug of tea across the counter to Angie.

How could it have gone? When she thought of Clacton and neighbouring Jaywick, it had always been there, solid, established, the place for happy families. Not her family – they couldn't have afforded it, but the perfect-looking family on the billboards, the girl with a blonde ponytail, a brother in shorts and a smiling mum and dad.

Angie had promised Danny a go on the paddleboats. She'd imagined them sitting on the little train and drinking soda floats in the bar. How could Butlins have been knocked down without her even knowing?

She found a table on the promenade. Danny's face was flushed, his hair sticky with sweat. He roused himself from the daze of sleep, when he smelt burger and chips. Angie broke off a quarter of the burger and passed it to Danny, who tried to squash it into his mouth whole, until Angie rescued it and tore off a bite-sized piece.

A seagull flew from the seawall and perched at their table with a caw. Angie threw a chip and the gull claimed it in a swoop. Danny chuckled and so Angie threw another chip and got the same reaction. Angie tried to coax Danny to feed the gulls but he wouldn't and so Angie cradled his hands and they did it together. Two gulls fought over the pickings and Danny squealed in excitement. How could something so simple as eating a burger and chips be so entertaining? Being a mum or a grandma was such a precious gift, her heart ached for what she had missed.

Danny jabbered away to the seagulls in Polish. Confident now, he fed the gulls himself breaking each chip into tiny equal parts. He wagged his finger at the gulls who took more than their share and tried to fling his scraps further away. Meanwhile Angie pushed pieces of burger into his mouth. The boy needed feeding up.

When the Styrofoam container was empty, Angie tossed it into a bin. 'We'd better be making tracks, Danny boy. It's still a little ways to Jaywick and then I have to get you back to London.'

The sun had gone. A few day trippers still straggled the promenade, half-heartedly playing ball. Others wound their way back to cars or buses, arms loaded with towels, coolboxes, and other paraphernalia. Back in the day, Angie and Lorraine were smug, privileged; *they* didn't have to go back to London. For six weeks in the summer they lived by the sea.

Danny was dawdling with steps so small it would take them till midnight to get to Jaywick.

'Hey, what we need's a bit of sugar. Didn't I promise you a toffee apple?'

A colourful seaside shop was preparing to close. A woman in an apron lifted a sandwich board advertising 99s with a flake and carried it inside. Angie followed her. Rows of seaside rock, honeycomb, and bags of candy floss lined the shelves. Danny twisted in her arms taking everything in.

'Mmm, can you smell sugar, darling? Sugar for my little sugar, eh?'

The woman smiled at Angie and Danny. 'Just in time. I was about to close the till.'

Angie bought a toffee apple and tucked it in her bag for later. It was a healthy snack, not all sugar. She tried to encourage Danny to walk but after a few steps he held up his arms to be carried.

'Come on, love, it's not much further. I have to get you back home tonight.'

Danny froze. His face went red as though he was about to explode.

'Okay, I'll give you a little carry.' Angie was dog-tired but she couldn't say no to the little angel. Lifting Danny was a struggle, as he tensed his body resisting.

Angie made soothing noises but it didn't work. Danny thrashed his limbs, jarring her back, and wailed. He was like a different child. It wasn't any wonder, the poor mite was overtired.

'I am sorry. I am sorry,' Danny cried between wails. 'Don't send me to the home for naughty boys.'

'Hush now.' Angie cradled Danny with a love that came from deep within. As though her love had been waiting for him for forty years.

She sat with him on the seawall. 'Let's see what Nanna has in here.' Angie rummaged in her bag and presented the toffee apple. 'Ta da!'

Danny's cry became a whimper, but his heart wasn't in it. His eyes were on the shiny caramel. Angie's mouth watered as the cellophane peeled off the sticky toffee with a smack.

'Mmm, you'll love this, Danny.'

He grasped the toffee apple with both hands and tried to take a bite. Angie laughed; his mouth was too small.

'Give it to Nanna.'

Danny watched as Angie broke the crisp candy shell with her teeth. The apple was soft. Soft and spongy. Urrgh it tasted of mold. Angie spat it out, disgusted.

'Do you really want this, Danny?'

She gave it to him anyway. It wouldn't be fair to throw away the toffee apple before he'd had a taste. Danny didn't think much of it either. Now Angie thought about it, toffee apples were always disappointing. It was the memory of them that enticed her to buy one. Funny how the memory held on to the taste of toffee and the satisfying crackle of those first bites – but forgot that nearly always a rotten apple was buried inside. Still, it had distracted Danny from his misery, poor mite. She took the toffee apple from him and threw it over the seawall. For some reason that made Danny laugh. And Angie laughed too. The pair of them giggled and giggled, although Angie wasn't sure why; just the joyous sound of Danny's chuckle – it released something in her. Eventually, when it hurt to laugh any more, Angie hugged him.

'We are *both* naughty,' Danny said, his face solemn again.

The welts on his back. Threatening to send him away. What kind of home did Danny come from? Angie stroked his hair. 'You're not naughty, lamb. You're a precious boy.'

Danny snuggled into Angie. 'You will look after me.' It was a statement not a question.

'Yes, Nanna will take care of you.' Angie rocked him in time to the waves' hush. Despite her exhaustion, Angie was calm and content. The warmth of Danny's soft body and the sound of the sea's breath – in and out. The black thoughts that had thumped a tribal dance in her head ever since her doctor said the C word had finally stopped. She had done the right thing coming back. And in this blissful state of mind Angie had a revelation. This was meant to be. She and Danny had been brought together for a reason. He was a gift to her – her salvation – and he needed her as much as she needed him.

10

The apartment, if you could call the room that, could not contain Nikoleta's nervous energy. She paced up and down, frustrated that she wasn't doing anything to find Danek. The woman who took him might be trying to find her; maybe she should go back to the station. Yes, that's what she would do. Kamil told her to go straight to the apartment but what good was that?

Cock-a-doodle-doo. Nikoleta grabbed her phone expecting Kamil but it was her little sister, Angelika, and her spirits lifted. Angelika was more excited about Nikoleta visiting London than she was herself. If Angelika could have stowed away with them she would have. That would have really upset their parents. Mum had been a bit frosty when she said goodbye. Dad made himself scarce. It still hurt; she was close to her dad and couldn't bear his disapproval.

'Hi, Angelika.' Nikoleta's voice sounded false, over-bright, but Angelika wouldn't notice.

'What's it like? Did you get on a red bus? Did you take Danek to the milkshake bar? I know which flavour I would

57

have – peanut butter and banana. No, let me talk first. It's Mum. She asked me to call you. I don't know why she can't phone you herself, but as she's paying for my mobile, I suppose I'd better let her.'

Nikoleta could imagine the exchange of looks between her mum and sister and it made her heart ache to be there with them.

'Nikoleta? You arrived safely?'

No, she didn't. She had lost Danek and her world was falling apart. 'I'm here in London, Mum.'

'We – *I* am proud of you, Nikoleta. I wanted you to know that. What you did leaving Poland, your family, and friends to make a new life with your man and his son was brave. It takes a strong woman – an independent woman – to leave her country and start afresh. I was afraid for you because I could not do it, but you can.'

Nikoleta swallowed the lump in her throat. 'Thank you, Mum, that means a lot to me. It wasn't easy. You know how much I will miss you all.'

'We are missing you already. You make sure that you phone me every day. I will pay your phone bill if that's a problem. Just make sure you keep in touch.'

'I'll do my best, Mum. How's Dad? Can I talk to him?'

'Hold on.' Nikoleta could hear her dad's voice. Her mum was trying to persuade him to talk. 'I'm sorry, sweetheart. Your dad's had to go out. Maybe next time you call – tomorrow.'

Nikoleta smiled. 'I'll try and call every day, Mum, but I'm not promising.'

'I knew you would forget us as soon as you left Poland.'

Nikoleta kept her mum talking as long as she could. She really wanted to tell her mum what had happened but Mum was so proud of her travelling to London on her own, she was ashamed to tell the truth.

When her mum hung up, the silence that followed was unbearable. Angelika's bubbling excitement, a ghost in the room. Mum might have forgiven her for leaving Poland but Dad hadn't. He didn't like Kamil and nothing Nikoleta could say would change his mind.

Nikoleta checked Twitter. Her plea had been retweeted twenty-eight times already, but she had to do more. It was no good sitting around feeling sorry for herself, she had to find Danek. She should never have listened to Kamil. It was crazy sitting there in the apartment waiting for him to get back from Paris to sort things. Even if the police did accuse her of neglecting to care for Danek, what of it? She *was* neglectful, but it wasn't Kamil's fault. Maybe she should get to the police first, so that they didn't blame Kamil. He was a good father.

Nikoleta almost ran down the stairs. She would tell Mrs Lisowski her plan, so that when Kamil arrived he would know where she was.

'Ah, Mrs Król, come in, come in.' Mrs Lisowski held the door open.

The apartment smelt of sandalwood and cedar, a mixture of spice and forest. Nikoleta's explanation faltered, as she took in the opulence of the room: a cut-glass chandelier, a painting of the New York skyline in bold colours and furnishings the like of which Nikoleta had seen in the pages of glossy magazines. Did people really live like this?

Nikoleta shook herself. 'Mrs Lisowski, I am going back to Liverpool Street Station to see if I can find Danek. I have an idea that he may be returned and I want to be there when he is. Please could you tell Mr Król when he arrives?'

The more she thought about it, the more sensible her plan. Where else would the woman go to return Danek? What if

Kamil's men couldn't get there in time? She never should have left the statue – even if it meant standing there all day. What was the matter with her running away like that?

'Of course I will. Have a drink first. I bet you've had no refreshment since you arrived. I told Kamil that I would look after you and I have been very neglectful. What will it be? A strong tea with lots of sugar like the English or a vodka like us Russians?'

Nikoleta wanted to say no thank you, but her upbringing was such that she thought it would be bad manners. A few minutes' delay wouldn't make a lot of difference and Mrs Lisowski was right, she needed something to revive her. A strong black coffee would have been her preference but that didn't seem to be on offer. 'A cup of black tea with no sugar or milk, if I may?'

'You may, but you will need to acclimatise. In England, all tea is black tea unless you ask for green tea or herbal tea. Here, black tea means without milk. Sit down and I'll fetch us a tray.'

Nikoleta perched on the edge of her seat, resisting the deep comfort of the suede sofa. The fragrance that permeated the apartment came from bottles and bowls holding reed diffusers. They looked expensive with orchids, shells, and other fauna trapped behind the glass. Mum would be crossing herself, believing Mrs Lisowski to be an informer: a person who sold their neighbours and friends to the Party police for rewards and favours. Nobody lived like this in Poland – except perhaps the very rich, and the rich were to be scorned and judged, if you listened to the older generation. Things had changed, but it was difficult to shift the weight of the past.

When Mrs Lisowski returned, her tray was laden with tea things as well as a bottle of vodka and two shot glasses. 'To steady your nerves,' Mrs Lisowski said as she poured a shot into each glass. 'To your good health and to finding Kamil's boy.'

Nikoleta didn't want the vodka; she needed to keep a clear head and hardly ever drank alcohol. Was it rude not to join the toast with her own wishes for Mrs Lisowski's good health? Nikoleta raised her glass. 'And to your good health.' She sipped the vodka, just a taste.

'Like this.' Mrs Lisowski knocked it back in one.

Nikoleta nodded and took another little sip. 'Maybe after my tea.'

Mrs Lisowski poured. 'Tell me how you met Kamil. I was surprised that he married. I never thought Kamil would settle down. You must be very special.'

'We're not married. I should have said. Not yet anyway. Kamil and I worked together before we became involved. I am his bookkeeper – well, I was in Poland. Kamil said that he has known you for a long time. How do you know each other?' Nikoleta's tea was too hot to drink quickly. She was very aware of the minutes passing when she should have been making her way back to Liverpool Street. She stood up.

Mrs Lisowski carried on as though Nikoleta had not just leapt to her feet. 'Ah, Kamil and I go way back. He knew my husband, a Polish gentleman with a big heart. Sadly, he died some years ago.'

Nikoleta felt bad trying to leave whilst her landlady was talking about her bereavement. She sat back down.

'Kamil is a great entrepreneur. He can get anything from anywhere – contacts all over the world.' Mrs Lisowski was talking about Kamil as though she knew him better than Nikoleta. Now she was looking at her as though trying to figure out what a great man like Kamil was doing with a little village girl with no experience of the world. One who couldn't even escort his son safely to London.

Irritated, Nikoleta started to give her apologies. 'I really do need to go.'

Mrs Lisowski poured herself another shot. 'You have not touched your drink. Maybe it is too strong for you.'

Nikoleta slung back the shot, to prove that she was no lightweight, and then regretted it. The alcohol burned her throat. The doorbell rang long and loud. Mrs Lisowski excused herself.

It was Kamil. Nikoleta sprung to her feet, making herself a little dizzy. She'd had nothing to eat for hours. There were some nibbles on the tray – olives and pretzels – but she didn't want them. They would stick in her throat.

'Lenka, how good to see you.' Kamil's voice was soft, caressing.

It was awkward loitering near the door, unsure whether to join Kamil or wait for Mrs Lisowski to show him in. Their voices were hushed. Nikoleta heard 'Danek' and 'police'. Before Nikoleta could reach them, Mrs Lisowski showed Kamil into the drawing room.

'Nikoleta was having a drink with me, will you join us?'

Kamil scowled as he took in Nikoleta's empty glass. 'No, thank you, Lenka. You have been very kind entertaining Nikoleta, but I cannot waste any more time in finding Danek. He's been missing for hours.'

Nikoleta flinched. Why hadn't she just stayed upstairs and let Kamil in herself? Now he was going to think her callous as well as irresponsible.

11

Angie's back ached, she was sweaty, her blouse was smeared with chocolate, and she smelt of wee, but she was happier than she had been in years. Angie nuzzled Danny's soft, sea-salted hair.

'Nearly there, my darling. We'll soon be home.' Angie meant Jaywick, not London. She hugged his soft weight and the void within her filled with love.

Fewer day trippers passed them now. A couple of dog walkers and a gaggle of kids on bikes shared the footpath that ran between beach and chalets. Locals.

'We're here, Danny. Welcome to Jaywick Sands.'

Danny woke up and bless him, he smiled. A dirty sleepy face, but a big smile.

'Look, Danny, the tide's gone out. I told you Jaywick has the best beach.'

The evening sun cast a golden light over sea and sand. Waves lapped gently on the still beach. It was the image Angie had treasured all the years between. This was her heaven. The place she'd been happiest.

Blancmange-like sand sucked the soles of their feet. Just a trace of heel and toe as their imprint dissolved. Angie tried writing her name in big looping letters but the 'A' had gone by the time she started the 'I'.

A gentle breeze ruffled Danny's curls.

'Ready for that swim?'

Cool sea lapped Angie's toes and tickled her ankles. It dragged the sand from beneath her feet. It was bliss. Danny hesitated, watching at a safe distance from the sea. Even in Clacton, Angie hadn't been able to tempt him into the water.

'Maybe you've not seen the sea before. Is that it, Danny boy?'

Danny found Angie's bag where she had dumped it before wading in. His head disappeared and then he pulled out a bucket and spade. 'Make a castle.'

They didn't have time to play. It was getting late. They had to get back to London that night. It was so tempting to fling off her clothes and have a swim. *This is the last time you will ever swim in the sea.* Angie caught her breath. She wasn't ready.

Danny held up his spade waiting for Angie to join him. 'Come here.'

'My darling, there is nothing I would like more than to play with you in the sand and swim in the sea, but we can't.' Angie paddled to the water's edge and beckoned Danny. 'Let me at least clean you up a bit, Danny boy. I can't take you back to London looking like that.'

Angie splashed her face with cupped hands of salty sea and then tried to do the same to Danny but he twisted away. 'Let's slip your shorts off so that you can have a little dip, get nice and fresh.'

Danny wasn't interested and Angie couldn't resist wading in deeper to cool down. She tucked her skirt into the legs of her knickers and unbuttoned her blouse, so that the sea breeze lifted it, cooling her armpits and belly. There was nobody to see, just the distant silhouette of a figure on the promenade. Danny squatted like an old yogi mesmerised by something. Angie paddled closer to see what was fascinating him – seaweed hair rising and falling on the cusp of each wave. He hadn't noticed the sea that was now licking his toes.

'Mind you don't get your pants wet.' Too late, Danny toppled onto his bottom. He looked up in surprise, just as a big wave broke and soaked his shorts. Angie roared with laughter. 'In for a penny, in for a pound.' The temptation was too much. She threw off her wraparound skirt and lifted Danny into her arms. 'Let's do it, Danny boy.' With her blouse tucked into her bra Angie strode into the sea.

Danny clung to her at first, a look of fear and then excitement creasing his face. A wave lifted them and Angie shrieked, 'Whee!'

Danny's arms relaxed around her neck as he searched for the next big wave.

'Is it coming? Is it coming?' Angie dipped down so that the sea reached their chests, ready to catch the next wave.

'Whee!' Danny whistled in her ear.

It was great fun. The cherry on the cake of a perfect day but somehow, they had to get back to London. They were both soaking wet, no towel or change of clothes, apart from a spare pair of knickers Angie kept for emergencies. It was past eight and she had no idea how she was going to get them back to Clacton, let alone London. 'What are we like, Danny boy? What are we like?'

Angie retraced the route she had taken so many times before, from the sea back towards Grammy and Gramps's chalet. But nothing was the same. What had happened to the pretty gardens? The handkerchief lawns bordered with marigolds and nasturtiums?

An abandoned fridge balanced against a low brick wall in one front yard, black sacks of refuse in another. A TV with a smashed screen and an old pushchair spilled onto the pavement from a garden strewn with debris. Angie swung Danny onto her hip. He couldn't walk barefoot here – not like the old days. She saw a supermarket trolley dumped in a garden and dragged it out onto the street. Shame she hadn't found it sooner. Angie swung Danny into the trolley; it would serve well as a pushchair.

What had happened to Jaywick? Angie kept expecting to turn a corner and see everything as it had been back in the seventies. But there were no wide clean streets. No neighbours sitting out, drinking tea and chatting. They reached the main street, the one they had to cross to reach Grammy and Gramps's. It was just as grey and dismal.

In the seventies the street buzzed with happy holidaymakers. Angie recognised the pub, a café, and the amusement arcade, but there was little else. Shops were boarded up and graffitied. There had once been a hairdresser and a toyshop. All that had gone. Tarnished and damaged.

Angie bit back her disappointment. She was a fool thinking that she could turn back time. The world was a dark and dirty place.

Angie sat on a garden wall opposite the Seashell Café – a closed sign on its door. At least their clothes had started to dry in the sun. At times like this Angie wished she owned a phone. She didn't have the energy to push Danny in the trolley back to Clacton and they were both too tired to wait for a bus. That's if there was a bus to Clacton that evening.

A car engine turned over, then died. Again – it whirred,

then spluttered. A girl with a funky haircut, longish one side and shaved the other, sat at the wheel. She tried again.

Angie peered into the car. 'You're not going to get her going like that.'

The girl glared. 'Fuck off.'

Angie didn't take offence; she'd have said the same thing.

'Want me to take a look?'

The girl sunk back in her seat. 'Fuck, fuck, and fuck!' She slammed the steering wheel and blasted the horn.

'Release the bonnet.' Angie knew everything there was to know about Ford cars produced between 1965 and 1980. She had a full set of Haynes manuals and had pretty much memorised them. Couldn't drive, but she could do basic maintenance and repairs.

The girl got out of her beaten-up Ford Fiesta. 'I've gotta get her going. I need a car for my work.'

'Watch Danny and I'll take a look. If I get her going the deal is you give us a lift to Clacton.'

'Sure.' The girl shrugged.

'There's nothing wrong with the battery or starting system.'

Angie rooted in her bag for the wet knickers, the next best thing to a rag. She prodded and poked. Cars had changed a bit since the eighties but not so much that she couldn't apply her basic knowledge.

'I reckon the compression in your engine cylinders is low. Have you got her wet or used dodgy fuel?'

The girl shrugged again. 'Yeah and yeah. Rain leaks in because of the rust and I've cadged containers of petrol when I've run out – so could be. But can you fix her?'

Angie wished she could get the car working that evening. It was their only hope of getting to Clacton. 'I'll do my best but if it's a broken timing belt or your valves are bust, you'll need to get the parts.' Angie didn't bother asking whether the girl had AA or RAC cover.

A trim, curly-haired woman came out of the Seashell, arms crossed over her apron. 'No luck, Zoe?'

Angie explained the problem, her head still under the bonnet. Danny pulled himself up inside the trolley and whimpered, holding out his arms. Soon he would build up into a tantrum and who could blame him? The little love was ready for bed.

'I'm sorry I can't fix it tonight. I'm pretty sure it's the valves but we need to replace them before I can get her going.'

The woman offered her hand. 'Josie, Zoe's mum. Thanks for trying. Can I get you a drink?' Josie lifted Danny out of the trolley and made soothing noises. 'Let's find something nice for you to eat.'

Restored by a glass of red wine, delicious pasta, and Josie's cheerful chatter, Angie relaxed on the sofa, Danny asleep at her side in an adult's T-shirt that served well as a nightshirt. He had gobbled a bowl of pasta in tomato sauce before dropping off.

'You're right, Jaywick's not as it was in its heyday, but it's okay. Who did you say your people are?'

'The Jeffers. We had a place on Sea Spray Avenue. Me and Danny came down for the day but reckon he's too tired to make it back to London tonight. Is there anywhere we could get a room?' Angie couldn't afford a fancy room but getting back to London that night was no longer an option.

'It's late. Why don't you stay with us tonight and maybe tomorrow you can fix Zoe's car? She's been offered a pub job in St Osyth but needs wheels.'

'Mind if I listen to the ten-o'clock news?' Josie's husband, Bill, poked his head around the door.

Angie's heart sank. So far, she'd got away with posing as Lorraine – the Jefferses' granddaughter. Danny was her grandson. He was spending the summer with her. Danny's dad – her son – married a Polish girl and lived with Danny in Poland. Josie had accepted the story without question. Having a connection to Jaywick seemed to have worked a charm. Angie was like family now.

But, in a moment her face would be on the TV – *Have you seen this woman?* The station CCTV cameras would have caught her boarding a train to Clacton and then she would have to come clean. The TV crackled. A newsreader was saying something serious to the camera but there was no sound. Bill fiddled with a remote and the newsreader's voice went from silent to full volume. Danny murmured in his sleep.

'Sorry,' Bill whispered, as he turned it down.

It was the national news but regional news would follow. The picture danced then broke into thin lines.

'Josie, it's doing it again,' Bill shouted to Josie, who was in another room.

'What do you expect? I told you not to buy it from Slippery Si.' Josie returned clutching sheets, blankets, and a towel.

'Here. I'll make a bed for you both on the sofa. Do you want to borrow something to sleep in?' Josie was so caring. What would she say when she found out that Angie had lied to her?

'Now the news for your local area.'

Angie felt sick. They watched together as the TV picture came good.

'There you go, it's working.' Bill looked pleased with himself.

69

Typical, she thought. *It starts to work when it's time for the regional news.* Angie sat very still. In a moment the warm conviviality would end and she would be exposed for who she really was: Weirdo Winkle.

People on beaches enjoying the sunshine, promises of more warm weather, and then the camera was on the weather girl. Bill switched it off and Angie let out her breath. She was safe for now.

Car headlamps arced across the ceiling. Someone kicked a can in the street. Years ago, she and Lorraine had fallen asleep to the sound of the bingo caller in the Club House and woke up to the sound of the Elsan man making his rounds in an electric cart to renew the chemical toilets at the back of each chalet. She wondered whether the chalets still had Elsans. Tomorrow they would have a look at Grammy and Gramps's place, then they'd better get back to London. But it had been a good day – one to remember. And no pain. Maybe the cancer would get better. She'd heard of that: positive thinking, swimming with dolphins, and stuff having a miraculous effect. Swimming with Danny. Angie drifted to sleep.

12

Nikoleta followed Kamil's rigid back up the stairs to their apartment. Anger and disappointment radiated from him, like a magnetic field. Kamil had not even said hello. Cursed Mrs Lisowski. She hadn't asked for that vodka; she didn't even like it. Kamil was warm and charming to their landlady – *Lenka*. When did Mrs Lisowski become Lenka? You'd have thought they were past lovers the way that woman purred at him. Nikoleta paused on the stairs. No, Mrs Lisowski was at least eight years older than Kamil.

Shame on her, blaming their landlady for Kamil's mood. Hadn't she just lost his beloved son on the London Underground? Of course he was angry. 'I am so, so, sorry, Kamil.' Words were inadequate.

'Have you a key?' He didn't turn to face her, just stood at their door, shoulders slumped.

At least he was talking. Nikoleta fumbled for the key then waited whilst Kamil threw open the door.

'There were so many people on the train and the platform.

I didn't know. I've only been to Warsaw once with my grandpa. How was I to know?'

Nikoleta had told Kamil that she wasn't confident taking Danek to London. She wasn't confident taking herself. She'd never been abroad before and had no experience of cities. Kamil didn't tell her that she was travelling during a busy period, that there would be so many people. To remind him of that would sound as though she was making excuses and there were none. She had lost his child.

Kamil loosened his tie and sank onto the bed. 'What was his face like when he saw the doors close? Did he cry? Was he screaming?'

'No, no, Kamil. Nothing like that. I don't think he noticed. It happened so quickly. But I told you, a kind woman looked after him. They told me at the station that she wanted to meet me to return him. That's why I know we will get him back. I wanted to go to the station now, before you arrived. What if she's already there waiting for me? What have you told the police? Are they at Liverpool Street? Maybe I should talk to them now that you're here. There must be things I could tell them that would help.' Nikoleta couldn't sit still. They should be doing something *now.*

Kamil sighed. 'There are men at Liverpool Street looking for Danek. Tell me everything, Nikki, every detail. I need to know.'

Nikoleta sat beside Kamil on the bed. She started at the beginning and tried to remember every detail: who was standing near her on the platform – that was difficult as she could only remember the grey backs of men in suits and the backpacks of travellers. The people on the platform, after the train pulled out, were easier to remember, as she had searched their faces looking for someone, *anyone* who might help but there were no sympathetic faces. As she spoke, Kamil found her hand and held it in his.

'How long was it between you hearing the announcement and getting to the statue?'

Nikoleta gulped. 'I'm not sure exactly.'

'Ten, fifteen minutes? It wouldn't take long to travel one stop. Was anyone following you?'

'Why would anyone follow me? There were masses of people all going the same way, I told you.'

'So how long?'

'Well, first of all I went to the wrong station. An old man told me the wrong way.'

Kamil released her hand. She could sense his body tensing.

'I don't know, about thirty minutes, maybe longer.'

Kamil stood up. 'That makes a difference. You should have said.'

'Kamil, let me talk to the police. If you had let me talk to them to begin with, I would have told them. That's why I think the woman may have gone back to the station. Or maybe she asked someone else, a guard or someone to mind Danek.'

'No, Nikki.' He sounded so weary. Defeated. And then Kamil noticed Danek's rucksack resting on top of her wheelie case and lunged for it, as though the rucksack were Danek himself. 'You didn't tell me you had his bag.'

'I did. It was because I was fiddling with the straps that...' Kamil tipped the contents from the bag. Underpants and T-shirts that Kamil had folded earlier that day, tiny in his big hands. 'Oh, Kamil. I'm sorry.'

'Where's his rabbit?' Kamil held a T-shirt to his face, as though breathing in the scent of his son.

It was a luxury to cry, one that she didn't deserve, but Nikoleta couldn't stop her silent tears. 'He was hugging it when…when the doors closed between us.' Her voice gave her away and Kamil whipped around.

'*Slonka.* I'm sorry. You were right, I shouldn't have asked you to go ahead without me.' He hugged Nikoleta to him. There was nothing else she could say.

Eventually Kamil stroked Nikoleta's hair from her face where it had escaped from her ponytail. 'I haven't told the police. They would take Danek away from me and send him back to Poland.'

'I will tell them it's my fault. We have to report Danek missing, Kamil.'

'Oh, *slonka*, I wish we could. But you don't understand they would lock you up, accuse you of neglect or child abuse.'

'No, Kamil. They wouldn't –'

'I wish it wasn't so, *slonka*, but we are always at a disadvantage here. We are Polish. I can't risk it. You know how hard I worked to convince the authorities to let me have custody of Danek? Years. Years knowing that he was being neglected by his alcoholic mother. Trying to sleep at night when my little boy could be alone, hungry, frightened? I am his *daddy* and there was nothing I could do. Except fight to get custody.'

It was heart-wrenching to see him like this. And it was her fault. She had to be strong. To support him. Nikoleta gulped back a sob. 'But you did, Kamil. You did everything that you could and the judge ruled in your favour. I remember how happy you were the day they said you had full custody.'

Kamil had taken Nikoleta out to dinner to celebrate. That was when he suggested they relocate to London. She had tried to talk him into waiting, give them all time to gel as a family first; she hadn't met Danek and although she knew that she wanted to spend her life with Kamil, they had only been together a couple of years. Going to London was Big. Something she had always dreamed of but never really expected to happen. That was what life was like with Kamil – a bigger canvas – bigger dreams and possibilities.

'We will find Danek, Kamil, I promise you.'

'If they find out that I entrusted my son to my girlfriend and left Poland as soon as I got custody – and then my girlfriend lost him in a big city – what is that going to look like? His mother might be a drunk but at least she managed to keep Danek safe. We have to find him before this gets out.' He stopped his ranting and took Nikoleta's hand. 'I'm sorry, *slonka*. I'm not blaming you. I'm just afraid. And angry.'

He had every right to be angry with her. She was angry with herself. Oh no, Nikoleta remembered the tweet she had sent earlier that day. *Please help us find our son, Danek. Missing in London.* Kamil would go crazy if he knew. It wasn't too late to delete it but she had to do something. If there was a chance it would help them find Danek, she was willing to risk Kamil's wrath.

Kamil was looking at her. 'What is it?' Why did every emotion have to show on her face?

'If you haven't told the police, Kamil, how are we going to find him?'

'As soon as I got your call, men positioned themselves at Liverpool Street Station and others close by. If Danek is within five miles of the statue, my men will find him. I'm waiting to hear if my contact in the London Underground has checked the CCTV footage. Make no mistake, Nikki. I will find the evil *suka* who stole Danek.'

Nikoleta didn't correct Kamil. She understood that he was distraught. 'He will be back with us tonight, Kamil. I know he will.'

13

The next day Angie promised Josie, over a full English breakfast in the Seashell, that she would hang around until Zoe got hold of new or almost new valves.

'Zoe's learnt from me in the café but she needs to expand her horizons. This pub job will give her more experience in catering. She's a bright kid.' Josie talked as she sliced cucumbers and tomato for the salads and sandwich fillings.

Danny loved his runny egg and toast soldiers. Angie shook her head. Were all little boys as mucky as Danny? She wiped his eggy face and he giggled.

'Thank you, Nanna,' Angie prompted.

'Thank you, Namma,' he repeated.

'I'll need to buy us both a change of clothes,' Angie said. Their clothes had dried, salt crusted and sandy.

'There's a boot sale by the seafront and a charity shop, end of the road.'

. . .

The glow of Josie's kindness and warmth insulated Angie from the disappointment of finding Sea Spray Avenue changed. It wasn't *all* bad; some of the chalets still had their charm, but these little white chalets with picket fences and pretty gardens were like a few remaining good teeth. Sadly, Grammy and Gramps's wasn't one of them.

The windows on either side of the front door were boarded; the front garden overgrown, but at least no one had used it for fly tipping. Angie lifted the gate and it came away in her hands, so she balanced it against the post.

'Well, it looks like it's empty, Danny. Shall we go and take a peek?'

Danny nodded, his eyes wide.

'This is where I spent my holidays when I was a girl, Danny.'

'When you was little?'

'Not little like you. But a very long time ago.'

Danny frowned; he was taking it all in. Sometimes he looked so serious – more like an old man than a little kid. He hadn't asked for his mum, not once. Angie noticed Danny listening when she spoke to Josie about minding Danny for his mum. He seemed to have accepted her as his grandma. It was wrong to hang on to him but Angie couldn't bring herself to give him back just yet. These precious days with Danny were her only chance of experiencing what it might have been like to be a mum or a grandma. It wasn't hurting Danny, they were having a great time, and if his mum really cared she would find him. In fact, Angie was surprised that the police hadn't already caught up with them. It just confirmed her suspicions that this little boy was not loved enough.

As Angie reverently crept through long grass at the side of the house, she felt as though she were visiting a beloved elderly relative in hospital. Grammy and Gramps would have died years ago. It didn't feel like the same place any more. They took such good care of their pretty chalet. The outside kharsie was still there. Angie pulled open the door to see cardboard boxes and black sacks of rubbish balanced on a chemical toilet. It wasn't the old Elsan; someone had replaced it with something more up to date. Angie threw the rubbish to one side to get a closer look. It was in good condition. Amazing, it hadn't been nabbed.

Danny wandered off to explore the backyard. Tall grasses made it a good place to hide. Angie pretended not to see him, then pounced on him with tickles. Danny squirmed and giggled, making Angie's heart swell with love. 'You see if you can hide from Namma and I'll come and find you.'

Angie peered into the grimy kitchen window and saw the same old cupboards and worktops. It had once been cheerful and cosy, a yellow checked cloth on the kitchen table. A shiny padlock secured the back door; Angie rattled it. If only Grammy and Gramps were inside. 'Hello! Guess who?' she would say.

Grammy would rub her eyes in disbelief. 'Is that our little Angie? Gramps come and see who's here with her grandson.'

They would love Danny – Danny, her grandson.

'Come and find me, Namma,' Danny called. He was squatting by a wire incinerator.

If I find the key to this padlock under Grumpy the Gnome then it will be a message from Grammy and Gramps. Angie knew that it was very unlikely that the old hiding place for the door key would be used any more. Grammy and Gramps would be over one hundred years old if they were still alive. The Jefferses had probably sold the place. But, it was a wonderful thought. She and Danny could hide out in the chalet. It would be as though she really were his grandma, like Grammy was to her and Lorraine. Just for a few days. Taking back what should have been hers. She should have been a mum and a grandma. This was her chance. *Please, Grammy, show me the key.*

'Where is that little scamp?' Angie said, peering around the incinerator.

'Here I am! Here I am!'

'See if you can find a gnome hiding in the grass, Danny.'

Danny screwed up his face.

'A little plastic man with a beard.'

They found Grumpy embedded in a tangle of weeds. The elements had stripped him of his jaunty jacket and breeches, but Grumpy was still on sentry duty where he'd always been. It was like finding an old friend and for a moment Angie felt as though Grammy was with them. It was too much to hope but Angie whispered, 'Please let the key be there.'

Angie prised Grumpy from his anchor of grass and an army of woodlice scattered across the exposed soil. Whilst Angie scratched at the earth, Danny crouched beside her and poked the woodlice.

'Pass me that stone, Danny boy.'

A bee buzzed. The smell of sap and nettles reminded Angie of her childhood; it had been a long while since she'd messed around in a garden. Danny decided another stone might be better and went off in search of one. Angie picked up the jagged stone and scraped away more soil. Nothing. She tore at the earth. *It has to be here.* Nothing.

Angie sat back on her haunches. It was a nice dream, but she was too late. Life had passed her by. She would have to return Danny to the police and find out what the hospital had to say. If only she had made different choices. Angie turned her face to the sun. Just being in Jaywick made her feel better.

Danny threw himself at Angie and they tumbled over.

They were scrambling up when the sun caught a flash of silver. 'Hold on, Danny. I think I've found the hidden treasure.'

Angie scoured the hard ground with a stone and revealed a key. *Thank you, Grammy!*

'Abracadabra! Come and see, Danny, a key. Now, will it fit the padlock?'

They were in. The place could do with a good clean and some furniture, but it would do very nicely. Grammy and Gramps had sent a message. *You are welcome to use our chalet, Angie. You and that grandson of yours must make yourselves at home. It will be good to hear the laughter of children again. You stay the whole of the summer if you like, love.*

'Home sweet home, Danny. Our little place by the sea.'

Danny ran from room to room. Two bedrooms, living room, and kitchen. Small, but perfect. The gas cooker was still there, but she would need a gas canister. Could she really do it? Her sick note was only for a few more days and sooner or later someone would come looking for Danny. But until then, why not? The night before she and Danny found each other, she had vowed to do the things she had missed out on before she died. There was no such thing as coincidence. The universe had heard her heartfelt plea and given her this chance. Angie had not had any breaks in her life and she wasn't going to look this gift horse in the mouth. It was as though Grammy had given her the key to her home and as good as said, *Use it, Angie.*

We will, Grammy.

'Come on, Danny. We have to do a bit of shopping so that we can fix this place up.'

Angie sat Danny in the supermarket trolley and headed off for the boot sale.

· · ·

There were several stalls selling new goods as well as blankets thrown down with offerings of plastic toys that had seen better days, mismatched crockery, plastic flowers, and holiday souvenirs such as a donkey in a sombrero and an egg timer with a leprechaun.

'Have a look at the toys, Danny boy, and choose something to take back with us.' If Danny's mum hired au pairs then the headless Chewbacca and faded lightsaber were not going to impress him.

Danny knelt by a basket of soft toys but his attention was on two little boys who were diving on video games. 'A *Super Mario*! Mum. Mum.'

'Put it back, Dexter. I'm not made of money.'

'*Legend of Zelda!*' his younger brother said. Their mum walked on and the boys reluctantly dropped the video games before traipsing after her. Neither of them noticed Danny and Angie felt sorry for him.

'What about these McDonald's toys?' Angie held up a Quality Street tin filled with plastic figures: a dinosaur, a troll with pink hair, a lobster, a green duck in a purple dress, and a Mario.

Danny beamed. He would have been happy with anything. Funny, you would think he would turn his nose up at second-hand toys. What had his life been like before she found him?

Angie settled Danny in the trolley with his new toys. They still had to find some basics for the chalet – a couple of sleeping bags, plates and cups. Good job she had the trolley.

'What do you want for this?' Angie held up a pair of tiny shorts.

'Fiver.'

Angie tugged at the seams and watched the thread unravel. Rubbish. Sullivan's made better quality than that crap. She threw the shorts at the stall holder. 'Forget it.'

She would look for an old sewing machine and run up a few things for Danny. The thought of making clothes for her boy made Angie's heart sing. Of course, that's what she should do. He would have the best wardrobe. A little Gruffalo suit with a hood and a T-shirt with dinosaur spikes down his back. Spotty shorts and…

'Oh my!' Angie stopped in her tracks. It was gorgeous. A silky red swimsuit that could have been worn by a 1950s star-let. It dangled from the stall's awning like an exclamation mark. A flutter of excitement – butterflies in her belly. She was fourteen again, falling in love with that broderie anglaise blouse. It was more than eight weeks of pocket money but how she longed for that blouse. It would transform her, make her look like the sultry, pouting model in the Miss Selfridge advert. The blouse represented a dream, just like the siren red swimsuit that beckoned Angie that morning.

Of course, she couldn't wear it. She was in her fifties – a grandma. It was years since she had worn anything beautiful. Something that made her happy. But, she reasoned, she would need a swimsuit and so would Danny.

'Shall I?' Angie caressed the soft fabric.

Danny nodded enthusiastically. 'Ye-es! It is pretty.'

A liver-spotted hand shot out and grabbed the other end of the swimsuit. Angie kept her grip as a woman who must have been in her eighties tried to snatch it from her. Angie glared at this octogenarian with her grey hair tied with red ribbon in a high ponytail.

'Here, Peggy-Sue, I've got something special for you, gal.'

The old girl released her hold on the swimsuit. 'What'll that be then?'

While the stall holder diverted Peggy-Sue's attention with a red glitter waistcoat, Angie took in the woman's outfit of white ankle socks – bobby socks – and a rock and roll flared skirt. If the old lady could pull it off, maybe Angie could wear the gorgeous swimsuit.

When Angie handed over fifteen pounds, the stall holder winked at her. 'You'll look cracking in that.'

Glowing with embarrassment and pride, Angie yanked the trolley across the turf. 'Over there,' Danny cried, pointing to a bouncy castle.

'First, let's buy the stuff that we need for the chalet, then you can play.'

Danny tumbled in the trolley as its wheels caught in the turf. It was perfect for ferrying everything home but not such a good idea to use on the uneven ground, churned up by cars and the traffic of people. Angie clenched her teeth and pushed, using all of her weight. The trolley broke free and they flew headlong into a man with a shaven head and a face full of piercings.

'Where'dya get that?' He stabbed an accusatory finger at her.

Surely, he wasn't after the ruddy swimsuit too.

'The trolley. It looks like the one that was nicked from my front yard yesterday.'

Angie felt her face flame. Caught red-handed. How was she to know it wasn't junk? 'They all look the same to me,' she blustered. The man was a little intimidating, the way he was squaring up to her.

'Oi, Mental Mickey, leave the lady alone.'

Her saviours were a couple in their sixties. They were riding mobility scooters that looked like Harley Davidsons the way that they had adapted the seats and raised the handlebars. The pair were dressed up in bikers' gear, a man and a woman, both wearing bandanas and covered in tattoos. Mental Mickey muttered something and after giving Angie a long look, skulked off.

'Thank you.' The McDonald's toys rattled in their tin, as Angie's hands shook on the trolley.

'Don't mind Mental Mickey. He'll have forgotten by tomorrow. Memory like a goldfish.'

'He wouldn't mess with Brewer,' the woman said. 'Brewer was the leader of the Harley Hell Raisers, before his hip gave him gyp.'

'Can't get me leg over now,' Brewer laughed. 'And the old lady's not much better.'

'It's me knees,' the woman said. 'Delila. Nice to meet you.'

Angie wasn't sure what was expected of her and so she shook hands.

With Brewer and Delila as escorts, Angie made her way to a stall of brick-a-brac in search of a sewing machine and other essentials. Danny rode shotgun with Delila, grinning at Angie – pleased as punch. There was an old sewing machine similar to the model that Angie had used at school but the mechanism was stuck. Brewer bargained and finally shook hands on a fiver.

'It's a heap of junk, he should've paid you to take it away,' Brewer said.

'I can fix it,' Angie said, already looking forward to the challenge.

When they got back to the chalet, Angie lifted Danny down from the supermarket trolley, which was full to the brim with their purchases, and they delighted over each item as they laid them out in the garden.

'I'll run you up some shorts and a shirt from that *Toy Story* curtain and I reckon I could make a little Gruffalo suit from that onesie.'

Bang. 'What the hell was that?' Angie spun around to see a bald, skinny man in a baggy suit and slippers brandishing a pistol. Her next-door neighbour.

Was he crazy? Ruddy Nora. First the thug at the market and now this lunatic. She'd had enough. But before Angie could give him a piece of her mind he disappeared into his outside kharsie. It gave her the opportunity to bundle Danny inside.

'Stay here and don't move until I tell you.'

Angie stormed out, her heart pounding, but it was anger more than fear. He could have shot Danny. This guy was going to be sorry he messed with her.

'What the hell do you think you're doing?'

Baldy reappeared and aimed his pistol at Angie. 'You're trespassing on private property.'

'And *you* are illegally using firearms. This is my family's place – my rightful home. *You* are trespassing on *my* land.'

The man lowered his gun. Before he could take it up again, Angie snatched it from him.

'Are you crazy or something? My grandson's in there. You could've killed him.'

The man shook his head. 'I'm sorry, ma'am, I've been keeping an eye on the place for Jeffers's boy. He didn't tell me that his folks were going to use it. Name's Higgins. I live next door.' He jerked his head to the right. 'You'll need to do a bit of work to make this place habitable – but it's not in too bad a state.'

Now he wanted to pass the time of day. Angie crossed her arms and shook her head in disbelief.

'I'll leave you to it then.' He shuffled off, stopping at his back door to check Angie wasn't watching, before retrieving his pistol from where she had propped it on a dustbin. It looked like a cheap replica or kid's air pistol.

She gave him the finger from behind her door. 'Lunatic.'

'It's alright, Danny, you can come out now.' But Danny stayed in the bedroom.

He was huddled in a corner facing the wall. His arms tightly wrapped around his knees, his head bent.

'Oh, Danny love, I didn't mean you to sit there like that. Come here to Namma.' She fell to her knees. The poor little mite. What did he think she was going to do to him? Was this how he had been punished in the past?

When Danny didn't move, Angie crept over to him and stroked his boney little back. 'I'm sorry, darling, I didn't mean to frighten you. I just wanted to keep you safe. Here, come and sit in my lap.'

Danny turned into her and buried his face in her chest. His little body trembled. 'Hush, darling. Namma would never hurt you. You're safe with me, I promise.'

14

They must have fallen asleep soon after sunrise, because Nikoleta awoke fully clothed with Kamil beside her. His fingers were curled around his mobile. Murmured conversations throughout the night, Kamil talking on the phone in Polish, Russian, and English depending on need, relaying information to Nikoleta: 'There was some footage of Danek on CCTV.' Then later, 'He was holding a woman's hand.' Later still, 'The woman has a ponytail' – Nikoleta. It was going to be a long process checking the CCTV cameras.

Nikoleta still thought that they should go to the police and told Kamil. 'It is taking too long, Kamil. The police know what they're doing. They would have found Danek by now. I'll explain that it's my fault. The court in Poland and your ex-wife may not even get to hear about this. Surely, it's better that Danek is safe, even if you have to go back to court.'

Kamil seemed to mull this over. At least he didn't dismiss the idea as Nikoleta had feared when she carefully chose her words and her moment. Then, his phone rang with another sighting, and Nikoleta knew that the moment had passed, and that Kamil would not go to the police.

Nikoleta slid away from Kamil, without disturbing him. She stretched to loosen her back and neck, before checking her phone. Her tweet had been retweeted two hundred and forty times.

'What is it? Have you got news?' Kamil sprang into action.

Maybe she should tell Kamil about her tweet. It wasn't good to keep secrets from one another. 'Do you think we should use social media to help us find Danek?' she asked.

'And tell the world that we are irresponsible parents who can't care for their child?'

Nikoleta shook her head. Not a good idea to tell Kamil. But he had said 'we are irresponsible parents.' He hadn't given up on her altogether.

If she had not made such a monumental mess of things, they might have had a chance at being a real family. Nikoleta was determined to put things right. She had lost Danek and so she would find him. When Nikoleta returned Kamil's beloved son to him he would see that she could be responsible, capable, and a good mother to Danek.

Kamil checked his pockets and put his passport on the table. 'Can you give me Danek's passport? I'll keep it safe, locked in my attaché case.'

Nikoleta rifled through her handbag; it was in there somewhere. For a few seconds, she thought that she had lost that too and she went into a cold sweat. 'Here it is!'

Kamil frowned. 'Maybe you should let me look after your passport too?'

He had a point. Kamil was much more organised than her and their passports would be safe locked in his work case; he never went anywhere without it.

'I have to go to Liverpool Street. I should have gone last night.' Kamil tucked their passports away in his case.

'I'll come with you.'

'No, stay here, *slonka*.'

Nikoleta didn't want to be left alone again. She felt useless sitting in their tiny apartment doing nothing. 'You haven't had anything to eat or drink since you got back from Paris. Why don't you at least have a shower and I'll go out and buy you something for breakfast – a coffee and something to eat?'

'I can't eat or drink. Not while my baby boy is missing.'

That stab of guilt again. Kamil's face when he thought she was knocking back vodka with their landlady hours after losing his son. 'What can I do, Kamil?'

Kamil shrugged his shoulders. Nikoleta hated herself for causing so much pain.

'Get some rest, *slonka*. I'll let you know as soon as I have any news.'

'Maybe I could talk to the guard who made the announcement. Someone must have seen me at the statue. If I'm there, I may jog someone's memory. Please, Kamil, let me help.'

But Kamil would not agree to Nikoleta joining him and so alone in the flat she checked her phone again. Two hundred and eighty retweets. There was a text from her sister, Angelika, wanting news of the big city. The need for comfort, her dad's voice, and her mum's optimism prompted Nikoleta to phone home. Maybe she should tell them what had happened. Her dad always knew what to do.

Although the mobile phone belonged to Angelika, it was kept in their farmhouse kitchen on the mantel. Nikoleta and Angelika had tried to explain that the point of a mobile phone was in the name. But the only time Angelika was allowed to carry it with her was when she went out in the evening and needed to phone Dad for a lift home. So Nikoleta was not surprised when her dad answered. It was so good to hear his voice.

'Dad, it's me, Nikoleta.' A lump in her throat. A throb in her temple. Don't cry.

He didn't answer immediately. Nikoleta could imagine him gripping the phone unsure whether to speak and break his silence or hand the phone to her mum.

'You got there alright.' Nikoleta could breathe again.

'You didn't say goodbye.' Why did she have to say that? It sounded like a recrimination when she meant that she was sad and needed his blessing.

'I was busy getting the tractor ready for harvest. I'll get your mother.'

It was a start, they were speaking but Nikoleta wanted more. 'Dad? I'll miss you.'

'Just take care of yourself.' After a pause he said, 'Remember what I told you? Always keep hold of your passport and make sure you have enough money for your fare home.' It was something. Not his blessing, he wouldn't accept Kamil, but at least he was talking to her.

When Nikoleta left the farm, her dad had been working on his old tractor and would not look up. No hug or kiss. It still hurt, as they had always been close. One of her earliest memories was of Dad rescuing her. She was playing and had wandered deep into a field of tall, spikey grass – rye, she was told. At first it had been fun, slithering on her belly, hidden from view. But when she tired of the game, Nikoleta couldn't see over the grass to find a way out. Nobody would know where to find her.

'So that is where my little kitten is hiding.' Dad reached down and hiked her onto his shoulders and the world looked different. The towering grasses that had scratched and poked were whiskers beneath her dad's boots. And Dad looked different from up there too. She was used to his big hands, which were rough against her skin, and his arms brown from the sun that could lift a pregnant ewe and heavy machine things in the barn. But up there she saw a pink scalp beneath his blond hair, sprinkled with freckles. It made her feel funny. Like she wanted to protect him, and that was silly, because he was much stronger and braver than she could ever be.

Dad didn't care about accountancy exams and new opportunities in London. Nikoleta had a perfectly good job working with her uncle in the cooperative of family farms. She had balanced the books for years, before she met Kamil and started working for him.

The trouble was, Dad listened to village gossip and there had always been rumours about Kamil. An international entrepreneur was a rarity in Toresnica, and Kamil, something of a legend. Of course villagers talked about how Kamil made his money. It was the old wariness of anyone who did well for themselves, a throwback to the communist days.

Dad and the farm, because Dad *was* the farm, had always been the centre of Nikoleta's world – the place where she felt safe and loved. But the world was changing – had changed. Dad's ideas were outdated. She really hoped that she would bring him around to her way of thinking, but Dad was stubborn and with him being so far away, Nikoleta was beginning to wonder whether they would ever mend the rift between them. She daren't tell him that Kamil bought her a one-way ticket to England.

15

The Seashell was doing a good trade when Angie popped in the next day to see if Zoe had got the valves for her car.

'Park your bum over there,' Josie said. 'I like your matching Toy Story outfits.'

'I ran them up last night. It's easy to make a sundress and there was plenty of material left over, even after making two sets of shorts and shirts for Danny boy.' She had worked until the early hours of the morning, using the sewing machine which she had repaired and then raised on a few bricks from the garden. It wasn't an ideal arrangement, but it would have to suffice until she could find a second-hand table.

Angie hadn't intended to stop for lunch; they couldn't afford to keep eating out. Before she could explain this to Josie, the waitress served her a salad with jacket potato and tuna.

'I didn't order this.' Angie eyed the green stuff suspiciously. She didn't do salad.

Too late – fish fingers, peas, and mashed potato were put in front of Danny. His eyes shone. 'What are these?'

'Fish fingers. Do you like them?' Angie said.

'Fishies' fingers?' Danny frowned. 'But fishies don't have fingers.'

'That's what you know. How do you think they tie their shoelaces?'

Danny giggled. 'Fishies don't wear shoes, Namma.'

'Really? Not even wellies?'

'What are wellies?'

Josie passed with a tray of sodas. 'It's on me, love.'

Danny gobbled up his fishies' fingers and declared that he loved them and that was all he wanted to eat from then on. Between mouthfuls they debated whether or not fishies needed fingers or indeed toes and whether Angie had really seen a fish wearing wellies as she claimed she once had.

Half an hour later, when the café had almost emptied, Josie took a break. 'Zoe reckons she'll have the valves this afternoon if you can stick around that long.'

'Me and Danny are going to stop in our old chalet for the summer.'

'Nobody's lived there since your brother moved out about eight years ago. It'll need a bit of work.'

Angie had forgotten Lorraine had a brother – Frank. He was older than them and too important to bother himself with his teenybopper sister and her friend. With a bit of luck, she and Danny would be long gone by the time he or Lorraine dropped by to check on the place.

'An old man next door fired a gun at us yesterday,' Angie ventured, as Josie cleared their plates.

'That'll be Old Man Higgins. You'd think he was hiding the Crown Jewels the way that he guards his place. We can't get his gun off him. Bill took away the bullets but he managed to find more. Social services won't go near his place – health and safety – but reckon that's the way Higgins likes it. When you leave, I'll wrap up some sandwiches for you to take to him. I try and keep an eye on the old boy.'

That wasn't the response that Angie had expected, but Jaywick folk constantly surprised her. If Josie trusted Higgins then so would she. They left the Seashell with a promise to visit later that day when Angie would repair Zoe's car. Before going home, Angie returned the shopping trolley to where she had found it and would have made a clean getaway, if a dog hadn't started barking from inside the house. A woman, about Angie's age, came out of the front door, struggling to keep hold of a pit bull terrier. Ruddy Nora, what now? Angie swiped Danny up; she'd read about vicious dogs mauling kids.

'What do you want?' the woman shouted.

'I was just returning the trolley,' Angie said, as she backed away.

'So that's where it went. Mickey lend it to you?' The woman pushed the pit bull back inside and pulled the door to, leaving it ajar.

'He said you needed it back.' Angie was relieved the dog was inside but his owner was a little scary.

'Too right. I need more supplies. Where is that boy? He's meant to be helping me this morning. We get busy in the summer.' She nodded at a handwritten sign in the window of the front room. *Ham and chips, sausage and chips, beans and chips, egg and chips – all one pound.* 'Still, decent of you to give it back. I've not seen you around.' The woman narrowed her eyes as she flicked fag ash at Angie's feet.

'Lorraine Jeffers. My family have had a chalet in Jaywick for years. We're staying for the summer, me and Danny.'

The woman's face softened. 'You should've said. I'm Sal.

Everyone knows Sal, Mickey's mum. Here, I'll get a little something for your boy.'

Sal was indoors when Mental Mickey stomped up the street. He clocked Angie straight away and from the scowl on his face recognised her as the trolley thief.

'Hey, what do you think you're doing? Come to fill *my* trolley with more booty from our yard? What do you think this is a fucking superstore?'

Angie pulled Danny close to her, covering his ears. The dog was going crazy inside; he must have heard his master. The door flew open, the dog jumped up at Mickey, and Sal brandished a frying basket. 'Michael O'Donoghue, apologise to Lorraine this instant and then get inside and start frying.'

Mental Mickey hung his head. 'I'm sorry, Lorraine, I didn't know you were Mum's mate.' Then he led the dog inside, stooping to kiss his mum on the forehead as he passed.

Sal handed Danny a Rich Tea biscuit. 'I'm sorry, he shouldn't have talked to you like that. He's a good boy, my Mickey, when you get to know him.'

Angie and Danny ambled back to their chalet. It was a beautiful day and Angie felt glad to be alive. In the past couple of days, she had almost forgotten about the cancer. Maybe there was nothing seriously wrong with her and the scare was just a wake-up call. It felt as though she had been given another chance, that the past forty years could be wiped out and she could start afresh.

'Don't tread on the cracks,' Angie said as she demonstrated how to step over the cracks in the pavement. If they got all of the way home without treading on a crack, Danny would stay with her in Jaywick. Nobody would find him. Danny didn't mind, he was having the time of his life and she was good at this, being a mum. 'That's it, hop like Licky. A hop, skip, and a jump.' Danny giggled and bounced alongside her.

'When we get back I'll get a chalky stone and show you how to play hopscotch.' They darted back and forth across the pavement avoiding cracks.

'We did it!' Angie hadn't stepped on a single crack – she was going to keep Danny. She would be his mum and his grandma. There was so much they could do together. She would teach Danny how to swim and read and write.

Angie was on her hands and knees marking out the squares for hopscotch when a woman with dark skin and black freckles passed by with a pushchair and a golden retriever. The pushchair was full of groceries and two boys, the same ones Danny had been fascinated by at the boot sale, ran alongside trying to keep up. The woman steered the pushchair into the road, ignoring Angie and Danny, but the boys hung back. 'What are you doing?' the older one asked.

'Playing hoppity socks,' Danny said.

Angie hoped that they might join in, but their mum didn't stop and so the boys chased after her.

Danny was quick to learn the rules, although they made them up a bit as they went along. It was Angie's go. She had completed the circuit and jumped round one foot on four the other on five to see Peggy-Sue hopping towards her. 'Two, three – mind out!'

Angie leapt to one side as Peggy-Sue passed by. Then she balanced on one leg and reached down to scoop up Angie's pebble.

'Your go,' she said.

'Okay.' Angie found another stone. It seemed that she was to play hopscotch with Peggy-Sue whilst Danny decorated the pavement with his chalk. She felt a bit silly when Higgins came out and sat on the wall to watch them.

'I've got something for you from Josie,' she said, glad of the opportunity to sit down. Her pelvis was beginning to ache and Peggy-Sue cheated.

Higgins munched his sandwich and Peggy-Sue took her leave. Angie tipped her face to the sun, not quite believing her fortune. Jaywick was a perfect fit for Angie, as though her shape had been cut from its cloth and she was now slotting back into a place that had been waiting for her. She belonged here.

Of course, it was Lorraine Jeffers who had been welcomed back into Jaywick – not Angie Winkle. Nobody knew what Angie Winkle had done. She had been given another chance, a new life as Danny's namma. This is what her life might have been like if she hadn't messed up big time. What if she didn't have cancer? What if nobody came looking for Danny? They could live here for years. Nobody would know that she wasn't his grandma.

16

'It's been three days, Kamil. I really think we should go to the police.' Nikoleta was irritable and restless. Maybe she was pushing for a row, to break the oppressive atmosphere. It was becoming unbearable, cooped up in that one room with the stifling heat. Kamil was constantly on the phone or tapping away on his laptop. He barely slept and was so wired, Nikoleta had crept around him, minding her words until she felt like screaming.

Kamil cast his laptop to one side and faced Nikoleta. 'Are you completely nuts? First, my girlfriend loses my four-year-old son and then I don't report it for three days. How's that going to look? I might as well hand Danek back to his alcoholic mother and forget ever seeing him again. Is that what you want?' Spittle glistened on his chin.

For a fleeting moment, she didn't like this man with his sulky moods and temper and that surprised her. Nikoleta reined herself in. 'No, Kamil, I can see that would not be wise.' She resisted saying that; if Kamil had not stopped her from going to the police as soon as she had lost Danek, he might be with them now.

Kamil's shoulders slumped and he stepped back. 'I'm sorry, *slonka*. I know you are trying to help. It is all such a mess. I thought we would know where he was by now. Why is it taking so long?'

'Tell me if there is anything that I can do. Anything at all.'

'There is something that you can do, *slonka*. While I'm spending all of my time looking for Danek, we're losing money. It would help our cash flow if you could work.'

Nikoleta was surprised. Kamil was a successful entrepreneur. Surely he could access enough funds to see them over the next few days. She screwed up her face. 'I would rather be doing something constructive to find Danek. It will take me a bit of time to find suitable work and by then Danek should be home.'

Kamil's face tightened, making a nerve on his temple twitch. She had never noticed that before. At work, Kamil was always calm and composed. But, she was seeing a different Kamil in London. Not surprising. She had lost his son. Mother of Jesus, of course the poor man was beside himself with grief.

'What did you have in mind?' Nikoleta said.

Kamil's face opened up; his brow cleared. 'Lenka has asked around and found you a little job in a grocery store. She had a word with Tavit, the owner, and he has kindly agreed to take you on. The money's not good but it will help to pay our rent. Lenka is an old friend but I don't want to take advantage of her generosity.'

How could she work at a time like this? It was irritating that Kamil had asked Lenka to find her a job, as though she were a schoolgirl. But, it would be good to get out of the flat. They were spending too much time together and a bit of money would give her some financial independence.

'Okay,' she said.

Nikoleta's first shift at the European Foods Emporium was two and a half hours. 'Just a trial run,' Tavit explained, 'while it is quiet. I won't be able to pay you as this is your training.'

Training consisted of telling Nikoleta that she was responsible for keeping her one pink nylon overall clean as the Emporium did not provide a laundry service. Only Tavit or his wife were to serve customers and operate the till. Nikoleta and Ana-Maria were required to keep the shelves stocked, the store room and shop clean, and unload deliveries. Nikoleta's first shift was very quiet.

Tavit was Armenian. They had three shops, he explained to Nikoleta. Another example of the opportunity in this country, if only she could get used to feeling like an outsider. Tavit was amiable enough. He would bark instructions and then laugh, revealing a broken tooth that made him look roguish. His wife, Liza, had a curvaceous figure and wore a tight skirt and close-fitting top, a little inappropriate for her age and size, but the way Tavit's eyes devoured his wife, Nikoleta could tell that there was still romance between these oldies. She couldn't imagine herself and Kamil at their age.

Ana had lived in England for eight years. A Romanian, she had found the job through her husband, an old friend of Tavit. It seemed that that was how things worked in England, Eastern Europeans helping one another out. Ana reassured Nikoleta that things would get easier.

There were very few customers and so when Tavit successfully sold a box of herbal tea he called enthusiastically for the girls to put out more. 'Come, come, there is more room here in front of these cans.' The cans that Tavit referred to were on the floor, snaking a line below the bottom shelf.

Ana and Nikoleta added a row of jars containing assorted condiments. A few of the labels were in Polish. Others in Russian, a few Swedish or Danish, she couldn't tell, Arabic, Chinese.

'More, more,' Tavit shouted from the till. 'There's plenty of room in the aisles.'

Ana pulled a face at Nikoleta. Customers would have difficulty picking their way along the aisle between the confectionary on one side: packaged cakes and biscuits including, bright orange and yellow buns with a sprinkling of sugar – Japanese? And tins of fish, octopus, fish roe, and other unidentifiable specimens on the other. The shift flew by. Nikoleta enjoyed working with Ana. She had made Nikoleta laugh when her heart was so heavy she had wondered if she would ever be happy again.

So, it was with a lighter step that Nikoleta turned into Lenham Avenue. As she approached 137, Nikoleta checked her phone. There was a reply to her tweet. Someone had seen Danek. Her heart raced. They had found him! Nikoleta couldn't type quickly enough. She needed more information. Where had they seen Danek? Who was he with? A tweet came back saying that they would send a photograph, so that Nikoleta could confirm it was the missing boy.

ngie was woken by a clanking and a clanging. For a moment she thought it was the Elsan man renewing the chemical toilets, but he would have to have been a ghost. According to Josie, the Elsan man hadn't purred along the avenue in his cart for many a year.

Whack. Something bounced off the outside wall.

Angie wriggled out of her mermaid sleeping bag; she had sewn the end into a tail and added some lurex. Danny was asleep on the floor beside her.

Crash. This time Danny stirred.

'Namma?' He squirmed in his customised dragon tail sleeping bag, disappeared, then reappeared squeezing Licky.

'S'okay, Nanna's up. What's going on, eh, Danny?'

They still had boarding over the front windows and so she hurriedly pulled the sleeping bag around her middle to look out of the front door. 'Stay in bed, Danny. Look after Licky while Nanna has a peek outside.

'Ruddy Nora!' Their front yard was full of junk. Had the whole town been using it as a fly tip? Discarded mattresses, a broken chair, an old sofa, a table. It must have been that Mental Mickey.

Angie's hands were on her hips as she searched for a guilty culprit. More than one person was responsible. Then she spied her neighbour, the one with the two boys, crossing the street and for once she didn't seem in a hurry.

'They've done good.' She nodded at the pile. 'Folks round here will give you the shirt off their back, if you're deserving, and I reckon you are.'

Angie didn't know what to say. She knew she was gaping, but she was still trying to make sense of what had happened and why.

'Molly Andrews.' The woman had a broad face sprinkled with big black freckles and a gap between her front teeth. She grinned. 'We live over there.'

'Why?' Angie asked. Why had her neighbours dumped furniture in her front yard? Why was she deserving? Why was Molly Andrews finally talking to her? So many questions, but all she could stutter was *Why?*

'Josie said how you could do with a helping hand fixing your place up. Seeing as how you've been keeping an eye on Old Man Higgins and sorted Zoe's car, well, you're one of us. I've left my kids on their own, so I'd best get back. I'll come by in a bit and help you get this lot inside. There's some good stuff.'

Bemused and a bit overwhelmed, Angie managed to nod. She had been ignored most of her life and wasn't used to strangers being friendly. So, her neighbours had found things they could spare, to help furnish her chalet. It wasn't rubbish – these were treasures. And Molly was right, with a bit of DIY she could fix them up. When she reached her chalet, Molly turned back to wave. And if she thought it odd that Angie had a green lurex mermaid's tail, she didn't show it. That's what Angie loved about living in Jaywick.

Furnishing the Jeffers's place had turned into a morning activity for most of Angie's neighbours. As they congregated in her front yard sorting through the 'gifts' and exchanging gossip, it reminded her of the old days in Jaywick.

Sitting on a dining chair that someone had retrieved from the pile, Old Man Higgins called out instructions. 'Shift that mattress over there and you'll see a table lamp. I might have a plug inside that'll do that.'

A couple of strong lads, Darren and Liam, hauled the heaviest furniture into the chalet. 'Where do you want this, Lorraine?'

When Angie didn't reply, they let the sofa drop so that they could take a breath. 'The sofa, Lorraine, where do you want it?'

Of course, they were talking to her. Angie gave the boys instructions, berating herself for being slow to respond. If she wasn't careful she would give herself away.

Between renewing mugs with tea and coffee, deciding where things should go, and keeping an eye on Danny and the Andrews boys, Angie was kept busy. Molly's two youngest, Dexter and Alfie, ran in through the front door, out into the backyard, round the side, then back in the front. Pickles the dog chased after them, followed by Danny, who was trying to catch his tail. Molly had three girls who were at school. They lived in a chalet the same size as Angie's – six of them and a dog.

'Behave,' Molly shouted, as the boys completed their third or fourth circuit. 'It'll all end in tears.'

Angie laughed. She was glad to see Danny playing with

other kids. 'Here, come and have a cold drink, boys.' Angie was pouring measures of orange squash when Josie's husband, Bill, poked his head around the door.

'A cold drink for the boys, eh? Got us a beer, Lorraine love?'

Angie was surprised to see Bill. She peered past him. 'Is Josie with you?'

'No, just Si. Josie asked us to drop in a gas canister for your cooker.'

Angie peeked around Bill to see a skinny man with lank hair. Was this the legendary Slippery Si, the one who sold Bill a dodgy TV? He certainly looked slippery. But *a gas canister* – she would be able to prepare proper meals for Danny. 'Wow, that really does deserve a beer, but I'll have to go and buy some – only squash and coffee here.'

'Want us to go?' Liam appeared from nowhere.

The word 'beer' seemed to bring everything to a stop. It was about time they all had a break – Angie included.

She unrolled her sleeping bag and dug around to find the envelope of money stashed in a corner. It wasn't much, just a hundred quid from her post office account to tide them over. When she glanced up, Slippery Si was watching her from the bedroom door. Angie hadn't heard it open.

'So, you're Frankie's little sister, Lorraine?' There was an edge to his voice that Angie didn't like.

She clambered up and faced him, feet firmly planted. 'Yes, Lorraine.'

Her eyes said, *Want to make something of it?* But she held her tongue. She couldn't afford to piss anyone off around here. Upset one and you upset them all, by the sound of things, and she'd had a close shave with Mental Mickey.

He smirked and then gave a knowing nod, before slinking away. Angie didn't know why he was nicknamed Slippery, but there was something distasteful about him. Skinny and unshaven with greasy, long black hair. It wasn't just his physical appearance, Slippery reminded her of a water rat. A man to be avoided. She just hoped he didn't know Lorraine – they could hardly be mistaken for one another. Even after all this time they would look very different. Lorraine was petite with small bones and straight hair, the opposite of Angie in every way.

'Ouch.' Angie doubled over in pain. It had been a couple of weeks since she felt it that bad. A deep searing pain, somewhere between her lower back and pelvis. Bloody cancer. 'Ow,' Angie cried again.

'What's wrong, love?' Molly's anxious face peered round the bedroom door. Seeing Angie doubled up in pain, she rushed to her side. 'Here, let's lower you onto the mattress.'

Angie gave in to Molly's ministrations; she was in no position to do anything else. It was easing. In a moment the pain would subside.

'Shut the door,' Angie whispered through clenched teeth. 'I don't want anyone to see me like this. I'll be alright, just give me a minute.'

Molly clasped her hand. 'Alright, love, if you're sure. Shouldn't you see a doctor?'

Angie shook her head. That was the last thing she wanted; her cover would be blown straight away. If Slippery knew she wasn't Lorraine, they had only a few more days of pretense. She had to hang on until then. The pain was already easing up a bit.

'Here, give Darren this. Tell him to go and buy some beers.' Angie still had the twenty-pound note in her fist.

Molly waited, unsure whether or not to leave Angie alone.

'Really, I'll be alright. Just give me a few minutes and I'll be out.'

. . .

There was quite a party going on in Angie's front yard. Now that most of the furniture was inside, Molly, Zoe, and Angie sat on the grass and the men gathered around Higgins, including him in their banter. It was too hot to work anyway. They all wanted to hear about Angie's son and her Polish daughter-in-law. Angie didn't want to lie more than she had to but found herself telling them that her son was a successful engineer and her daughter-in-law was a nurse. 'Of course, having such busy working lives they rely on me to look after Danny in the school holidays when his nursery closes.'

Danny crawled into Angie's lap and she stroked his hair. 'I like it best when Namma looks after me,' he said.

'Don't you miss your mum and dad?' Dexter, the eldest of Molly's boys, said.

'Namma is my mummy,' Danny whispered.

Dexter laughed. 'No she's not!'

Danny joined in with his laughter and the three boys tumbled together like bear cubs.

But, Angie was curious. She had tried to get Danny to talk about his home life but he would go quiet and become clingy. Something wasn't right there.

'I have to get going; the girls will be back from school soon. Dexter should've been in school but the monkey said he had a tummy ache.' Molly rolled her eyes. 'Wouldn't believe it the way he's been tearing around all morning.'

Angie took Molly's hand to pull herself up. 'It was good for Danny having your boys to play with. If you want to leave Dexter and Alfie with me, I'll take them all to the beach.'

Dexter whooped. 'The beach? Great. Can we go, Mum? I want to show Danny my bodyboard.'

'Only if Lorraine feels up to it.' She threw a questioning look at Angie, who nodded, anxious to change the subject.

'I'll take Pickles too. Let him have a run, if you like?'

Higgins had been helped back inside. Darren and Liam said goodbye.

'We'd better be going too, before Josie sends out a posse to find me.' Bill aimed an empty can at an open rubbish sack.

'I can't thank you enough. *All of you.* Our place looks quite homely now and I'm so excited that I can use the cooker. Bill, I must pay you for the gas.'

'Don't you worry. There'll be a time when you help us. That's how things work.'

As Bill and Slippery Si walked to the van, Slippery looked back over his shoulder, 'Goodbye, *Lorraine.* I'll tell Frankie I saw you. Reckon he'll be surprised, don't you?'

18

The sighting of Danek turned out to be false. The photograph tweeted back was of a boy older than Danek, who bore no resemblance to the angelic four-year-old. Although Nikoleta was disappointed, it had given her the confidence to take things into her own hands. Kamil alternated between mooching around their flat, as though he had flies up his nose – her mum's favourite expression – or would disappear to goodness knows where, apparently on another mission to find Danek.

Things were still strained between them. Kamil's USP – unique selling point – was that he could get anything for anyone. He boasted to Nikoleta that when he was in his twenties, he supplied alcohol, rock music CDs, and even a few iPods to local kids, a scarcity in the mid 1990s as the country adjusted post communism. But, his reputation for making things happen was failing as far as Danek was concerned. Nikoleta would find him. In fact, she already had a plan.

Ana and Nikoleta were taking their break together. The shop was never busy and with Tavit and Liza out front a lot of the time, there wasn't really any need for help, but the girls were not complaining, they needed the work.

'Do you want some of these Hungarian pot noodles? I don't know what's in them but they don't seem too old.' Ana was pouring boiling water over said noodles.

'Okay.' Nikoleta wanted a bit of uninterrupted time to talk to Ana. They had worked together for only a short time but they had shared information about their families, life before London, and for Ana, her life since emigrating. Ana had two girls aged five and seven. Her husband worked shifts and so they managed the child care between them.

Nikoleta sipped from her mug of noodles, stealing the courage to tell Ana what happened when she first arrived in London. It was too hot, but it smelt – interesting. She put the mug down. 'Ana, I want to tell you something but first, promise me you'll keep it a secret.'

Ana nodded, her eyes wide. 'Go on.'

Nikoleta told Ana everything. Even the false sighting on Twitter. Ana didn't look shocked when Nikoleta told her about being separated from Danek. But, she pulled a face when Nikoleta told her Kamil's instructions to go straight to 137 and not talk to the police. Nikoleta explained about the custody battle but Ana didn't seem convinced.

She tilted her head and frowned. 'Is that the only reason he doesn't want to involve the police?'

Something in Nikoleta stirred. A flicker of uncertainty. The nagging worry that Kamil's explanation did not justify his refusal to involve the police. But, Kamil knew best. He couldn't risk losing custody after all that he had been through. Irritated by the uncertainty that Ana's question aroused, Nikoleta said, 'Why else would he keep Danek's disappearance a secret?'

Ana shrugged. 'I don't know. Maybe I've seen too much,

since moving here. It makes me suspicious of people. I'm sure you're right.'

It wasn't fair, the way everyone wanted to judge Kamil. Ana hadn't even met him. But Nikoleta couldn't brood; she needed Ana's assistance. 'I'm telling you all of this, Ana, because I have a favour to ask.'

Tavit shouted from the front of the shop, 'Ana-Maria, Nikoleta, customers!'

'He means you've had a long enough break,' Ana laughed. 'Of course I'll help you. Tell me later.'

19

Angie and Danny worked together wrapping cutlery sets in paper napkins. Danny concentrated hard, glancing at Angie every few seconds to check he was doing it right.

School holidays started next week, but already Jaywick's population had doubled. The caravan parks always did a good trade with East Enders visiting for the summer. Zoe and the part-timer had worked every day that week and even the Saturday girl was working evenings after school. Josie had finished taking food orders for the day and a few customers lingered over empty mugs. The warm weather slowed everyone down like drowsy bees.

Josie slumped into the seat opposite Angie and Danny. 'Well done, that should keep us going for a few hours.'

'I am going to the beach with Liam and Dexter,' Danny said, puffing out his little chest.

Angie was thrilled that Molly's boys were making a fuss of Danny. The day before Angie had taken all three boys to the beach and this morning she walked Molly's dog, Pickles.

Josie smiled. 'It's hard to believe you've only been back in Jaywick a few days.'

Angie grinned. Being part of this wonderful community was like being swaddled in a blanket. All of these new friends, people who cared about her and *needed* her. Molly and her kids, Old Man Higgins, even Josie. They must never know her true identity. If Josie found out Angie had lied to her, she would never forgive her.

Angie gave an awkward smile. 'I know it was only because you put in a good word for me that everyone helped us out.'

'Is that so?' Josie clicked her tongue. 'Folks round here help each other, once they get to know you, that is. I might've had a word here and there. We're a suspicious lot. Don't take to outsiders. But, with you being a Jeffers.'

Josie's words hung in the air as Slippery Si came in. Bill followed mid-conversation, but Angie had all of his attention. He narrowed his eyes and she felt herself pinned like a beetle in a display case. Angie ducked her head to fiddle with the cutlery tray.

'Just goin' for a quick pint with Si.' Bill pecked the top of Josie's head.

Angie felt sick. Slippery knew she wasn't Lorraine. How long before he spilt the beans? They would all hate her. A stabbing pain near her pelvis. *Not now, not now.*

Angie rocked back and forth. Sod that bloody cancer. It wasn't fair.

'You can stop folding, there's more than enough.' Josie covered Angie's hand. She'd rolled another cutlery set. 'Can you take some leftovers back to Old Man Higgins and Molly?' Josie heaved herself up.

Angie took a deep breath; the pain was ebbing away. She forced a smile. 'Of course, although I know as well as you that they aren't leftovers. Admit it, Josie, you've a heart of gold.'

Bill slipped back in. 'That's my woman – heart of gold. Si's van won't start so we're taking my car, love. Just getting my keys.'

She had to confront Slippery now, see what he knew. It was better than waiting for him to pounce. 'Josie, could you keep an eye on Danny for five minutes? I'll have a look at Si's van.'

Danny tried to clamber out after Angie. 'I go with you, Namma.'

'Oh dear, then who's going to help me in here?' Josie sighed.

Danny frowned. 'I am sorry, Namma, I have to help Aunty Josie.'

Slippery turned the engine of his Transit. It barely spluttered. Angie knew his type; other people's dirty secrets were just another commodity he could trade. How did he know Frank Jeffers? Surely, he wasn't a friend of Frank's? From what she remembered, Frank had been a decent sort of bloke, but so was Bill and he seemed taken in by the snake. 'Slippery' suited him well.

He saw Angie watching him and climbed down. 'Ah, Frankie's sister, Lorraine. How was Australia?'

Angie's face flamed. 'Fine. I didn't know you were still in touch with my brother.' Her heart thudded.

Slippery regarded her. They both knew she was lying but Angie wasn't going to make it easy for him. If Slippery hadn't seen Lorraine or Frankie for years, he might be persuaded that Lorraine had put on weight and dyed her hair.

He stepped closer to Angie. His breath smelt like an ashtray, his clothes of stale beer. 'It's been a while but I was thinking it was about time I visited my old mate Frankie. Tell him I've been catching up with his sister.'

Sweat pooled in her armpits and trickled down her spine. 'I'll mention it to him when we next speak.' She didn't know how she had kept her voice even.

His lip twitched before settling into a sneer that revealed a gold cap on his incisor. 'S'alright. I'll surprise him.'

Angie stepped away from Slippery as Bill approached. She hadn't fooled him. He would hotfoot it to Frankie and then it would all be over. It was time to give back this borrowed life. Angie Winkle didn't have friends. Angie Winkle was an outsider. *Weirdo Winkle.*

'Here, we'll go in mine. I'll jump-start you when we get back – must be your battery,' Bill said.

Slippery gave Angie a long and steady stare, before following Bill.

Angie loathed him but in a burst of foolish pride called out, 'Check your fuel injection pump.'

'Oh yes, Lorraine can help you. She got Zoe's car back on the road. Nice one, Lorraine.' Bill thumped Angie on the back.

'Another thing I didn't know about Frankie's sister,' Slippery muttered.

'Our dad worked at Ford's – you must remember that,' Angie replied. That much was true, both her and Lorraine's dads worked at Ford's. 'I'm not a mechanic – just picked up a thing or two. If you do change the fuel injection pump, make sure you clean out the fuel system too.'

When Slippery told Bill and Josie that she was an imposter, it would all come out. Lorraine's brother, Frankie, would throw her out of the chalet. And the worst thing was, Frankie knew what Angie Winkle had done all those years ago. Her shameful past would be exposed. How could she go back in there and make small talk with Josie, the kindest woman she knew?

20

A drowning person will grab at a straight razor, but Nikoleta had to do something. The mysterious woman who had kidnapped Danek haunted her dreams. The transport officials at Liverpool Street must be able to give them some useful information. Danek was small for his age, so the woman may have concealed him beneath a shawl. Kamil's men were taking too long; they must have missed something.

Nikoleta had told Kamil she was going to work before slipping out to meet Ana at Earl's Court Station. She knew that she had blushed and stumbled over her words. Hopefully, she wouldn't have to lie to Kamil again and this was just a white lie as her intentions were honourable. *A lie is a lie* – her mum's voice. Was London turning her into a bad person?

'You just want me to ask if we can speak to the guard who made the announcement so that we can thank him personally?' Ana said.

Nikoleta shrugged. What else could they do without giving

themselves away? 'Just so that we can get a description of the woman, maybe even a shot from the CCTV cameras.'

If only it were so easy. The station felt as chaotic today as the first time Nikoleta visited and she was glad to have cool, calm Ana at her side. Ana asked to speak to someone in charge without any hesitation in her voice, as though she were there on official business. Within a few minutes a big woman with hair extensions emerged from a back office and invited them to step inside. The office was cramped but a one-way mirror gave the impression that they were sitting on the concourse as travelers jostled by, oblivious to the observers just a few centimetres away. Ana explained the purpose of their meeting.

'Did you know the woman who found your son?' The officer's eyes narrowed and Nikoleta darted a look at Ana.

She took too long to reply. Nikoleta's palms itched. Kamil would go crazy if the police got involved now. 'It is my son,' Nikoleta said before Ana could respond. 'We just want to say thank you to the guard who made the announcement.'

'Was your son safely returned?' The officer looked at Nikoleta and then Ana, as though trying to read their faces. Ana was frowning. Nikoleta willed her own face to relax.

'Of course, all ended well,' Nikoleta stumbled over her words.

Thankfully, Ana remembered the script and added, 'He gave us all a scare but thanks to your excellent station guards and the kindness of a stranger there was a happy ending.'

The officer turned to a computer. 'If you give me the date and time I'll see if I can find the guard concerned.' Nikoleta's heart found its regular rhythm and she unclenched her fists.

'Unfortunately, he's not on duty today but if you come back on Friday after ten-thirty, I'll see what I can do.'

It was something. One step closer to finding Danek. Nikoleta thanked Ana; she was a good friend. 'I will persuade

Kamil to go to the police. I know that's the right thing to do, Ana.' Ana was a mother and Nikoleta could sense her disapproval but she hadn't let her down.

'Let's go and stand at the statue and ask passersby. Someone might have seen Danek,' Ana said.

More grabbing at straight razors, but they were there and there was nothing to lose. Ana read the inscription under the statue of the refugee children. 'It is called *For the Children*. It's a tribute to those who helped rescue ten thousand Jewish and other children escaping Nazi persecution through the Kinder-transport.'

They studied the faces of the boy and girl waiting to be collected. Those children didn't know who would collect them or what life would be like in this country. Like Nikoleta, they had left their families behind. At least Mum, Dad, and Angelika would be at home waiting for her.

They split up to ask anyone who would stop to listen whether they had been in the area on the morning Danek went missing. Nikoleta asked an elderly couple who were on their way to visit a recently widowed friend in Southend. They were interested in Nikoleta's impressions of London and if she hadn't hurried them along, they would have stayed chatting until their train arrived.

'Come here,' Ana called over to Nikoleta. She was talking to a young Polish woman. 'This lady says that there's another statue of refugee children at this station. It's up the escalator outside the Broadgate entrance.' Nikoleta's heart sank. Could she have been waiting in the wrong place? Danek might have been just metres away when she left the statue. 'Let's take a look,' Ana said.

The statue was of five bronze children, three girls and two boys. The youngest girl propped a teddy on her lap and Nikoleta thought of Danek cuddling his toy rabbit. There was no knowing which of the two statues the woman had meant.

'"Whoever rescues a single soul is credited as though they had saved the world,"' Ana read from the inscription beneath the statue.

'There's another inscription on the wall,' Nikoleta pointed out. They walked together as though in a museum or church. Around them, people rushed and bustled, not seeing the children or thinking about their plight.

'Does that say Hope Square?' Nikoleta asked.

Ana smiled. 'It does. We are in Hope Square. This dedication says, "To the children of the Kindertransport who found hope and safety in Britain through the gateway of Liverpool Street Station."'

They rested at the statue for a few more minutes. They may not have got any closer to finding Danek but Nikoleta found a grain of peace, remembering the children in Hope Square. She said a prayer for Danek and for children everywhere who were far from home and dependent on the kindness of strangers.

Kamil opened the door to Nikoleta before she put her key in the lock. 'Where have you been, *slonka?*'

'It's hot out there. I need a cold drink and then I shall tell you my news.' There wasn't any time to think of a clever reply and she had done enough lying for one day.

'I went to the Emporium and Tavit told me that you had this afternoon off. I thought you had left me. I know I've been difficult to live with. Let's not wrap the truth in cotton, I've been a miserable *taki*. I wouldn't blame you if you did leave me.'

Nikoleta felt a surge of love. Kamil looked so lost and

unsure of himself. 'You are entitled to be miserable, but I have some news that might cheer you up.' She slipped past Kamil and kicked off her sandals. 'I wouldn't get very far with just thirty pounds in my pocket and no passport.'

'Ha, then I'm glad that I locked it away for safe keeping. I don't want you running away. But – if you really are fed up with me.' Kamil hung his head.

Nikoleta stroked his back. 'I'll let you know when you become unbearable.'

Kamil took a bottle of beer from the fridge and a Sprite for Nikoleta.

'So, where have you been?' Kamil's voice was soft and uncertain.

Nikoleta poured her soda into a glass. 'I'm sorry I lied to you, Kamil. You are right, I didn't go to work this afternoon. You are going to be angry with me – but first, let me explain. I went to Liverpool Street Station to try and talk to the guard who took the message from the woman.' Nikoleta didn't tell Kamil that Ana had gone with her. It wasn't a ploy to make her seem braver than she was, although she could tell Kamil was surprised and that gave her a boost. It was because she self-ishly wanted to keep a little bit of her life separate from Kamil. Her friendship with Ana and the easy banter with Tavit and Liza – it wasn't much, but it had become very important in this city so far from home.

Kamil took a slug of beer from the bottle. 'And?'

'He wasn't on duty, but he will be on Friday. You could talk to him, Kamil. Find out who this woman is. We don't even know what she looks like, how old she is, nothing.'

'Oh, *slonka*, my little sunshine, you did that for me? To help find Danek? I don't deserve you. I'm sorry I've been so wrapped up in myself, I've been shutting you out. Today, when I went to your work to take you out for a treat and I heard that you weren't there, I thought the worst.'

'Where were you going to take me?' Nikoleta smiled. He loved her. They would get through this, somehow.

'Anywhere you wanted. You've been in London for five days. You've been working to help pay the rent and have put up with my moods. I thought we could go to one of the parks in London or just go out for a drink. It was a warm evening and to be honest I was sick and tired of this room.'

It was as though Kamil's emotional outburst had cleared the air, a downpour of rain on a humid day. Nikoleta took his hand. 'Don't you think it's time we involved the police?'

Kamil gazed at her and smiled. 'You really are the best thing that ever happened to me, *slonka*.'

Nikoleta sighed with relief. It was all over. They would go to the police and with God's good grace they would find Danek before it was too late.

Kamil got up and fetched his attaché case. 'I should have told you, *slonka*. We found the woman on CCTV. She's an old woman – like a grandma. Here, take a look at these shots.'

'Do you know where she took him?'

'We know enough. I have a man who is close on her trail. It won't be long before he makes contact with her. Don't worry, *slonka*, the evil *suka* will pay for all that she has put us through.'

'And Danek will be safe, thank God. Could I keep this photograph?' Nikoleta could at last put a face to the wretched woman who had caused them so much misery. It would have been better if Kamil had agreed to involve the police, but it sounded as though his men were making some progress.

That night they made love for the first time since arriving in London.

21

'It'll be hard for you to give Danny back to his mum,' Molly said, as the boys dug a trench in the sand.

Angie's scalp prickled; it was as if Molly had read her thoughts. Had she spoken out loud?

'Will he get some time with his mum before he has to start school?'

Angie let out her breath. If she wasn't careful, she'd give herself away with no help from Slippery. 'His mum's going to collect him in a couple of weeks. We've had a lovely time, Danny and me. You're right, it's going to be tough saying goodbye.'

'Tough' didn't begin to describe how hard it would be giving Danny back. Angie always knew it couldn't last, even if Slippery didn't do the dirty, she couldn't care for the little mite. It had been stupid, kidding herself that she was getting better. She had cancer and she was dying. It might be a few months if she was lucky but as she got worse she would have to give the boy back. In the past few days, Angie had tasted what life might have been like as a mother and a grandma, but it wasn't enough. She wanted more. Was it too much to ask, to steal a few more precious days as Danny's namma? Hadn't she paid for her past? A life sentence of not belonging – watching the world from the sidelines?

Danny staggered towards them trailing a long-handled spade. A sandy Licky dangled from his other hand. 'Namma, look after Licky. We're making a fork.'

Angie loved his mispronunciations and didn't bother to correct him. She took the raggedy rabbit and shook the sand from him. Pickles thought it a game and jumped up barking.

'Pickles, behave!' Molly stood and brushed sand from her shorts. 'No, boy! Come back here.' Pickles ran off with Licky between his teeth. You'd think it was his toy not Danny's the way that dog was obsessed with the rabbit.

Danny never complained. He shrieked with laughter and ran after Pickles. Dexter and Alfie joined in the chase. She was going to miss all of this so much – Molly, her boys, Jaywick.

'Namma, Namma, we got Licky.' It was Alfie. She'd become Namma to Molly's boys as well as Danny. 'Namma', not 'Nanna.'

Angie took Licky and tucked him safely in her bag away from Pickles. She found the sun cream and squirted Alfie's back. He stood still for a few seconds, barely catching a sprinkle, before charging off to join Dexter. Danny had wandered away from the fort building operation and was busy searching for something or other. Every so often he crouched, chatting away to himself. Angie caught his voice on the breeze; he was talking in Polish as he did when absorbed in his imaginary world.

She must have dozed because Danny woke her when he sat on her belly. Angie loved the way he climbed and crawled over her as though she were a piece of furniture. Danny was sorting his collection of pebbles into two piles.

'These are the children, and these are the mummies and daddies,' he said, his voice grave. 'We need to find a mummy and a daddy for all of the children. We might need to make more houses, Namma.' Bless him, he sounded so serious.

'Namma has lots of boxes saved up for you. We'll make more houses when we get home.'

'Some of the children can live in the same house like Dexter and Alfie.'

'What about some sisters? Dexter and Alfie have Rosie, Petal, and Daisy.'

Danny considered this. 'I don't think so. They can live in another house so that there are not too many peoples.'

If only life were as simple as that. Angie stood up. The boys were still busy with their fort. Molly had taken Pickles for a run to burn off some energy – the dog's, not Molly's. Lord, the woman needed all of her energy to manage five kids. At least the girls were a bit older – eight, nine, and ten, and close enough in age to get along. Well, most of the time. Molly said that they had terrible fights.

Angie wandered over to the boys. They were digging a trench from where the waves broke up to the moat of their castle. It seemed a very long time ago that Angie had built those first sandcastles with Danny. Just a few days and yet she felt like a different person.

'It's a fort and here is where the sea will come in.' Dexter stabbed the sand with his spade. 'It *is* coming in, isn't it, Namma?' This was said with a little less confidence.

'Yes, it is.'

The sea breeze carried Pickles's bark. It was a joyful bark, excited. She'd never noticed, until that summer, how different barks meant different things. Angie shielded her eyes and squinted. Molly was strolling back, flip-flops swinging from one hand. Pickles cantered back and forth in the surf, barking at the waves and chasing seagulls. You couldn't help but smile.

With her back turned on the boys, Angie didn't notice the stranger who had reached them and was now watching them at play. It was his voice that made her turn. He was talking to Danny in Polish. With a sweep of her arm, Angie swiped Danny up.

He wriggled like a fish. 'Let me down, Namma. Let me down!'

'You have a fine grandson there,' the man said. 'He was explaining to me the science of the sea.'

Dexter joined them. He scowled, no doubt put out that Danny had been the one to explain about the tide filling their moat. 'The sea's coming in. You'd better stay up there if you don't want to get wet.'

The good old Jaywick rebuff to keep out strangers. Alfie stood close to his brother. 'What were you saying to Danny?'

Pickles's bark was getting closer. Angie didn't turn but she could imagine Molly quickening her pace when she saw the man.

Danny clasped Angie's face between his hands. 'Put me down. I'm not a baby.' He pressed her cheeks together to give her a fishy mouth and chuckled.

The man removed his sunglasses and extended his hand. He had nice eyes – a warm brown, and a salt-and-pepper beard. 'I'm sorry to have startled you. My name's Tomasz.' There was something familiar about him that made her skin prickle. Where had she seen him before? And what was he doing in Jaywick? He wasn't a day tripper or a holidaymaker that was for sure.

Ignoring the man's hand, Angie blew raspberries on Danny's tummy before dropping the giggling bundle of boy. 'We'll need to make tracks soon, boys.'

'Are they all your grandsons?'

He was a good-looking man for his age, but he could bugger off because his charm wasn't going to work on her.

'I'm their namma,' she said to put him off, and it was true. She wasn't going to answer any more questions. Where was Molly?

Danny said something to Tomasz in Polish and Angie's heart quickened. She didn't want Danny talking to him any more. *Please don't let him be in Jaywick looking for Danny.*

At last Molly joined them. 'Hmm, only left you for a few minutes and you found yourself a gentle-man-friend.' Molly sung the last three words. 'Who is he?'

'A busybody who asks too many questions.' Angie hoped to trigger the Jaywick defense mechanism, but Molly had other ideas.

'Looks to me that *he likes you.*' Molly walked over to Tomasz and Angie reluctantly followed.

'I haven't seen you around Jaywick. Are you visiting for the day?' Molly asked.

'It's true that I'm new to the area but not on a social visit.'

Angie's heart sank. Could Danny's parents have hired a detective? One of their own?

'I'm what you call a community development worker,' Tomasz said. 'We are trying to make Jaywick a better place to live. Why don't you come to the Club House tonight? It will be fun. A chance for the community to get together. Like a party. The council are providing refreshments.' He was looking directly at Angie. When he smiled Angie noticed little crinkles around his eyes. She turned away, immune to flirtation.

'Will there be beer?' Molly asked.

'There will be beer, wine, and fish and chips,' Tomasz said.

That sold it to Molly. 'I'll put word about. We all like a bit of a knees up around here.'

'Let me take a selfie of us for the website, all of you, your friend and the boys.' Tomasz was determined to take the wretched photo, despite Angie hanging back and doing her best to be excluded. 'The bosses like to see photographs of the community.'

In the end it was easier to give in and Danny loved the silliness of crowding together with his friends, making daft faces. But Angie wouldn't be going to the Club House. The Club House was where she and Lorraine had entered a fancy-dress competition, where Grammy played bingo every Wednesday evening, and where they had gone on that last night in Jaywick. The night her life changed.

'I'll see you both this evening then.' Tomasz grinned and raised his hand in farewell.

The boys had lost interest in the fort and were now prodding a dead crab.

'Handsome for an old guy.' Molly raised her eyebrows. 'About the right age for you.'

Angie tutted. Men her age went for younger woman, especially the good-looking ones. Not that she was interested. She changed the subject. 'You're not really thinking of going to this get-together malarkey at the Club House, are you?'

'Why not? It's a night out and we don't get many of those. I'll ask Zoe to babysit the kids.'

'I'll babysit and then Zoe can go to the party.'

Angie knew that she was a coward but she couldn't go back to the Club House.

Danny padded up the beach with a bucket full of stones. There were already enough littering their chalet to build a rockery.

'You'd better leave some on the beach, sweetheart.'

'But they need mummys and daddys too.' Danny pulled Licky out of Angie's bag, spilling his socks and underwear so that they were covered with sand. Angie was about to complain, when Danny stroked her face with his rabbit. 'Licky is giving you a kiss, Namma.'

Bless his little heart, he could tell when she was feeling blue. How could she feel sorry for herself when she had been blessed with the love of this beautiful boy?

Angie slipped Danny's sock over her fingers. 'Stinky is looking for Danny's toes.' She tickled him with the sock puppet. They laughed and played as Angie dressed him.

Above them the clouds gathered, packing together like dense cotton wool. The sea crept up and over the fort. When Dexter and Alfie cheered and waved their spades high, Danny scrambled up, impatient to join them.

Molly put an arm around Angie. 'I'll miss Danny too. And you, Lorraine. It won't be the same when you leave us.'

They sat in silence.

'We'll miss you too,' Angie croaked.

Angie watched as the sea swept away the boys' fort. They'd already lost interest and had made a game of chasing Pickles.

A rumble of thunder, then torrential rain. Molly and the boys shrieked and whooped. The storm would break the oppressive humidity. But as they ran to take cover, Angie's heart was heavy. Soon she would have to say goodbye to Danny, even if Slippery didn't give her away, she didn't need a doctor to tell her that the cancer was getting worse. She couldn't keep the boy, however much she longed to. It was just as before.

22

1974

The Club House stank of stale beer and cigarette smoke. Angie's bare legs stuck to the plastic of the red banquette where she sat nursing a rum and coke. They shouldn't have been drinking alcohol. Angie wasn't used to it, didn't even like the taste, but Lorraine was determined to make the most of their last night in Jaywick and was at the bar flirting with a couple of boys. Barry was kind of squat and wore a tonic jacket. It looked as though he was about to lose a button where the two-tone fabric stretched across his belly. Len was like a giraffe; he seemed to have grown too fast and was stretched out of proportion. The two of them could have come from the House of Mirrors; maybe they were reflections of two average-size boys.

Lorraine sashayed over to Angie, glancing back to see if she still had the boys' attention. Their eyes followed her every move and Lorraine tossed her hair.

'Come on, Ange. We're having a laugh. They've bought us a couple of drinks, we ought to be nice.'

Angie didn't want the drinks, she would have been happier with a plain Coca-Cola. 'We promised Grammy that we'd be home by ten and I need to pack my case. Can't we go now?' Angie knew that she was whining, that she sounded like a baby, but she didn't understand why Lorraine wanted to spend their last night talking to those stupid boys.

Lorraine clicked her tongue. 'Well, don't spoil it for me. If you want to sit here on your own that's up to you. Don't say that I didn't try and include you.' Then she waltzed off leaving Angie feeling self-conscious and stupid.

When Angie looked up from trailing her finger in a dribble of Coke, he was looking at her. She had noticed the man when they first arrived. They both had, because he looked a bit like David Essex, with his long curly hair and earring. The man grinned and Angie felt weak; he was gorgeous. She twisted around to see who he had spotted but there was nobody behind her just a portrait of the Queen.

The man was still watching Angie and so she dipped her head. Oh no, she was going red, really red – her face must be beetroot. She shook her hair hoping to close a curtain over her face, but the frizz stubbornly remained rigid.

'Mind if I join you?' His knee nudged hers under the table and Angie jumped. What was she meant to say? She mumbled 'no,' and bit the inside of her cheek.

'Your friend's left you all alone and I've been stood up by my girlfriend. I thought maybe we could keep each other company.'

Angie relaxed a little. He was just feeling lonely and Jaywick was one of those places where people talked to each other. That's what Grammy and Gramps loved about living there – the friendliness of their neighbours. This man probably knew Grammy and Gramps. As soon as her face was a normal colour, she would ask him.

'My name's Pete, what's yours?'

Angie had to look at him now. He was really, really good-looking. She felt a little star-struck, as though the real David Essex was sitting there. It was like the comic strip love stories in *Jackie*. Pete could have been one of those heart-throb boys, but Angie wasn't anything like the girls they met with their flowing hair. Still, she could daydream.

'Angie,' she said. Angie glanced to the bar to see if Lorraine had noticed who she was talking to.

'Angie – Angel. You have a kind face. I was feeling sad but then I noticed you and I thought, there's a girl who wouldn't stand a boy up. There's a girl you can trust. Do you have a boyfriend, Angel?'

'No,' Angie giggled. Didn't he know that she was only four-teen? Well, nearly fifteen.

'When you do get a boyfriend – and I'm sure that you'll have many, you are really pretty – don't be cruel. Don't go making promises and then break them. I'd been looking forward to this evening.'

He did look sad. Angie was pleased to be able to comfort him and asked gently whether his girlfriend might have misunderstood where they were to meet or the time. She couldn't believe that any girl would turn down a date with Pete.

Without noticing, Angie had finished both of the rum and cokes. The room was starting to spin, like when the credits go up at the end of a film. She felt as though she was seasick. Angie hiccupped and then – it was mortifying – burped.

'Let's go and get a little fresh air, Angel.' Pete steered Angie towards the door.

'I need to tell Lorraine where I'm going.'

'Your friend looks as though she's having a good time. She won't miss you. Come on; let's go down to the sea. I love watching it at night.'

Pete was right, the sea was beautiful in the moonlight, with the white crests of waves illuminated so that they seemed fluorescent. It was soothing watching the waves creep up the deserted beach.

'Are you on holiday or do you live here?' Angie said, feeling a bit braver talking to him when he couldn't see her face.

Behind her, Pete rested his chin on Angie's head and wrapped his arms around her middle. 'Warmer?' She felt the scratch of his denim jacket on her bare skin and the masculine scent of Brut aftershave and tobacco.

It was exciting and frightening at the same time, a lurching in her belly, like when you are about to go on stage for the school play and you're terrified but a bit in awe too.

'I've got a summer job on the pier.' His voice was low and deep, close to her ear, and Angie's arms tingled with goosebumps.

'Come on, I'll show you where I work. I can get us free rides.' Pete pulled away and Angie felt the loss of his warmth as the sea breeze licked her neck.

Clacton was two miles away. They wouldn't get there and back before ten. Grammy would be waiting up for their milky drink and gossip. Angie wanted to go with Pete. He was kind and funny, they were having fun, but she knew it was wrong. 'I can't. I'm sorry. I have to get back and I can't leave my friend without telling her.'

Pete fumbled in his pocket and pulled out a pack of cigarettes. He flicked his wrist to release one into his palm and offered the pack to Angie, who shook her head. As Pete stooped over the flame shielding it from the breeze Angie noticed the stubble on his chin. Pete was a man – he shaved.

Maybe she should tell him that she was only fourteen. The boys Lorraine was talking to were seventeen, but Barry's brother worked at the bar and he had slipped them shots of rum to pour into their Cokes. Pete must have thought that she was eighteen because she was drinking alcohol. Maybe she wasn't so plain. Pete had said that she was pretty and a good listener. That she was kind and thoughtful, not vain and self-absorbed like other girls. He had been miserable when they started talking and she had managed to cheer him up; it would be mean to leave him now. The waves crashed on the shore louder in the dark, as though shouting for attention.

'Alright,' she said, 'but we'll have to be quick so I'm not late home.'

23

Tavit was outside the Emporium yelling and swearing when Nikoleta arrived for work. She couldn't think what had riled him and then she saw the ugly white paint daubed across the windows.

Ana joined Tavit with a bucket and a mop. 'You go inside, Tavit. Nikoleta and I will clear this up.'

'I try and help the locals. Didn't I offer to take on a couple of their schoolkids for summer work, when I don't need extra hands? I search for the food that they "tried on holiday and would love to buy here". Ridiculous descriptions, can't even remember the country half the time. But I am always patient. Too patient. And now this! Don't tell Liza, she will go crazy.'

Eventually Tavit was persuaded by Ana to make a pot of coffee for them all.

'What does it say?' Nikoleta asked, but she could guess.

'"Go home. Not welcome here." It's not the first time, but I thought things were improving. Tavit and Liza donated money to help fund the Christmas festival and Liza goes to meetings for Keep Our Streets Neat. I guess we will always be outsiders.'

Nikoleta was sad for Tavit and Liza. Did they mean all of them weren't welcome? It was a horrid thing to say.

They worked together soaping and scraping. 'This was done by one person, a coward,' Ana said, reading Nikoleta's face. 'Despite all of this, I love living in London.'

'I'm not sure that I'll ever get used to it.' Nikoleta wrung out her cloth.

'Give it time. Things will settle down, once you have Danek home. Did you tell Kamil about our visit to Liverpool Street?'

Nikoleta updated her as they finished the job. Eventually, there was no trace left of the spiteful words. 'There, good as new.'

'Oh, don't go thinking that. Tavit will want us to make the window shine now!' Ana teased.

When Liza arrived later that morning, there was no clue as to what had happened. Tavit and the girls batted banter in an unsaid agreement to bury the nastiness, but then a customer came in for a tin of mango puree and an inquisition on the graffiti culprit.

As soon as he left, Liza started shouting in Armenian and then Tavit joined in. There was nothing Ana or Nikoleta could do to calm them, so on the pretense of unpacking a new delivery, they hid in the storeroom.

'I do miss my mum and dad, my brothers and their families,' Ana said. 'I phone home at least once a week. My mum would chew my ear off if I didn't. At least it's cheap and easy to have a video call now, not like ten years ago when we first arrived.'

'My mum doesn't think so. We use my sister's mobile. When we tried the video option, all I could see was the inside of Mum's ear. I was going to buy my parents a mobile as soon as we arrived but with everything that's been going on and with Kamil not earning…' Nikoleta shrugged.

'We get paid today. It's not much but hopefully it will help.'

That was good news. Nikoleta had used what little money that she had brought with her and hated being financially dependent on Kamil. It wasn't as though he was mean, but she hated having to ask for things. It was like being a child.

'I suppose we had better unpack a box or two. See if it's safe to venture out.' Ana broke the seal on a cardboard box stamped with Arabic script and logos. The rush of spice, sharp and pungent, filled the air and Nikoleta sneezed.

Tavit and Liza were cuddling behind the till. It was just as well they had few customers, there was far too much drama in the shop to find time to sell things.

'Give them a few more minutes,' Nikoleta said.

Ana took out her phone and showed Nikoleta some photographs of her brothers and their families. Then she remembered that Nikoleta had mentioned Twitter. 'What's your name on Twitter?' she asked as she scrolled and typed.

Nikoleta told her and then pushed the box of spices to the doorway. 'I'll go and unpack these.'

'Hold on, Nikoleta, have you seen this?' Ana was excited about something.

Nikoleta stepped over the box and took Ana's phone. It was a photograph of a blond child sitting on a fire engine, a fairground ride. Nikoleta used her fingers to zoom in. There was no mistaking Danek. The photographer had focused on a little girl sitting in a pink Barbie car behind the fire engine. Beneath the photograph was a message. *Could this be the child in your photo? It was taken at Clacton Pier.* Six days ago!

24

Nikoleta had two hundred and eighty pounds in her purse and a photograph showing Danek's whereabouts the day that he went missing. Her prayers had been answered. At last she could do something useful – pay some of their rent and tell Kamil that she knew where the woman had taken his son. If his men really did know where Danek was they had done nothing to get him home. Nikoleta's pace slowed. She had been walking fast, in a hurry to share the news but the enormity of this knowledge – what it meant to her and Kamil – stopped her in her tracks. They were going to get Danek back, maybe even tonight. They would be a family. She would have to stay at home for a while until Danek was settled, but she was getting ahead of herself. Kamil would be overjoyed and – she stole herself to be a little proud, although it was a sin – amazed. His *slonka* had found Danek. Nikoleta did a skip as she resumed her pace. He wouldn't believe it! Of course, she would have to confess to using social media. Kamil couldn't be angry when he saw that it had worked.

Nikoleta pushed open the door to 137. It would change

their life in London – well, her life certainly. She hardly knew Danek, what if he didn't like her? She was only twenty-four. Was she ready to be a wife and mother? It was a bit late now to be having second thoughts. Of course she was ready – *Kamil's wife*. The legendary Kamil, the most successful man in her village. She was just unsettled by the past week. They would all need a bit of time to adjust to their new life. Nikoleta squeezed her phone. Kamil was going to be so, so happy. She took the last few stairs two at a time.

'Kamil!' Nikoleta called as she closed their front door. She was bursting with her news. There was no reply – Kamil was out.

Nikoleta kicked off her shoes and sunk onto the bed. She flipped the cover of her phone and opened the tweet again. Danek's face became grainy as she stretched it between thumb and forefinger. It was difficult to judge his mood, not knowing the boy very well or having much experience of children, but at least he wasn't crying. Nikoleta zoomed back out and scanned the photo searching for the woman who took Danek. There were no adults in the shot. The photo was taken a week ago, Danek may have been taken elsewhere. Where *was* Kamil? They needed to act fast, talk to the police. Nikoleta phoned him – engaged. She didn't want to spoil the surprise by leaving a message.

Two hundred and eighty pounds. That was a lot of money for just five days' work. If she paid two hundred pounds towards the rent, then she could keep eighty pounds for housekeeping. Her own money at last. Nikoleta hated being dependent upon Kamil.

His phone was still engaged. Too restless to sit waiting, Nikoleta decided to go downstairs to offer their landlady a contribution towards the rent.

Mrs Lisowski opened the door in a silk affair, a dressing

gown resembling a kimono. Her luxuriant hair fell about her shoulders. 'Come and join us,' she said, waving Nikoleta into the drawing room.

Nikoleta hesitated, she had obviously disturbed something and was not ready to meet Mrs Lisowski's friend. Then she heard Kamil's voice and her heart bumped. What had she walked into?

There was an empty wine bottle on the table and two glasses, stained red. Mrs Lisowski seemed unfazed by Nikoleta's arrival, which either meant that she had nothing to hide or didn't care that Nikoleta had caught her with Kamil.

'Can I get you a drink?' Mrs Lisowski gathered the glasses and tray. As if noticing Nikoleta's discomfort for the first time, she said, 'Oh, I was sunning myself in the courtyard when Kamil called.' She flashed a navy bathing suit beneath her kimono.

Kamil wandered into the doorway, his phone pressed to his ear. He acknowledged Nikoleta and continued his call. 'There was an unavoidable disruption to business. No, no, nothing like that. What can I say? We have surveillance – the best, I promise you. When have you known me not to deliver? The boy...' He glanced at Nikoleta and then lowered his voice before slipping through a door out of earshot. Was he talking about Danek? No, the conversation was about a business transaction, Kamil must be talking about one of the boys who was working for him. When they were in Poland she had some idea what Kamil was working on, but now it was a mystery to her. The overseas connections always had been.

'I hope that my friend Tavit is not working you too hard,' Mrs Lisowski said. 'A vodka?'

Nikoleta shook her head and Mrs Lisowski disappeared through the same door as Kamil. Even if it wasn't what Nikoleta had first feared, she was still irritated. Kamil had been downstairs drinking wine all afternoon whilst she was out working. He said that he couldn't work because he was too busy searching for Danek and yet she – Nikoleta – had found Danek *and* managed to work full-time.

It was a few minutes before Kamil returned followed by Mrs Lisowski, who had at least put on some clothes. 'This is a nice surprise, *slonka*. You're home early.'

'No, I'm not. I was surprised to find you here.' Her voice was harsh and accusatory. This wasn't how she had imagined their evening.

Kamil glared at Nikoleta. She shouldn't have snapped at Kamil in front of their landlady; he was a proud man.

Mrs Lisowski exchanged a look with Kamil, raising her eyebrows.

'We were discussing business.' Kamil's chest expanded and he grew a few centimetres taller, but red wine whiskers spoiled the effect.

'Well, I'm home now. Are you coming upstairs?' Nikoleta had no intention of offering the two hundred pounds today. She just wanted to get out of there.

'Thank you for your help, Lenka. I don't know what I would do without you.' Kamil kissed Mrs Lisowski's hand.

Nikoleta fumed. Kamil had only kissed her hand once and that was when they first met. She had thought it sweet and old-fashioned and had been enchanted with the gesture.

'What are friends for, Kamil? It has been a very pleasant afternoon.' Kamil was still holding her hand as though he didn't want to let go. If he was trying to annoy Nikoleta he was doing a good job.

Nikoleta stomped up the stairs ahead of Kamil. She was furious but what was the point in starting a row? They had to live together in a cramped space; there was no room for friction. Besides, she knew where Danek was and getting him home had to be their priority.

Kamil spoke first. 'Lenka has been very helpful. It was rude of you to snap at her like that. You embarrassed me.'

Nikoleta cringed, maybe she had overreacted. 'I'm sorry, Kamil. I didn't mean to be rude. I was just disappointed that you weren't home. I had something I wanted to tell you.' *But not like this*, Nikoleta thought.

'With Lenka's help we should have Danek home in just a few days. I had to say thank you.' He sorted through their mail, mostly junk. He didn't ask about her news.

'Why? What did she do?' Nikoleta snapped, angry again. She had found Danek, not their cursed landlady.

Kamil threw the mail to one side. 'I don't really want to talk about this now. You don't understand how things work in England. Lenka does and I trust her.' There was that twitch in his temple again.

Nikoleta fished a couple of carrots from a drawer in the fridge to start making dinner, but she couldn't carry on as normal. The silence in the room was loaded.

'Are you saying that you can't trust me?'

'For heaven's sake, Nikki, does everything have to be about you?' He raised his voice and Nikoleta wondered whether he was drunk.

'All I'm saying is, you can trust me too. Do you know where Danek is being held?' She would tell him and then they would forget the silly row and find a way to get Danek home.

'I said that I didn't want to talk about it.' This time Kamil shouted.

Nikoleta dropped her knife and gave in to the tears that had been threatening since Kamil kissed their landlady's hand.

'That's all I need! It's like having two children to take care of. I should never have trusted you to look after my son. What was I thinking?' The door slammed.

When it became apparent that Kamil was not coming home, Nikoleta gave up on preparing a meal and took herself to bed. Outside it was still light and the voices of children playing in the street reminded her that life was going on as normal. Nikoleta buried herself under the duvet like a wounded animal. Kamil had never shouted at her like that, not even when she had lost Danek. If anything, they had been closer then. Kamil's outburst had shown Nikoleta that he could never forgive her for losing Danek. *Danek* – they could have brought him home this evening, if only they had got help from the police. Nikoleta knew, deep down, that Kamil would never have agreed to that. It didn't make sense. But then nothing made sense any more. Her head was pounding. She ought to get a glass of water but did not have the energy or will to drag herself out of bed.

Nikoleta awoke some hours later to find Kamil curled around her, his hand cupping her breast. She covered his hand with hers and he wriggled closer, squeezing her tight. 'I'm sorry, *slonka*. I was just tired. It's been the worst week of my life. Danek will be home in a few days and things will be better, I promise.' He kissed her neck and then gently snored.

Nikoleta lay awake for an hour or so, comforted by Kamil's embrace. She loved him so much. Kamil was trying to forgive her for losing his son but it would always sit between them destroying any hope for a future together. Nikoleta knew what she had to do. She would find Danek herself and return him to his daddy. At least she would have put right her wrong.

25

Despite being exhausted, Angie had lain awake until the small hours, after babysitting Molly's kids. The get-together hadn't gone entirely to plan, according to Molly.

'There was fish and chips and plenty of booze, probably too much, because it ended in a punch-up.' Molly paused whilst she rounded up the girls and Angie wondered at the council's poor judgement in providing alcohol; they'd been asking for trouble.

'There was a good turnout, once word got about that there was free fish and chips. Shame really. Peggy-Sue was jiving with Albert, and Scotty was doing some kind of Highland fling, when bloody Councillor Radford turned off the music and started to pontificate. That pissed everyone off for starters.'

'Well, it was a council event, what did they expect?' Angie yawned. She hoped Molly would leave so that she could go to bed. Danny had fallen asleep on the sofa and Dexter and Liam were overtired. It had been too much really, minding six kids.

'You haven't heard what he said,' Molly yelled, waking Danny, who struggled up to see what was going on. 'Sorry.' She lowered her voice. 'He tried to persuade us to move into social housing, so the council can bulldoze our homes. Can you believe that? It all kicked off then. He was lucky to get out of there in one piece. Poor old Thomasz copped it too.' Molly held up a denim jacket. 'Mental Mickey grabbed hold of him, but thanks to Bill he only managed to rip off the sleeve of his jacket. Anyway, I said you'd fix it. It weren't Tomasz's fault, he didn't know the councillor was going to use the meeting to pull a fast one.'

It was eleven-fifteen when Molly eventually left with five half-asleep kids. Danny settled down straight away, but Angie lay awake for hours, thinking about the last time she went to the Club House. Was there a clue, something that might have warned her not to leave with Pete? She had been so careful since, trusting her instincts and reading the signs, but it was too late – closing the door after the horse had bolted. What if she hadn't left with him that night?

The following morning, Angie was only half awake when there was a rap on the door. 'Finish your cereal,' Angie said. 'I'll see who's there.'

It was Tomasz looking as fresh as a daisy. His face pink and smooth, his shirt crisp and clean, and he smelt of lemons. Angie felt crumpled and shabby in comparison. Why was he staring at her like that?

'I think you have something caught in your hair.'

Angie patted at her tangle of frizz, embarrassed by what she might find. Her hand came into contact with a foreign body and she tugged. Her toothbrush, that's where it went.

'There's something else in there.' Tomasz tilted his head

154

and peered into the labyrinth. His hand wavered near her hair, as though unsure whether or not to go in. He grimaced and wisely dropped his hand. 'It, uh, looks like a green duck.'

Danny would insist on walking his toys across 'the jungle'. It wasn't the first time an action figure had got buried in her hair. Angie's fingers closed over the duck but it was going to take more than a twist and a tug to free her from that tangle.

'Molly said you might fix my jacket, but don't worry if you're busy, I was just passing.'

Of course, Molly had left the torn jacket last night. 'If you don't mind waiting I'll do it now,' Angie said, leading the way to the kitchen, as she tried to tease out the duck, which was still clinging on. Best fix his jacket; it would take two shakes of a puppy dog's tail and if she didn't he would only be back.

Danny smiled shyly at Tomasz, delighted to have a visitor. At last the ruddy duck gave up the fight and Angie thrust her at Danny. They hadn't been expecting a visitor and were both wearing what Angie called their dressing-up clothes. Angie was wrung out from the exertion of the evening before; she had a nagging pain in her pelvis and was tired. Once she got rid of Tomasz, they could veg out. Shame they didn't have a TV, she was too tired to play imaginary games.

Angie threaded the machine which sat at one end of the table.

'Is Namma going to sew you some shorts? You can have a dinosaur soup if you want, with spikes and things. Shall I show you mine?' Danny slid off of his chair.

'Did your grandma make that Gruffalo suit you're wearing?'

Danny nodded. 'It has horns, look.' He bent his head to show off the stuffed horns protruding from a furry hood.

Angie kicked the machine into action. It whirred, as she

guided the sleeve, then backstitched and broke the thread free. 'Done.'

'Look.' Danny pulled a cardboard box from beneath the table. 'Tell Namma what you want and she will make-ed it from these.'

Tomasz peered into a box of clothes that Angie had bought from the charity shop and boot sale. 'You are clever, transforming these. Did you make that patchwork gown you're wearing?'

It wasn't so much patchwork as a mismatch of old skirts, dresses, and shirts, fashioned together to make a long gown with an Empire bodice and flared sleeves.

Danny fanned out the skirt of Angie's dress. 'That's Namma's princess dress. Do you want to see my sleeping bag with a dragon's tail?'

Tomasz looked to Angie.

'Feel free.'

As Angie busied herself clearing away the breakfast things she heard Danny and Tomasz talking in Polish. It took some getting used to, having people dropping in whenever they felt like it. Nobody visited Angie in Dagenham. Come to think of it, she hadn't had any visitors since her mum died six years ago. The Dagenham house felt dead. Here, voices and laughter breathed life into the Jeffers place: the scratch of Pickles's paws on lino, the tumble of boys and giggles of girls. It was as though the place had a heart and she was at its centre: preparing meals, sewing clothes and kissing bruises better.

She should have had four or five kids. How many grandchildren might she have had then – sixteen? Twenty?

Tomasz chuckled, a deep throaty sound, and Angie crept to the door to listen in. She imagined that they were Danny's grandparents. Tomasz would take Danny fishing and they would return with their catch – a nice big cod and a bit of mackerel – in a bucket of water.

'See what you can do with these, Nanna Angie,' Tomasz would say, dumping a bucket on the table.

Angie would swipe him with a tea towel. 'Take that filthy bucket outside and bring me the fish once you've cleaned and gutted them.'

He would squeeze her and nibble her neck. 'Don't nag, woman,' he would say, and she would pretend to be cross.

'Angie, how long is Danny staying with you?' Tomasz interrupted her thoughts and Angie felt herself go red.

'A few more weeks, why?'

'It's good having someone to talk to in Polish. I expect you've learnt a little Polish from your daughter-in-law.'

Angie didn't like the way the conversation was going and he was looking at her in a quizzical way. Had Danny told Tomasz about his home life and if he had, did Tomasz think Angie was partly to blame for his mistreatment? She couldn't bear it, if Tomasz thought her capable of harming her darling boy.

'We get by,' she said.

Tomasz struggled up from Danny's sleeping bag. 'You're doing a good job. Danny is lucky to have such a clever and imaginative grandma. This sleeping bag is a work of art.'

'Namma has one with a mermaid's tail,' Danny said.

'Wow! That's really something.'

'I like taking things apart and putting them back together to make something different. I never got to do that in the factory and Danny loves everything that I make for him.'

Tomasz followed Angie back into the kitchen. 'I can tell you love being a grandma.'

'It's the best thing in the world, next to being a mum.'

'Does Danny have a grandfather?'

Angie hadn't given that part of her story any thought. She didn't want to spin more lies by inventing a husband who had died or left her, so she said, 'Not really.'

'What is a grandfather?' Danny asked.

'Like my gramps. I told you about Grammy and Gramps. Well, I'm like your grammy but you don't have a gramps.'

Danny thought about this for a moment. '*You* be my gramps.' He pointed at Tomasz before tipping his McDonald's toys across the floor.

Angie was reaching into a cupboard to stack their bowls and cups, but she felt the air change. It became heavy, pressing into her back. She pretended to be absorbed in the task of cleaning the worktop, whilst she stole a glance at Tomasz and caught his unguarded expression – a deep sorrow that she recognised as though a reflection of her own soul.

'Do you have any kids?' she asked.

Tomasz didn't reply for what felt like minutes. He inspected his jacket, turning the sleeve, glanced up at Angie, bit his lip, and smoothed the new seam. Eventually, he said, 'I did. A little girl. Lydia.'

Angie could feel his heart breaking and wished that she hadn't opened that wound. Tomasz shrugged on his jacket. 'She was what they call stillborn. Her eyelids were paper thin and her fingernails, perfect little shells.' He looked away and then shook himself. 'I don't know why I told you that.'

Angie gently squeezed his arm and Tomasz's hand covered hers.

'Can Tomasz come to the beach with us?' Danny said, breaking the tension.

'Tomasz has to work.'

'I'm not working tomorrow,' Tomasz said. 'If your namma will have me, I would love to spend the day on the beach with you both.' He stepped away from Angie but his gaze lingered, as though reluctant to break the spell.

'Namma can teach you how to swim.'

At the door Tomasz's lips brushed Angie's cheek and she felt a frisson of electricity that was nothing to do with the static in her hair.

'Bring your bathing suit,' Tomasz said and his eyes crinkled.

26

I t had been a mistake agreeing to spend the day with Tomasz. Angie didn't need the warning of a single magpie, which sat on Higgins's dustbin mocking her; she had known it was a bad idea from the moment she opened her eyes. What had she been thinking? There was the dilemma of a suitable swimming costume, for one thing. The silky red number that had seemed so appealing the day she wrestled it from Peggy-Sue at the market would look ridiculous and she would need more time to run something up on the machine, even if she did have the right material. Tomasz had caught her at a weak moment. She would have to make an excuse.

Danny waddled into the kitchen wearing swimming trunks over his pyjama bottoms; a deflated water wing encased one arm and a pair of goggles dangled from his wrist. 'Put these on, Namma.'

'Shall we have a quiet day at home, Danny, just the two of us? We could make some houses for your pebble people.'

'No, I am going to swim with Tomasz. Put these on *you*, Namma.'

Angie couldn't disappoint Danny, she would just have to be careful. She didn't know anything about Tomasz. He had shared his sorrow with her and in that moment, she had felt close to him, but he was still a stranger. A handsome, gentle stranger who seemed to have a good heart but she had got that wrong before.

'If we are going, you had better get dressed, you can't wear your trunks over your pyjamas.'

'Dexter and Liam wear their trunks over their clothes.'

'No, *under* their clothes.'

Angie resigned herself to a day on the beach with Tomasz, despite the warning flutter of butterflies in her tummy. She glanced in the bathroom mirror as she washed Danny. Something about her had changed; she was no beauty but there was a certain glow – the kiss of the sun or just being happy?

Danny bounced alongside Angie as they made their way across the beach to the agreed meeting place, close to Sal's takeaway service. They could buy refreshments later and Tomasz didn't need to know that it was Mental Mickey's place. After the tussle at the Club House he might be a bit wary.

'Is the tide in or out?' Danny said.

'Is there a lot of sand or a little?'

'Nearly a lot.'

'Then the tide is out.'

'Is it coming in?'

'I'm not sure. It will be a surprise.'

Danny stopped in his tracks. 'There is Tomasz.'

Angie wanted to run in the opposite direction. She couldn't do this. Why did he want to spend the day with them? Danny was the attraction, not her. She had to get a hold, not let her imagination run away with her. Danny hid behind Angie's legs.

'Go and meet him then,' she coaxed, but Angie was as shy as Danny.

It took only a few seconds for Danny to find his nerve. He stumbled across the sand without a backwards glance, hesitated, and then ran towards the lone figure striding towards them. Angie remembered the goggles around her neck and the water wings on her forearms like some kind of orthopedic aid and shrugged them off. She wanted to make a better impression on Tomasz this time. At least there was nothing lurking in her hair; she had given it a close inspection before leaving the chalet. Why was she worried about what he thought? This was what she was afraid of – getting carried away – he wasn't interested in her.

Tomasz raised an arm to show he'd seen them and Angie's tummy did a flip. He was wearing sunglasses, like the first time they met on the beach, and just as then, Angie had a fleeting memory of meeting him another time – another place. She tried to retrieve the memory and then gave up; maybe he just reminded her of someone on the telly.

Tomasz dropped to one knee, ready to greet Danny, and fanned his face with a panama hat. His shirt billowed and then parted to reveal a tanned chest and flattish stomach. He'd kept in good shape. Now she was close enough to see the crinkles around his eyes as he smiled.

'You came,' he said after shaking hands with Danny.

He sounded unsure of himself and Angie was glad that she hadn't made up an excuse to cancel. Now that she was here, she would make the most of the day. Whatever Tomasz's reason for wanting to spend time with them, it was a new experience for Angie – the company of a handsome man and one who knew how precious it was to care for a child, her beautiful boy. Just for one day, she would pretend that they were a family. She had to stop worrying about what might go wrong and live in the moment.

Angie unpacked an Aztec throw she'd taken from the sofa and a couple of towels. Today she had suntan lotion and a bottle of water. So different to that first day when she and Danny had staked their place on the beach.

The morning sun reflected off the sea, a kaleidoscope of glistening diamonds. A gull glided on the sea breeze; its cry loud in the stillness. Angie turned her face to the sun and closed her eyes.

Tomasz and Danny were talking together in Polish. Tomasz's sentences were short but Danny was talking quickly and confidently. Angie ached to know what he was saying; she missed so much, not speaking his language. He sounded older, more confident, talking in Polish. She concentrated on the rhythm of their voices, one soft and low, the other a breathless chirrup.

'Like this?' It was Tomasz. She opened one eye to see him pouring water into the moat of a fort. He caught her. 'Ah, you are awake. Come and see our castle.'

Tomasz pulled Angie gently to his side and kissed the top of her head. He did it so naturally, as though they'd known each other for years. *Nobody* before had treated her with that kind of loving affection. Not even her parents. They were caring, but in a practical no-nonsense way. Tomasz's unselfconscious gesture overwhelmed her. She wanted to say something, to show him that she wasn't reading anything into it, but she couldn't speak.

Tomasz stepped back to hold Angie at arm's length. She

hoped he wouldn't notice the silly tearing of her eye. 'Danny has promised me that you will teach me how to swim.'

Why did he have to look at her like that, as though she mattered? If he knew that she was Angie Winkle, he wouldn't waste his time with her. A goblin whispered in her head, *You're no good, Weirdo Winkle. You should have stayed where you belonged. Nobody wants you.*

'You and Danny have a swim. It's too cold for me.' She cringed at the silky swimsuit beneath her dress. What had she been thinking?

Tomasz spoke to Danny and Danny shrieked, 'Come on, Namma, come on!'

'What did you say to him?'

'That Namma was a scaredy-cat and didn't want to swim.'

Danny chattered to Tomasz.

'What did he say?' Angie asked.

'He said that Namma is really a mermaid. Are you afraid that your legs will turn into a tail?'

'Come on, Namma,' Danny trilled.

I am not going to hide in the shadows any more. Angie blasted the thought goblins. She had given them too much headspace for too long. *Make the most of every moment.*

Angie whipped off her dress and ran. The wind snatched up the floral nylon so that it billowed like a banner from her outstretched arm.

'You're beautiful!' Tomasz's exclamation glided on the breeze.

Angie felt beautiful, for the first time in her life. When she reached the sea, Angie stopped. She stood tall and strong; for a heartbeat she was part of the sand that rooted her feet and the sky beyond her touch. Free from thought. The tide was coming in, four strides and a wave took hold of Angie. She let herself go, allowing the current to lift and rock her. Nerve endings tingled – she had never felt so alive. Angie lay on her back; above the sky was blue, not a cloud in sight. Everything was sharper, brighter, and more beautiful, at this end of her life, like looking through a telescope, seeing every detail. Today was perfect. If it all ended now, it would have been worth it.

Tomasz had taken off his shirt. He was rubbing suntan lotion onto Danny's back and shoulders. The slight slackening of muscles in Tomasz's lower back, a reminder of his age, made him more beautiful to Angie. He grinned when he saw her approaching. If Angie wasn't careful she was going to fall for this dear man.

'Was it cold?' Tomasz held up a big towel, then wrapped her up as though she were six, and Angie basked in his attention. He stroked the hair from her face. 'Any ducks or trolls hitching a ride today?'

'I don't think so, but it's like a Jamboree bag up there, you never know what you might find.'

'What is this Jamboree bag?' Tomasz pulled Angie down onto the throw beside him.

'When I was a girl we bought Jamboree bags from the sweetshop. You would get a surprise gift and some sweets in a coloured paper bag. I loved tearing open the bag, not knowing what I would find inside.'

Danny was busy collecting pebbles in his bucket and so Angie allowed herself to lean against Tomasz, who wrapped his arms around her. 'I bet you were a pretty child with that wonderful hair.'

'If I was, nobody told me.' Angie thought about Tomasz's daughter, Lydia. He would have made a good father.

As if reading her thoughts, Tomasz said, 'Lydia's mother

died six months after we lost our baby girl. There hasn't been anyone special in my life since. It's easier being on your own, you don't have to worry about providing for anyone and you can travel wherever you choose. But it can be lonely.'

In the silence that followed, Angie rehearsed a number of replies. Tomasz hadn't asked for her story, but that was how it worked, wasn't it? She was new to this, but his honesty touched her and she wanted to be honest in return. But how much could she tell him?

'Has Danny told you anything about his home life?' she said. If Danny had confided in Tomasz then she would tell him about her concerns regarding his ill treatment and admit that he wasn't her grandson.

'He told me that he wants to live in Jaywick with his namma forever. He really loves you.'

'And I him. But there is something that I must tell you, Tomasz.'

A ball skittered across the throw and Tomasz caught it. 'Hold on, Angie.'

He jumped up and kicked it back to a group of teenage boys. There was a bit of banter and then the ball was returned to Tomasz, who headed it. There followed a bit of toing and froing of the ball.

A deep, sharp pain seared through Angie's side. Bugger. Even if she was brave enough to confess to Tomasz that Danny wasn't her grandson, she couldn't tell him that she was dying. He would be sympathetic and kind but she didn't want his pity.

When Tomasz jogged back, a big grin on his face, Angie was fighting a cold sweat.

'I was quite good in my day. You were about to tell me something.'

Angie scrambled onto her knees and bending over to

control the pain, rooted around in her bag, as though searching for something. 'Why don't you and Danny see if Sal is frying chips today or could make us a cuppa? I like to support the locals – help them make a bob or two.'

'We could wait and go together.'

'No. I'll get dressed and catch you up.' She tried to keep her voice light.

The pain was passing, it always did, but these pains were becoming more frequent, a reminder that she was on borrowed time. She couldn't keep Danny boy, even if that was what he wanted. If only she could have a few more days like this – her, Danny, and Tomasz. Tomorrow she and Molly were taking the kids to Clacton Pier to celebrate the start of the school holidays. She would bring things to an end after that. Just one more day as Danny's Namma.

27

1974

Pete, the boy who looked like David Essex, had walked to the pier with fourteen-year-old Angie. The light of his cigarette danced like a firefly, as he waved his hands describing how he jumped from car to car collecting fares on the dodgems. Angie imagined all of the girls making eyes at him, but he would only have eyes for Angie – his angel. If only they had one more day in Jaywick, so that Lorraine could see how this handsome man had singled her out – *Angie Winkle*.

The music, loud and throbbing, reached them long before they could make out the illuminated rides. The pier was a different animal at night, as though it had shed its cloak of respectability. Lewd and raucous, it bewitched the throngs of teenagers who gathered at its mouth shouting obscenities and revving their bikes.

Pete took Angie's hand. What was she doing with this man at eleven o'clock at night? She should be home with Grammy and Gramps; they would be worried sick. Maybe she should tell Pete that it was all a mistake, that she was only fourteen and shouldn't have come. Angie tried to tell him but it was too noisy and he kept turning away to talk to his mates. The men he was talking to were old – maybe twenty-five. One of them looked her up and down and smirked. It must be because she was wearing a miniskirt; they weren't fashionable any more. They were laughing at her. Angie tugged at the hem of her pink brushed denim skirt. Maybe she should just slip away and run back to Jaywick. The thought of walking home alone so late at night terrified Angie.

Pete slung an arm over her shoulder. 'Me and my angel are off to find somewhere a bit quieter. Get away from you degenerates.'

That was when she should have told him, but Angie had lost her rum-induced confidence and was too timid to speak up.

'You don't want to go on those kids' rides,' Pete said as he led Angie past the pier.

Angie thought that was the reason they had walked to the pier, for Pete to show her the dodgem cars and for them to have some fun. It had been a silly idea – stupid. She wanted to go home. 'I ought to get back, really,' she squeaked, her voice failing her.

'Come on. I'll show you my special place.' Pete led Angie under the pier.

He took off his denim jacket and lay it against the boulders, releasing a rank, animal smell of sweat. Angie recoiled as he put an arm around her. She wanted to gag.

'What's the time?' Angie couldn't see her own watch. She'd never been up after midnight before, except once on New Year's Eve, and then Mum had woken her up from where she lay on the couch so that she could see the year in with the grown-ups before going to bed.

'Who cares about the time? We have all the time in the world.'

Angie didn't. She had to get back, but Pete was holding her tight. Then, Pete leant in and kissed her. A hard, bristly kiss that bruised Angie's lips where they clamped against her teeth. And then his tongue, a cold slug prodding and poking at her molars. She couldn't swallow and so saliva, his and hers, pooled in her mouth until she thought that she would choke.

Pauline Plunkett had told Angie and Lorraine about French kissing when they were on the school bus. Angie hadn't really believed that people put their tongues in each other's mouths. It sounded disgusting and now she knew that it was.

Now was the time to tell him that she was only fourteen and had never kissed a boy before. 'Pete.' It was hard to breathe, let alone speak, with his body crushing her. 'I've never had a boyfriend.' She wanted to cry. How had she got herself into this situation?

Pete didn't seem to hear as he fumbled with her blouse. It fell open, exposing what Mum called her baby fat and her Tweety Pie bra.

'Please, Pete, I want to go home.'

He was rubbing against her now and grunting like a pig. Then he pushed up Angie's bra so that her breasts were exposed to the cold sea air. She wanted to die of shame. He was breathing heavily as he dipped his head to lick her nipples. His hair smelt of chip fat and the bristle of his chin scratched her ribcage.

When it was all over, Pete smoked a cigarette. Angie couldn't find her knickers in the dark; he must have thrown them out of reach. She groped around with a trembling hand, stifling the sobs that wracked her body.

'You've done that before,' Pete said, a nasty tone to his voice. Angie just wanted him to leave.

At last, she found her knickers and pulled them on. They were wet and sticky. If only she hadn't been wearing a miniskirt she would have thrown them away. Her matching Tweety Pie set. Buying what the girls considered to be racy lingerie in Etam's, they had giggled at the thought of a boy ever seeing their underwear. It felt as though that was a different Angie.

28

Nikoleta sat on a bench, looking out to sea. Around her seagulls cawed and children shrieked. If things had been different, she could have been eating ice creams with Danek, paddling in the sea – having fun. The woman who had snatched Danek had stolen that joy. *She* had watched Danek on the merry-go-round, claiming memories that should have been Nikoleta's. Why had she taken Danek? Would knowing help Nikoleta forgive her? *Please, God, let Danek be alive and well. Help me find him today and I promise that I will search my heart to find some forgiveness for this woman's evil deed.* The waves rolled in, true and steady, knocking down sandcastles, they wiped the beach clean. Would there be any trace that Danek had once been on this beach? Now that she was here, Nikoleta had no idea how to go about finding him.

She'd had to wait until Saturday, two days after receiving the tweet, to get away without Kamil. At first, she thought he would want to spend the day with her but fortunately he kept to his plan of meeting with business associates in Kent. Nikoleta had no idea what business Kamil was dealing in nowadays. It certainly wasn't sourcing machinery for Polish farms as he had done in the past. But then Kamil dealt with all sorts of commodities. At least he was working and so there would be a bit more money coming in. Nikoleta still had just over a hundred pounds after paying her train fare and was reluctant to hand it over to Mrs Lisowski because it felt like handing back a little bit of independence. Hopefully, everything would change when she arrived back at 137 with Danek that evening.

The pier was to her right. Like a child's construction of a racetrack, a roller coaster seemed to teeter, midpoint on the pier, confirming the presence of a funfair. Nikoleta set off in that direction.

It was no good looking for a blond head, she had to ask whether anyone had seen Danek. Nikoleta tried to stop a couple who were walking arm in arm. 'Have you seen...' They ignored Nikoleta and she was left wagging her phone at their backs. It was as though she were invisible.

A woman with a Labrador dog at least pretended to glance at Nikoleta's phone but she didn't stop walking. Maybe it was hard to see the photograph in the sun. She had brought the printed photo of the woman and tried showing this to passersby. The response was a bit better, as at least they glanced at the photo before saying no.

The boardwalk to the pier was busy with people strolling. In London they had paced with a purpose, eyes set on the way ahead. Here, they meandered without direction, easily distracted by anything and everything, eating burgers or pink spun-sugar, not looking where they were going. Happy music, happy people – the place was buzzing with excitement. Nikoleta imagined the funfair through Danek's eyes. Was he entranced by the colour, the frenzy of activity, sights and sounds that had you twisting your head one way and then the other: the pirate ship rocking back and forth, tipping its screaming cargo, blue and orange boats that begged tots to get on board and sail across an enormous paddling pool, a Wild West shooting range? Did he forget Nikoleta and the plans that they made on the plane? An American milkshake and discovering their new flat paled in comparison to this.

Nikoleta gave up on showing the photograph of Danek. Competing against the blaring pop music was hard and she suspected people thought she was showing them a photograph of her son, because several smiled and said, 'Yes, he's lovely', or words to that effect and gave her a wide berth as though she were a bit of a simpleton. The photograph of the woman at least made people stop, as they seemed curious to know why she was looking for the woman – not that Nikoleta satisfied their curiosity.

Nikoleta meandered through an amusement arcade full of Grab machines with brightly coloured soft toys, then back into the sun on the boardwalk, where there were more rides. Angelika, her sister, would love it here. There were several amusement parks in and around Krakow but they rarely visited the city. She was having a conversation with Angelika in her head, telling her about the pier, when she saw the bounce of blond curls. It was him. It was Danek and he was alone.

29

They were all together. Angie was absolutely sure, because she kept on counting their heads, but she must have had her eye on the wrong one because Rosie cried, 'Where's Danny?' They had only been in the amusement arcade for twenty minutes. Daisy, Petal, and Rosie were playing the Grab machines, whilst Alfie and Dexter tried their luck at *Shoot the Zombie*, the flashing lights and electronic sounds stimulating the boys more than a bag of Haribo sweets. Angie was with the girls because Danny had fallen under Rosie's spell and followed her like a puppy dog. They had moved on when the kids ran out of pennies. Danny had insisted Rosie take his twenty pence for a final go at grabbing a Peppa Pig, which she *really, really*, wanted. As on the last five goes, the grab hand dropped the prize just when they thought they had won. That was five minutes ago and now Danny was missing.

Angie's heart stopped. *Keep calm, he could not have wandered far.* They scattered, as though blown apart, wandering in circles. 'Don't lose the others, Molly. Stay put and I'll find Danny.'

'Should we contact security?' Molly winced even as she said the word. Police and security were taboo to Jaywick folks, even when you needed them.

'No, he won't be far.' Angie tried to sound confident, but she was worried sick. It had all been too good to be true and now she was going to have to pay. *Please let Danny boy be safe.*

A pain shot through her pelvis, a reminder of her stolen time, and Angie crumpled. It would all end here – on the pier of all places.

Angie clutched her side. *Think the pain away. You can't die here in front of Molly and the kids. Not with Danny missing. Breathe. Breathe.* Bent double, Angie was close to the industrial carpet, littered with fag ends, spilt drinks, and gum. A child was crawling amongst that filth. As Angie was mentally berating the parents, she watched the child slide an arm up the chute of a machine. It was Danny!

Angie found renewed strength. She had been given another chance, but this might be the last. It was a sign. She had to give Danny back and go home to die. Leave the wonderful Tomasz with his gentle ways and crinkly eyes and her precious boy, who was now trying to poke his head up into the machine.

'Hey, mister. What do you think you're doing?' Thank goodness he was safe.

Danny extracted his arm and turned, shame-faced to Angie. His little mouth pulled down. 'I am sorry, Namma. I wanted Rosie to have a Peppa Pig.'

'What did you plan on doing – climb into the machine?'

Danny tilted his face, his brow a zigzag, as he thought through that possibility.

'How many twenty pence would I need to grab myself a Danny-boy?'

Danny giggled. 'Lots!'

'Maybe not, because Namma knows a trick. Shall I show you?' She had always been good at this. It just needed a bit of concentration, skill, and know-how. On the third attempt Angie won a Peppa Pig.

'Yey! Namma catched a Peppa Pig. Namma catched a Peppa Pig.' Danny jumped up and down.

'Okay. You can give this to Rosie but first, promise me that you will never run away from me like that again.'

Danny hung his head. 'I am sorry, Namma. I love you.' That boy knew how to twist her around his little finger.

They were all on a Dumbo ride, Angie and Danny in the front of one, with Alfie and Dexter in the back seat, and Molly in another with the girls. The ride had just come to an end when Angie noticed a man who looked like security, talking to the ride operator. They were talking about her, she knew it. Couldn't she just have a break? Get through this day with no more drama.

The security man stopped Molly, whilst Angie was scrambling out of Dumbo. It was so undignified being cautioned whilst sitting in a giant pink elephant. They waited for her.

The security man held out some ride tokens. 'Where did you get these from?'

Bloody Bill. Of course, it was too good to be true. Angie relaxed her face and widened her eyes, all innocence. 'A man in a pub gave them to my husband. Why, is there something wrong with them?'

'I'm sorry to say that they are counterfeit. There have been a lot of them in circulation. I hope that your husband didn't pay for them.'

Molly was handing over the rest of the tokens, when the

DEBORAH KLÉE

security guard got a call on his radio. There was urgent business he had to attend to. A woman acting suspiciously. Lots of complaints. He took off, leaving Molly and Angie gobsmacked.

'Slippery. It has his name all over it,' Molly said. Angie agreed.

The kids hadn't taken any notice. 'One more ride and then home. But I get to choose,' Molly said. 'And I choose the helter-skelter.'

Angie wasn't surprised to see that Molly had kept back some of the tokens. The last ride. Her last ride *ever.* They were organising themselves at the top of the helter-skelter – Danny and Alfie had to share a mat with an adult – when Angie saw the security man. He was escorting a young woman with a ponytail off the premises. She reminded Angie of Danny's mum or au pair. Then, Angie was off down the slide, shrieking with laughter, the girl forgotten.

'That's Slippery's van. Looks like he's our driver. Good, I'll give him a piece of my mind. I know it was him that gave Bill the dodgy tickets,' Molly said.

Slippery was leaning on his transit when Angie, Molly, and the boys reached him. Shepherding the straggle of weary kids a couple of hundred metres was no mean feat. Angie didn't have the energy for a confrontation with Slippery, not about being Frankie's sister or the counterfeit tickets. Let Molly have it out with him.

Slippery held open the back door to the van. 'It's messy in there, but clean. Sit on the tyres, you'll be alright.'

As Molly organised the kids, Slippery pulled Angie to one side. She really didn't need this.

'Okay, I'm not Lorraine, what of it?' Angie snapped. Molly's head was in the van, so she couldn't hear.

'I don't give a toss,' Slippery said. 'But, I thought you should know, someone else does.'

Ice chilled Angie's veins. 'Who?'

'Some Polish bird showed me a photo of you holding Danny. Could have been from a CCTV camera. Who is she, the Old Bill? Detective?'

'What did you tell her?'

'Nothing. What do you think I am, a grass?'

Angie let out her breath. 'Thanks, Si.'

'Reckon I owed you one, with you sorting my motor. Here, she gave me her address, in case I saw you. You might want to keep low for a while.'

Molly joined them. 'Me and Lorraine in the front then?'

'I'll walk. It'll give you more space and I could do with the exercise. Can you mind Danny? I won't be far behind.' She had to be alone. It was time to give Danny back and she didn't know how she was going to do it. Facing the end of her life was easier than saying goodbye to him. And then there was Tomasz, and her friends in Jaywick. She had to leave before they found out she wasn't Lorraine Jeffers. But first, she had to make sure that Danny was going to be okay.

30

Nikoleta burned with humiliation and shame. She had started that morning with such hope, to find Danek and bring him home. Kamil must never know of her foolishness. To be escorted off the pier by two security men, it was unthinkable. Maybe she had pounced a bit too enthusiastically on the lone child. Convinced the blond head belonged to Danek, she had flung her arms around what was a little girl. As soon as she realised her mistake, she backed off, but the child's mother screamed something at her and everyone stared. There was no time to explain. The security men appeared as though they had been watching her, and maybe they had. A few people had eyed her suspiciously when she was asking if anyone had seen the woman in the photo.

Maybe Kamil and Mrs Lisowski were right to mistrust the English and their police. To think that she had been proud of herself for travelling to Clacton on her own. She was, as Mrs Lisowski's looks implied, a naive village girl. *Pride comes before a fall* – her mum's voice. *Then I will get back up*, Nikoleta retorted in her head. If she got home before Kamil, he need never know.

Nikoleta opened the door to 137 and crept up the stairs. If Mrs Lisowski caught her, then Kamil would soon know everything. It was her Catholic upbringing that made it so difficult for Nikoleta to lie and Mrs Lisowski had a way of worming information out of her.

She made it into their flat without being spotted. Kamil wasn't there. It occurred to Nikoleta that he might be downstairs with *Lenka*; she would never call their landlady by her first name. Nikoleta dismissed the thought. She wasn't going to add jealousy to her list of sins. Kamil was working in Kent.

Angelika would cheer her up, even her mum with her words of wisdom – never eat with your hands or drink from a bottle, it's bad manners, and don't go jumping at the sun with a hoe. That was exactly what her mum thought Nikoleta had done when she took off for London with Kamil and Danek. A new country, new job, taking on another man's child – if that hadn't been jumping at the sun with a hoe, she didn't know what was. Mum was probably right on that one.

The phone rang four times and then there was a red, bristly jowl on the screen followed by a nostril. 'How do you turn this thing off?'

'Dad, Dad. It's me. Look at the phone.'

A close-up of her scowling dad. She wanted to hug him. Video calls were alien to Dad. He regarded her image, on the kitchen table or wherever Angelika had left her phone, as though it was sorcery.

'Dad. It's so good to see you.'

Her dad's face composed itself, as he looked straight at the phone camera. Such a dear, dear face. 'Your mother is at the market. Angelika left her phone. That damn ringtone. I was trying to turn it off.'

'I'm glad you didn't. I miss you, Dad.'

He looked away and then rubbed his bristly chin. 'I haven't shaved. I was working on something.'

Dad hated talking on the phone and that was without a camera and the awkwardness between them.

'So, you thought you had the place to yourself. I bet you have a beer there.'

Dad gave a sheepish grin and lifted his grey stone tankard to the phone. The one he had used forever. 'You know what your mum's like. She goes to market on the bus with her basket and returns hours later with an empty basket and a head full of gossip. She'll be gone all day.'

'You do the same at your farmers' club. I've seen you and your cronies sitting around a table sorting out the troubles of the world.'

'They are work associates and we are talking business, not idle gossip.'

'If you say so.' For a couple of seconds her dad forgot himself and they grinned at each other. She was back in the family kitchen as though she had never left. Desperate to keep him talking Nikoleta brought up his favourite topic. 'Mum said you are finally going to buy that tractor. Have you got your eye on anything special?'

'There's a Zetor that's good for the price. I was just looking at the figures – with a grant and part exchange, we might stretch to it, but there again...'

'Dad, you have to invest for the business to grow. I told you that when we looked at the figures together. That old tractor is going to pack up any day. Why don't you let Kamil source you one? He could get you a good price. It would be better than buying one second-hand that is not much better than the one you have now.'

'I would not buy anything from that gangster. He would

sell his own mother for the right price. To think you left a decent family to set up with that crook. Please tell me, Nikoleta, that you haven't given him your passport.'

Her dad had gone too far this time. She had made allowances for him up until now – his old-world suspicions, his limited experience of life, and low expectations – but this was too much. How dare he criticize her future husband?

Nikoleta took a deep breath and her hand trembled. Kamil was her partner and the time had come to show her loyalty to him over her dad. It was hard, but she was no longer a little girl. Dad had to respect her as a woman and her choice of a husband. 'Kamil and I have moved to England to start our life together. We would have liked your blessing but I can see that is never going to happen. I trust Kamil as you trust Mum. Yes, Kamil has my passport. And for your information I don't have a return ticket. We live in England now, Dad.' Nikoleta tried to swallow but her mouth was dry, and she had a lump in her throat.

'Nikoleta, open your eyes. Don't let that man make a fool out of you.' Her dad sounded exasperated and sad.

Nikoleta didn't know what else to say. It felt as though they were saying goodbye forever, but she couldn't back down. 'Bye, Dad,' she whispered.

Nikoleta poured boiling water onto a teabag. There was nothing in the fridge for supper and Kamil would have expected her to prepare a meal as she had the day off work. Convinced that she would return home with Danek, Nikoleta had envisaged a celebratory meal at a restaurant or a takeaway. Now she had to explain to Kamil where she had been and that she had failed. Unless she rushed out now and threw something together. All she wanted to do was collapse in a chair with a mug of coffee. She was emotionally wrung out from the disappointment at not finding Danek and then that confrontation with her dad. The row had been simmering for months now. It started when she left the co-operative to work for Kamil. 'There are more opportunities for me, Dad,' she had argued. 'I want to get my accountancy exams and work for an international company, see the world. Don't you want me to do well?'

Her dad had surprised her with his words because it wasn't like him to be philosophical, that was Mum's habit – a saying for every situation. Thinking about it now made her melancholy. He said, 'It is not about what you achieve in this life but the person you become. Remember that, Nikoleta.'

Now she was being sentimental. Dad was always going to find it hard to let her go. She was his little girl, his kitten. Getting a good job, making her way in the world, would make her a better person. How could you develop as a person without experience of life? Growing up on the farm was all very well. It was safe and secure, but if she stayed there, married a local boy, and never progressed beyond managing the books for the family business she would stagnate.

Mum and Dad were stuck in the past. Maybe that was her problem too. She had left Poland but taken with her her parents' values and beliefs. That was why she was finding it so difficult to adapt to a new way of life. Phoning home whenever she felt down, seeking comfort from her parents, it had to stop. She had been brainwashed by her upbringing, that's why she always heard her mum's voice. No wonder Kamil thought her a child, incapable of looking after herself. If she wanted to be taken seriously, she had to grow up.

Putting Kamil before her family was a big step and Nikoleta felt as though she had crossed a threshold. She was an independent woman. Her parents had given her a strong foundation, but it was time to take responsibility for herself. Today had been a disaster, but she had gone about it the wrong way. Kamil had told her to trust him and that's what she should have done. Kamil and Danek were her family now. Kamil was confident that Danek would be home very soon, and she had to have faith in him.

Nikoleta drained her coffee, and fired by indignation and a sense of purpose, she set about buying and preparing supper.

31

Thick padding between her legs – she must have had another bleed, unless she was in hospital and had had an operation. No, a duvet covered her, one that smelt of hyacinths. Angie had been walking home from the pier when the pain in her pelvis got bad – really bad. That's all that she could remember.

Angie struggled up. 'Where's Danny?'

'Hey, Lorraine, you gave us a scare. Lie still and I'll get Mum.' Zoe's voice came from across the room, Zoe's room.

Josie was at her side within minutes. 'How are you feeling, Lorraine? Have a sip of water.' Angie took the glass from Josie with a shaky hand.

'Could you eat a little something? Some soup?'

'What is today? I was meant to collect Danny from Moll. How long have I been here?' Angie remembered the note with Danny's home address. The girl had come looking for him. She had to give him back.

Josie sat on the edge of the bed. 'Don't fret. Danny stayed at Molly's last night. We were really worried. You wouldn't get in the ambulance at first because you didn't want to get admitted to hospital.'

Angie vaguely remembered. If they had taken her to the hospital she would never have come out – not alive anyway.

'You must have mentioned the Seashell because I got a call. They brought you here but on the condition you saw your GP and took his advice. Old Dr Morris popped by when you were asleep. He thinks you should go to hospital, see a specialist.' Josie clutched Angie's hand. 'I think it's bad, Lorraine.'

Angie knew it was bad; she was dying. If she had kept her hospital appointment she might have a clue how long she had left and what to expect. It could be weeks or months. The pain had been bad though, maybe she was near the end. Please God don't let her die now, not in Zoe's bed. Danny would be taken away and everyone would know that she had lied to them – Tomasz, Josie, Molly.

Josie looked so mournful, Angie felt like she was already dead, watching her funeral, except when she did die – as Angie Winkle – she would die alone with nobody to mourn her wasted life. 'I look worse than I am. It's okay, Josie, I know what's wrong. It's endometrial cancer – cancer of the womb.'

Josie gasped. 'Are you sure, babe? Have you seen a proper doctor?'

Angie smiled, as if she could dream up something like that. 'Yes, I have a specialist in London. I'll go and see her today or tomorrow.'

'You won't go anywhere until you're strong enough,' Josie said.

There was a rumbling, like a herd of donkeys had been set loose in the house. Their hooves pounded on the stairs and then the door flew open. Dexter, Alfie, and Danny tumbled into the room. 'Namma, Namma,' they all cried.

Zoe followed them in. 'Sorry, I tried to get them to wait until you said it was okay, Mum.'

'She's *my* namma,' Danny said.

Angie opened her arms and all three scrambled onto the bed.

Molly followed them. 'Careful, boys, you'll hurt Lorraine.' She looked tired and Angie felt bad for burdening her with another child.

'Just a few minutes, Lorraine needs to rest.' Josie looked at her watch.

Dexter and Alfie climbed down but Danny snuggled into Angie, his arms around her neck. 'Are you better now, Namma? Are you going to come home?'

Angie hugged Danny close. 'Fill me up with cuddles, Danny boy. It's the best medicine.'

Danny screwed up his face. His English was improving, but this was a new word.

'It will make me better.' Angie looked to Molly. 'Thanks for looking after Danny.' She couldn't imagine how Molly had squeezed another body into that chalet. They must have slept three to a bed.

'Danny's no bother. I wish my kids were as good as him. He eats everything on his plate – and toilet paper!' She laughed. 'Two squares. That's all he'll use. You should see what the girls get through. I'm always telling them they'll block the toilet. So polite too.'

'I made you a card.' Danny extracted himself from Angie's hug.

Molly found Danny's drawing in her bag. It was of two stick men – one small, the other tall. Both had big heads. Eyes, nose and mouth were a bit random, giving the impression of an abstract painting. 'That is me and that is you. Super Namma! You are winning all of the toys. And I made you a base-let with Rosie's beads.' Molly supplied a loosely threaded string of red beads.

'It's beautiful, thank you.' Angie slipped the bracelet on.

The boys then shared their presents. Dexter, a treasured rock that he believed was a real fossil, and Liam, the remainder of a honeycomb he had started to nibble. He'd bought it with his pocket money the day they spent on the pier. Angie knew how precious these gifts were and cherished them.

'Okay, that's enough. It's time Lorraine had something to eat.'

Danny didn't want to leave her side. 'I could stay and cuddle Namma, because cuddles will make her better.'

Reluctantly, Angie persuaded Danny to go with Molly. 'I'll be up tomorrow and maybe we can go back home.'

Who would look after Danny when she had gone? *His parents*, the goblins hissed. Maybe she had invented an unhappy home life as an excuse to keep Danny. Angie squirmed; she did have an overactive imagination. But she wasn't going to give him back until she had made sure. Angie reached for her bag; she remembered tucking the girl's address in the front pocket before she started the walk home.

'Stop fussing with your bag, I've brought you a bowl of soup.' Josie returned with a loaded tray.

Josie was a good friend, Molly and Zoe too. She had been blessed with their love and friendship. What would they say when they found out that Angie was an imposter who had tricked them into trusting her by borrowing Lorraine's identity? She would have to make plans to return Danny and go home before she was exposed.

Josie settled on the edge of the bed and Angie knew that she would watch and wait until she had eaten every mouthful, but it was hard to swallow with a lump in her throat.

Satisfied that Angie could eat no more, Josie took the tray. 'There's something I have to tell you, Lorraine, but you're not going to like it.'

Angie couldn't think of anything that Josie could say that would make things any worse than they already were.

'I didn't ask because I knew you'd say no,' she continued.

She's told Tomasz, Angie thought.

Josie was looking very serious. 'Dr Morris had your brother Frank's phone number. He's phoned him to say that his sister is very unwell and needs help getting to the hospital in London. I'm sorry, babe, but it seemed like the best solution.'

32

1974

A ngie couldn't remember walking home from the pier that night. Pete had left her as soon as the deed was done. He said that he had to go to work and thanked her. *Thanked her.* She remembered that. What she said to Grammy and Gramps when she arrived home – oh she ached everywhere and felt dirty, as though she stank of him – what she said, she couldn't remember. She remembered that the shower was not hot enough to scrub him away.

Mum noticed something was wrong. She was kind and attentive in the first few weeks after the holiday. 'You must have come down with something,' she said when Angie was too lethargic to get out of bed.

Angie dreaded the start of school. Everyone would be able to tell what she had done. She never told Lorraine, it was too shameful. School wasn't the same any more. She couldn't concentrate, even in her favourite classes like physics and maths. Mum was called into the school to discuss why Angie was slipping behind and she lost a day's pay. Things weren't good at home, money was tight, and her parents were squabbling more than usual. Angie wanted to tell someone what had happened, but she knew that it was her own fault.

When Angie missed her periods, she wasn't particularly worried. They had come suddenly, just a few months before her holiday and so it didn't seem strange that they had stopped just as suddenly. Maybe that's how it happened, until you grew into them.

Then one day her mum said, 'Do you need more sanitary towels? I haven't bought you any for at least three months. You should have said, Angie. Have you been buying your own?'

'It's okay, I haven't had a period for a while.' Mum's jaw dropped and when their eyes met Angie experienced a bolt of fear. She was pregnant.

33

Nikoleta swung her grocery bag as she walked home. Tonight, she would start as she meant to go on – being a good wife to Kamil. The birds were happy too. Birdsong was different here than on the farm. It sounded as though there were lots of birds, although Nikoleta could not see them. Majestic brick buildings bronzed by the evening sun crowded the horizon. So different to the big uncluttered skies of home. Everything was different. This was her home now, and Kamil and Danek were her family.

The European Foods Emporium stocked tinned sauerkraut and vacuum-packed Polish sausage. Nikoleta bought these, some of the spices – paprika, caraway seeds, and allspice – dried mushrooms and prunes, but she had to shop elsewhere for fresh pork, beef, cabbage, and a few other herbs and spices. It was expensive, not like at home where lots of the ingredients were in the store cupboard and they used up what meat was in the fridge or on offer at the co-operative. The return journey to Clacton and today's shop had eaten into Nikoleta's wages. The cost of living was high in London and what had seemed a generous wage was not looking so good. It would be extravagant to buy a bottle of red wine but it would taste good with the stew and on special occasions her mum would pour some in for extra flavour. Nikoleta wanted Kamil to love her bigos. He deserved a treat and she could at least provide a decent meal, if nothing else.

Kamil had sent a text to say he would be home by seven. The bigos would take one to two hours to cook. If she got a move on, they could eat by eight. It tasted better the next day but Nikoleta wanted to spoil Kamil tonight. She hadn't been very supportive, insisting all the time that they go to the police. Tonight, she would listen to him properly without judgement and give him credit for what he had achieved in finding Danek.

When Kamil arrived, Nikoleta was adding diced pork to the pot. A pan spat fat, ready to brown the diced beef and sliced sausage.

'Wow, that smells good.' Kamil hugged Nikoleta from behind. 'Is that kielbasa sausage? Fantastic. Please tell me you're making bigos.'

Nikoleta removed the pan of hot fat from the heat and turned into Kamil's arms. 'It is. I can do more than heat microwave meals.'

Kamil inspected the bottle of red wine, reading the label. 'What's the occasion?'

'I just wanted to do something nice. I've been a bit of a misery.'

'We both have. It's to be expected, with Danek missing, but your celebratory meal is well timed, *slonka*. One of my men is watching Danek; he should be home soon.'

Nikoleta's first reaction was to yell, 'Then what are we

waiting for?' But she stopped herself. Instead she said, 'That's fantastic, well done, darling. When are we going to collect him?'

Kamil went to nab a piece of sausage and she swiped him away. 'It's a delicate situation. We need to get Danek without arousing suspicion.'

Nikoleta didn't get it – they hadn't done anything wrong. 'How do you plan to do that?' She tried to keep her voice neutral.

Kamil kissed the nape of her neck. 'Don't worry about the detail. Danek will be home this week. Is there enough bigos to stretch to three?'

Nikoleta guessed what was coming. She didn't want to share their evening with anyone, especially not Mrs Lisowski. But what could she say? It was a big pot of stew. 'There is plenty but it will not be ready until quite late.'

'I'll ask Lenka to join us, after waiting patiently for our deposit and rent, it's a way of saying thank you. I'll go and ask her now before she makes other arrangements.'

Nikoleta noticed that Kamil took the bottle of wine with him. As the meat fried so did Nikoleta's temper. What chance did they have of starting a life together if the cursed Mrs Lisowski stuck her nose into everything? Nikoleta flung the meat into the pot, a few chunks missed and skitted across the floor. The stew needed to simmer for one to two hours – the perfect time for her and Kamil to share that bottle of wine and talk. Instead, he was downstairs with that *kurwa*. He had been gone for fifteen minutes. Should she go and join them? Suggest they have a drink together, whilst waiting for the stew to cook? She knew what her mum would do; she would go downstairs and rant at them both. Not very sophisticated or worldly. If she was going to show Kamil that she could be patient and supportive then it would be best to wait a bit longer. She didn't want to seem insecure or needy. Instead, Nikoleta used the time to freshen herself up. A quick wash, a squirt of perfume, lipstick reapplied, and hair brushed. Kamil was still downstairs. He would be telling *Lenka* his plans for getting Danek back. The plans that he couldn't share with Nikoleta – his partner, Danek's guardian and soon-to-be mum. At least Danek was coming home. She should be happy with the news instead of seething with jealousy.

Nikoleta was on the landing, ready to head downstairs in search of Kamil, when she heard voices. They were on their way up – no bottle of wine, she noted.

'Did they show any interest in the boy?' Mrs Lisowski said.

Nikoleta couldn't hear Kamil's reply. It infuriated her that he confided in their landlady, telling her about his work transactions. Kamil must be helping a youngster get started on his career. He was a good man, using his contacts to help other Poles find work or start up in business. Anxious not to be caught spying, Nikoleta ducked back into the flat and was stirring the bigos when they sauntered in.

The bigos worked beautifully: the meat was tender, the spices perfectly balanced, although there had been no red wine to add to the broth.

Kamil made all the right noises. 'This is better than my mother's bigos and that is saying something, *slonka.*' Nikoleta beamed. She stole a glance at their landlady, who concentrated on cutting a chunk of meat that was small and tender enough to eat whole.

'What meat did you use?' Mrs Lisowski said.

'Pork, beef, and Polish sausage.'

'My mother-in-law made a fabulous bigos. She always used boar and venison.'

Nikoleta gritted her teeth. 'Kamil tells me that he knew your husband.'

'My dear Filip passed away three years ago. He and Kamil were like that.' She crossed her fingers and winked at Kamil. How did that woman always make Nikoleta feel like the outsider, even in her own home? Except it wasn't 'her home', it was Mrs Lisowski's. The sooner they found a place of their own the better.

'I don't think there could be any improvement on Nikki's bigos,' Kamil said. Nikoleta wanted to cheer him.

'It is kind of you to invite me to share your meal.' Mrs Lisowski's voice was formal, no more dripping honey.

'You have been very patient waiting for your rent and for finding Nikki work. It is the least we can do to express our gratitude. When Nikki gets paid at the end of the month we will be able to settle our debt.'

'You are very welcome. You know that you are a very dear friend, Kamil. But surely Nikki has already been paid? Tavit usually pays weekly in cash.'

Nikoleta struggled to swallow the beef that should have melted in her mouth. They were both looking at her.

'Yes, I forgot to say, Kamil. I have some money towards the rent.' Nikoleta handed over the remainder of her wages and with it her independence.

34

A ngie was sitting in an armchair by an open window, flicking through one of Zoe's *Hello* magazines, when Josie walked in, her arms crossed.

'Who exactly is Angie Winkle?'

Angie's heart stopped. It was too late. Josie knew who she was. If Frank hadn't told her then Slippery had. It was all over. If only she had given Danny back when the girl came looking. She could have said goodbye to her friends and then died in hospital. Now, the authorities would come and take Danny away and she would be despised by Josie and Bill. She had taken advantage of their kindness. They had trusted her. Angie Winkle was a fraud. A good-for-nothing miserable fraud who deserved to die. She had just borrowed the past ten days pretending to be someone else.

Josie's words hung in the air. *Who is Angie Winkle?* Who indeed. A breeze pushed the curtain into the room. It billowed and then collapsed. Somewhere outside, a boy called to his friend.

'Someone I wanted to forget.'

Josie shook her head and Angie felt her disapproval.

'I thought Zoe tidied her room before I made your bed up.' Josie reached under the bed and dragged out some dirty laundry. 'Well, if you wanted to forget Angie Winkle, you're out of luck because she's downstairs in my café, looking like she has a smell under her nose, all fake tan, phony designer bag, and *I'm too good to slum it here* attitude. Do you want me to throw her out?'

She had been given another chance – more lives than a cat. There was only one person it could be – Lorraine. Angie hadn't seen Lorraine in forty years. 'No, show her up, if you don't mind, Josie. Or I could go down to the café. It's time I started getting out and about.'

'If you're sure, I'll help you downstairs. I can keep an eye on you down there. Don't want that madam upsetting you.'

At first, they both stared at each other, searching. And then Angie found Lorraine in her hazel eyes and rested in them, drawing to her the shared memories, the close friendship they once cherished.

'You didn't give me away?'

Lorraine sniggered. 'I knew it had to be you when Frank phoned me to check I was okay. He got a freaky call from Dr Morris saying Lorraine had collapsed. Who else would pretend to be Lorraine Jeffers and stay at the old homestead?'

Angie covered her face. 'I'm so sorry, Lorraine. It was a terrible thing to do. It's just that we were here, me and my grandson, Danny. I wanted to show him the Jaywick I remembered from the old days, but it's changed. It was all spur of the moment. I hadn't booked anywhere to stay, there's nowhere around here, only Clacton. It was empty, looking a bit sad, and the key was under Grumpy. I'm not making excuses, it was wrong. It felt like home and I thought if Grammy and Gramps knew I needed somewhere to stay they'd make me welcome.'

'You're right about things being different around here. I must admit I've not visited Jaywick for a few years and the chalet has been a bit neglected.'

'I'll pay you for the time I've spent there and get out.'

Lorraine waved away Angie's offer. 'It's okay, you can help me get it ready to put on the market. Now I'm here, I might as well make the most of it. Now, tell me *everything*. It's so good to see you, Angie. Why did you call yourself Lorraine?'

Oh, it was mortifying, having to explain her deceit. 'You know what people are like around here. Maybe you don't, they weren't like this when we were teenagers. Now, everyone is so suspicious of strangers. I thought that they would accept me if I came from around here and I was right, they did.'

'That explains why your friend keeps giving me the evil eye.' Josie was watching them, as she wiped the counter.

'Tell me about your family, Lorraine. What happened to Grammy and Gramps?'

'You remember that last holiday we had here?' Lorraine said. 'Well, on our last day, or maybe the day after we left, Grammy had a stroke. They went back to Harold Wood and never used the chalet again. She kept going for a while. Gramps did everything for her but they're both dead now.'

'Did Grammy have a stroke while we were out on that last night of our holiday?' Angie couldn't bear to think of Grammy suffering. What if she had stopped them from going to the hospital?

'I really can't remember. You have a better memory than me. Fancy remembering what we did on our last night.'

'You don't remember me leaving you at the Club House and then getting home late?'

'No.' Lorraine shrugged as if it was nothing.

'I thought that was why we fell out,' Angie said. She meant the whole thing. Her mum told her that Lorraine's grandparents were shocked at Angie's sluttish behaviour and never wanted to see her again. She had cried herself to sleep many a night thinking about their disappointment in her.

'I don't remember us falling out as such. You left school early, before the exams. I thought it was because of your dad going off with the barmaid from the Sports and Social. Didn't they go and live in Spain?'

It was like being hit by a cricket ball. She didn't see it coming and this information knocked Angie sideways. All those years Mum had told Angie that Dad left because he was ashamed of her, that she had broken up the family. The barmaid at the Sports and Social? Angie's jaw dropped and she nodded dumbly.

'Shame you left school. You were the clever one. My dad was right impressed that you wanted to be an engineer. You were good at maths and science. It was always, *Why can't you be like Angie*.'

Angie had forgotten her aspiration to become an engineer. Lorraine was right, she always did well at school. Pete had stolen so much more than her virginity.

35

Lorraine's unexpected appearance unsettled Angie. It was as though they were both fourteen again and Angie felt the past jar with the present. Except, the past was not as she had remembered it. For years, Angie had believed that Dad left because she had disgraced the family. Mum and Dad had rows, terrible rows. Shouting about what Angie thought was her shameful behaviour but now she wasn't so sure. The burden that Angie had shouldered for more than forty years did not belong to her. It was Dad who had broken Mum. He hadn't left them because of Angie. Maybe in time she would feel lighter, find a way to cast aside the guilt. It wasn't that she didn't want to let go. It had become part of her and she wasn't sure who Angie Winkle was, if she wasn't that girl.

Josie hadn't taken to Lorraine. Angie wondered whether it was because Lorraine was considered an 'outsider'. What would Josie say if she found out Lorraine was the real Jeffers? Bless Lorraine for keeping schtum. To her it was a great joke, but Angie knew that Josie would feel betrayed if she knew the truth. Lorraine's arrival got Angie off the hook. She was able to persuade Josie that Lorraine would look after her in her own home and when she was fit enough, Lorraine would travel with her to London.

Time was running out and Angie had to get a move on; she was not going to get better, only worse. So, after reassuring Lorraine that she was well enough to travel, and calming a distraught Danny who didn't want to be left in Lorraine's care, Angie set off for Earl's Court. The hospital could wait – she had to check out the madam who was looking for Danny before she gave him back. Right from the start she had her suspicions that Danny was being mistreated, the welts on his back and the way that he clung to her, the poor little mite. Then there was his talk of the school for naughty boys and what he said to Molly's kids about Namma being his mum, as though he didn't miss his mum at all. It wasn't right. Maybe she ought to hand Danny over to the police. It was hard to know what to do for the best. The only way to settle it was to visit the address that the girl had given and see for herself.

Lenham Avenue was a smart street. Danny's parents were probably more interested in themselves and their lifestyle than their child. A child who was farmed out to a string of au pairs. No wonder Danny didn't miss them. Before handing Danny over, she would give them a piece of her mind.

Angie jabbed the doorbell. She couldn't tell if it was working and so bashed the knocker for good measure. They were likely to be in the Mediterranean on their yacht or on safari. Did they even know that Danny was missing? Angie was simmering with rage when a tall woman, dressed in crisp white trousers, auburn hair caught back in a scarf, opened the door. The smile that she must have prepared, expecting someone else, anyone but Angie, froze. She recoiled as though a heap of manure had been dumped on her doorstep. Before she could slam the door in her face, Angie barged past. It wasn't hard, she was twice the woman's weight.

'You and me need to talk,' Angie bellowed.

There was a flicker of fear in the woman's eyes before she regained control. Angie had nothing to lose. This was all about Danny. Let the silly bint quake in her ridiculous jewel spangled flip-flops. Her son had been missing for eleven days and she was fannying around here like Lady Muck, with no thought for her son's whereabouts or what had become of him. Danny deserved better than that.

They faced each other in a stand-off. Angie glared the woman into submission and she stepped back. 'What do you want? I haven't got all day.'

Angie thrust the note that Slippery had passed to her, under the woman's nose. 'I have the boy that your au pair was looking for. Did you even know your son was missing?'

The woman plucked the scrap of paper from Angie. 'Who gave you this address?'

'Your girl came looking for Danny in Clacton. I know where he is but you're not getting him back until I tell you a thing or two.'

'You had better come in.' The woman led Angie into a spacious – no, palatial room. There was more floor space in that one room than the whole of Higgins's shack. It was wrong that some people lived like this, whilst other good people were crammed together like rats. Didn't mean it was a better life. Children needed love, not money.

'I was potting some orchids in the conservatory. I am sorry if I didn't hear the doorbell. Now, can I get you some refreshment, Mrs…'

She could play the high and mighty but Angie wasn't going

to be intimidated. 'I'm not stopping. I'll say what I have to say and then I'll be on my way.'

'In that case I had better invite Danek's mother to join us.'

Oh no, she had got it wrong. Angie sank into a deep sofa. The woman kept her eyes on Angie as she made a call from her mobile. Did she think she was going to steal something? At least the icy madam wasn't Danny's mum. Angie unfastened the Velcro on her sandals. Her feet had swollen in the heat and the sandal strap was cutting into her bunion. Sand scattered across the carpet. It felt good to get some air to her feet. Angie was rubbing her bunion when the girl with a ponytail joined them.

Nikoleta heard a woman shouting downstairs and crept out of her flat to peer over the bannister. The woman was a little scary with her wild hair and big voice – like an angry Ronald McDonald in a flowery dress. Nikoleta wondered whether a vagrant had got in from the street. Maybe she was going to rob Mrs Lisowski. Then Nikoleta heard the woman say that she knew where Danek was, only she called him Danny. Nikoleta's heart thumped. This was the woman who stole Danek, but where was he? Had she hurt him? Was she going to ask for a ransom? Nikoleta wished that Kamil wasn't out. Nikoleta's mobile rang as she dithered outside the door, trying to decide what to do.

Mrs Lisowski seemed flustered when she showed Nikoleta in. No wonder their snooty landlady had lost her cool, the woman with wild hair was resting her bare feet on Mrs Lisowski's suede footstool.

'Oh, it's you,' the woman said. 'Somehow I didn't believe you were Danny boy's mum. Thought his own mum might have taken better care of him.'

Mrs Lisowski smirked and Nikoleta guessed that her land-lady was already rehearsing the story that she would tell Kamil.

Nikoleta's face burned. 'It wasn't my fault. Why didn't you wait?'

The woman struggled up and put on her shoes. 'If you are Danny's mum, we need to talk.'

'Go ahead,' Mrs Lisowski said. 'We are waiting to hear what you have to say.'

'What I have to say is between me and her.' The woman poked a finger at Nikoleta. 'Do you live with this woman?'

Nikoleta shook her head. 'No, we live upstairs.'

'Then let's go upstairs and talk in private.' Nikoleta loved the way the woman put Mrs Lisowski in her place. She had never seen her lost for words. 'Well?' the woman said, and Nikoleta led the way up to their little apartment.

The wild woman's straightforwardness put Nikoleta at ease. She might be a bit crazy but Nikoleta didn't think that she was a threat. Funny, her mum would approve of this woman more than she would Mrs Lisowski. Nikoleta invited the woman to sit down and then she said, 'Please tell me that Danek is safe and well.'

'Danny is fine. I've taken good care of the boy. I'll give him back once I am satisfied that you are his mum and there's no funny stuff going on.'

Nikoleta didn't understand what she meant by 'funny stuff'. There was nothing humorous about Danek's home life. She frowned.

'Okay. Start by telling me why you didn't come and collect Danny from me at the statue. I heard the announcement. Me and Danny waited a good hour.'

Nikoleta had dreamt about this moment. What she would say to the evil woman who stole Danek. In her imagined confrontations, she had been the one demanding answers. The woman was waiting. 'When I got to the statue you had gone. I was desperate to get there, to find Danek, but it was difficult for me. We had just arrived in England from Poland and I was frightened – in a panic. When I was told about the announcement I tried to find the statue but I went to the wrong station. It was the statue of two children at the entrance to the Tube. Is that right?'

The woman nodded. At least she had been waiting at the right one. Nikoleta's throat tightened as she remembered the horror – how everyone had ignored her and all the while Danek was travelling further and further away. 'The English are so cold. Nobody would help me. It was as though they could not see me. It is different at home.'

Angie got up and fetched a glass of water for herself and one for Nikoleta. She seemed to make herself at home, as though Nikoleta was a child that needed taking care of. Her kindness made Nikoleta want to cry, when she should be the one in control. She swiped her eyes with the back of her hand. The woman wandered over to their bedside table and returned with a box of tissues in one hand and a photograph of Nikoleta's family in the other.

'Are they Danny's grandparents?' Now she sounded sad.

Nikoleta took a tissue and blew her nose. When had she started to cry? 'That's my mum and dad and my little sister, Angelika.'

'Are you a close family?' The woman sat down, the photograph in her lap.

'I come from a very close family and community. At home everyone cares for one another. It is so different in London.'

'What's life going to be like for you and Danny in London? Has he got a father?' The woman glanced around their tiny apartment. 'It's a bit cramped here. Where are Danny's toys? Where will he play?'

Nikoleta explained that Danek was not her biological son and that she had moved to London with Danek and his dad, Kamil, to make a better life for them all.

'How will it be better?' the woman said.

Nikoleta didn't know what to say. It was what her mum and dad had asked. Then, she had been full of answers: better work opportunities, higher salary, being in a city where things happened, not stuck on a farm in the middle of nowhere. It all sounded a bit hollow now. 'More opportunities,' she said, but it sounded more like a question.

'Are you going to carry on living here?' The woman seemed concerned that Danek had nowhere to play. Nikoleta hadn't considered that before.

'I expect we will move once Danek is home.' It was irritating; this woman had put her and Kamil through hell. How dare she ask about their plans? Who did she think she was? Then it occurred to Nikoleta that this woman might be making enquiries on behalf of the Polish courts. Had they seen her message on Twitter? 'Why did you take him?' she asked.

The woman sighed. 'Do you mind if I take off my shoes?' Nikoleta shook her head. 'I'll be straight with you. I don't have long left to live. Don't look like that. It's a fact. I'm not looking for sympathy. I wanted to know what it was like being a mother or a grandmother. I had a son. Todd.' The woman took a sip of water. 'I had to give him away.'

Nikoleta didn't understand what the woman meant, *give him away*. 'Why?'

'When I was a young girl – fourteen – an older boy took advantage of me. I got pregnant. My mum arranged for me to go to her sister in Northamptonshire, until I gave birth. I wasn't allowed to keep him.'

Nikoleta nudged the box of tissues towards the woman. 'What happened to Todd?'

'I never saw him again. Anyway – that's why I took Danny. It's not an excuse. It was wrong and I'm sorry.'

They sat in silence. Eventually Nikoleta said, 'How old was the boy that raped you?'

The woman shrank, her eyes fearful, like a scared teenager. 'Pete was in his twenties. I shouldn't have gone off with him like that. I was stupid.'

Nikoleta lay her hand on the woman's fist. She was clutching a ball of tissue, her knuckles white. 'What is your name?'

'Angie.'

'Angie. You were fourteen, a child.' Nikoleta took the photo frame from Angie's lap. 'My sister, Angelika, is fourteen. If a boy in his twenties raped my little sister I would kill him.'

Angie nodded and wiped her eyes. 'I never really thought of it as rape. We didn't talk about things like that when I was a girl.' She blew her nose and recovered a little. 'Tell me about your family. It must have been good growing up in a close community. Until I went to Jaywick with Danny I didn't know what that was like.'

Nikoleta told Angie about growing up on the farm. Angie was enthralled; she had lived most of her life feeling as though she didn't belong and couldn't understand why Nikoleta, who had a strong sense of belonging, could give it all up.

'Before I give him back I need to ask about the marks on his back.'

Nikoleta didn't know what Angie was talking about. 'What marks?'

'It looked like someone had given the boy a thrashing.

Now, tell me the truth because I'll know if you're lying. I have good instincts for these things.'

Nikoleta believed her. 'I probably shouldn't tell you this but Danek's real mother is an alcoholic. His dad, Kamil, had to fight the courts to get custody of Danek. We don't know what life was like for him living with his mum, but we guessed he wasn't being cared for properly. That's why we didn't go to the police. We were afraid that the courts would revoke the custody because we – *I* – couldn't protect him and keep him safe. Angie, I am so ashamed. I promise that I will be a good mother to Danek.'

Angie seemed to give this consideration. Eventually she said, 'Promise me that you'll make a home for Danny where he feels safe and secure. It's important to feel that you belong and matter. You're not his real mum and I'm not his grandma, but I think I did a decent job. Someone else brought up my son. It's a big responsibility and a privilege. A gift. Don't let Danny down.'

Angie's words moved Nikoleta. More than anything, she wanted this woman's approval, and she vowed to Angie that she would love Danny as though he were her biological son.

It was agreed that they would meet the day after next at 11.00 am in Liverpool Street Station. At last, her little family would be reunited and maybe then they could put the past eleven days behind them.

36

I t wasn't much of a leaving party, just Molly and the kids, Josie, Bill, Zoe, and Slippery. Lorraine had been invited but declined and Higgins rarely left his home nowadays. Josie turned the Seashell sign to closed and wiped the dust off a bumper bottle of Lambrusco for the girls, whilst Bill found some cans of lager.

'We'll all come and see you in the hospital,' Josie said, as she tipped a bag of crisps into a bowl. 'Won't we, Moll?'

Molly looked a bit unsure; she had probably never been to London. 'It's okay, I don't expect you to visit me.' Angie didn't say that was the last thing that she wanted. Nobody need ever know that she wasn't who she said she was. Danny would be returned to his family, where he belonged, and she would get in touch with the hospital to find out how long she had left to live.

'What did the specialist say, babe? They can cure cancer now, it's not like it used to be. You see you'll be back down here in a few weeks ready to party.'

If only – it was a wonderful thought. 'Let's see,' Angie said.

'Oh, Lorraine, look who's outside,' Molly said. Tomasz knocked on the door. 'I didn't tell him.'

Josie shrugged. 'What?' She winked at Angie and then unlocked the door to Tomasz, who was carrying a bouquet of pink roses.

Angie wanted to hide. How could Josie tell him? So far, she had managed to hold it together, but seeing Tomasz's sad face above the most beautiful bouquet she had ever had – the first in fact – brought tears to her eyes.

Tomasz kissed Angie's cheek. 'You should have told me, Lorraine.' He delivered the roses into Angie's arms and everyone cooed. 'I know it's not very practical with you leaving tomorrow but I wanted you to have something beautiful.'

Angie had to tear her eyes away from Tomasz. It was too much. That was why she didn't want him to know. It was hard enough saying goodbye to her friends.

Tomasz swung Danny up and kissed the curl on his fore-head. 'You look after your namma for me.' Danny buried his face in Tomasz's shirt.

'He's going back to Poland,' Alfie said.

Tomasz raised an eyebrow at Angie. She couldn't correct Alfie because that was what everyone thought. Angie had explained to Danny that he wasn't going back to his mum in Poland but to stay in London with his dad and new mummy, but Danny's reaction to this wasn't much better – he didn't want to leave Angie or Jaywick. Well, neither did she.

As Angie's hand smoothed Danny's hair to try to convey some reassurance, it brushed against Tomasz's shirt and she felt electricity tingle her veins. 'Danny's going to go home to his mum and dad whilst I'm in hospital.'

'I don't want namma to go to hospital,' Danny cried.

'There now, big guy,' Tomasz wiped away Danny's tears

with his handkerchief. 'Blow.' Danny let Tomasz wipe his nose.

'I was naughty,' Danny cried. 'Don't send me back, Namma. I'm sorry. I'm sorry.'

Angie wrestled a writhing Danny from Tomasz. 'Hush, sweetheart. You've not been naughty. You know that I was only minding you for the summer. I love you, Danny boy. I'm your namma and as long as I live, you will have a special place in my heart. But Namma is sick. I can't take care of you until the doctor makes me better. I have to go to the hospital and you have to go home to your daddy. He needs you too, sweetheart.'

The party fizzled out as nobody was in the mood. Bill and Slippery went to the pub and Molly told the boys to say goodbye to Danny.

'Let me travel to London with you,' Tomasz said.

'There's no point. I'll drop Danny off and then I should go back to the hospital. But if you could give us a lift to the station tomorrow morning it would help.'

Angie and Danny were both miserable when they curled up together between the two sleeping bags. Tomorrow they would leave their friends in Jaywick and return to their real lives. Angie knew what lay ahead for her – she just hoped that Danny would be safe and happy.

37

1975

The weight of Todd's warm body in Angie's arms, his milky, vanilla scent and the downy softness of his skull against her cheek, it was the first time that she had held her son and Angie knew that she would never forget this moment.

Mum put an arm around Angie. 'How are you feeling, sweetheart? You did so well in there.'

Angie tucked the cellular baby blanket back from Todd's face and they both stared in wonder at the little miracle. To think that she had created this tiny, perfect little treasure. She had been in labour for five hours and gave birth with just gas and air. Mum had been there with words of encouragement, wiping Angie's forehead with a cold flannel.

'I'm going to call him Todd,' Angie said. It was as though something in her soul had unfurled, something magnificent that had always been there dormant and unknown. This little boy made her complete.

'Could you leave us alone for a few minutes?' Mum said. The nurse and social worker left the room.

Angie reached for her mum's hand and squeezed it. They were both crying; Angie's tears were tears of joy – complete and utter happiness. She no longer cared how Todd had been created, he was her son and she was in awe of the fierce love that consumed her for this tiny perfect being.

'I'll go back to school when he's old enough for nursery,' Angie said, unable to take her eyes off Todd, whose little mouth was contorting with a yawn.

'Can I?' Mum took the baby from Angie. She stood up, holding Todd close to her chest. Angie remembered the comfort of lying her own head against Mum, a rough apron or nylon overall and the smell of Wright's Coal Tar Soap and Nivea cream. Todd started to cry and milk surged in Angie's breast, a strange but not unpleasant sensation. She had read about breastfeeding but hadn't yet tried. Todd was not yet a day old – there was time.

Mum turned her back on Angie to look out of the window.

'I'll take him back now,' Angie said. She couldn't bear for her son to be out of her sight.

'We talked about this, Angie.'

Angie's heart went cold, as though something dark had entered her soul. Todd cried and her breasts ached with milk.

'You can't keep him, Angie.'

When did they talk about it? Todd was *her* baby. 'Give me back my son.' Angie spoke with authority – she was a mother herself now.

'It's for your own good. One day you'll thank me.'

Before Angie could reply they came in – the social worker, a nurse, and the ward orderly. The ward orderly stood close to Angie blocking her view. Todd cried and her milk surged, a pain in her breasts as it fought to reach him. And then he was gone. They slipped through the door, leaving Angie bereft as though he had been ripped from her womb. They might as well have torn out her heart. She screamed and cried until sedated, but it made no difference, she never saw Todd again.

38

M rs Lisowski had, as Nikoleta guessed she would, pounced on Kamil the minute he was through the door to tell him about their visitor. She could hear their hushed voices downstairs and didn't care. She, Nikoleta, had found Danek and arranged for his safe return. Her heart sang – a chorus of restless birds.

Kamil was full of concern when he greeted Nikoleta. 'Lenka told me about some madwoman who threatened you. Are you alright, *slonka*? You shouldn't have brought her up here alone, anything could have happened. Lenka tried to phone me but I was in a meeting.'

Nikoleta beamed. 'Lenka need not have worried.' Saying her landlady's name, Nikoleta felt, for the first time, just a little bit bigger than the formidable Mrs Lisowski. 'I am meeting Danek and Angie, the lady who has been taking care of him, at eleven o'clock Wednesday morning at Liverpool Street Station.' Nikoleta tilted her chin. It was a sin to be proud but she couldn't help herself.

Kamil's mouth fell open. Nikoleta was smug; he couldn't

believe that his little village girl had achieved what he and his men had failed to do. 'How did she find you?' Kamil dropped into a chair. She really had taken him by surprise.

Explaining her deceit was not going to be so easy. If she didn't handle this carefully, Kamil might get angry and spoil the moment. Nikoleta took a deep breath.

'Are you happy that Danek is coming home?'

'Of course I am, *slonka*. Come here.' He opened his arms and Nikoleta perched on his knee.

'You know how guilty and miserable I felt when I lost Danek?' Nikoleta sought Kamil's eyes. It was important he understood why she did what she did.

'I never blamed you, *slonka*, not really. I blamed myself for not being with you. Danek was, *is*, my responsibility.'

'I know. You were so kind and forgiving. I couldn't bear to see you miserable, knowing it was my fault. So, I did something stupid. Well, I thought it was stupid at the time.' Nikoleta prayed that Kamil would forgive her for the tweet, now that she had found Danek.

'Go on.'

'I posted a tweet of Danek. I did it without thinking. Then I realised that I shouldn't have, because Danek's mother might have seen it or the courts in Poland.'

Kamil hugged her. 'Oh, *slonka*, I didn't mean to frighten you with my paranoia. Are you telling me that this tweet helped you find Danek?'

She could breathe again. 'Yes. I was sent a photograph of him on Clacton Pier. I spent the whole day on the pier, giving my address to people in case they had seen Angie – that's the woman's name – or Danek. And it worked. The woman who visited me yesterday has been looking after Danek and will hand him back to us tomorrow.'

Kamil nudged Nikoleta off his lap and leapt to his feet. 'I'm going to buy a bottle of bubbly to celebrate. My clever, clever Nikki. Thank you, *slonka*.'

When Kamil was at the door Nikoleta said, 'This is our moment to celebrate, Kamil. Just the two of us.'

Since Angie's visit, Nikoleta had been reflecting on her childhood. The close community in which she grew up. It was only because she felt secure and loved that she had been able to make this leap of faith, to set up home in a foreign country. Now, it was down to her to create the same environment for Danek. With Kamil's resourcefulness and strength and her optimism and faith, their little family was going to thrive.

They barely slept the night before collecting Danek. Their first night in that flat, they couldn't sleep for misery and now it was excitement at Danek's return. Nikoleta insisted that they find somewhere else to live, as soon as they were reunited as a family. 'There's not enough room for Danek to play,' she said. They had to get away from Mrs Lisowski before Nikoleta throttled her.

Kamil was insistent that Nikoleta pursue her dream of working as an accountant. He talked about day school and boarding school for Danek – getting an au pair, anything to help Nikoleta. He had promised her the world, pears on a willow, before they left Poland and wanted to make things up to her. If she did sleep that night, it was to catch one or two hours between whispered conversations – 'Are you asleep?' 'No.' 'I was thinking…' and so it went on until dawn. The day that Danek was coming home.

Nikoleta squeezed Kamil's hand. It was nearly time.

'I'm going to wait in that coffee bar,' Kamil said. 'I want you to meet Danek on your own.'

'Why?' Nikoleta didn't understand. Kamil had been so excited to see him.

'I know that this woman seemed okay but we don't know that she hasn't contacted the police. Give me your phone, *slonka.*'

Nikoleta passed Kamil her phone. She frowned. 'Why?'

'When you have Danek leave by that exit.' He pointed behind him. 'There will be a black Audi waiting. Get in the car and I'll join you later. I don't want anyone tracking your mobile.'

Kamil *was* paranoid. Never mind. Once they had Danek, things would settle down. He was funny, really. Nikoleta smiled and agreed to do as he asked. Then the train pulled in and Kamil disappeared.

Danek was subdued, but then he hardly knew Nikoleta. Angie had done a good job; he was clean and tidy and carried a bulging plastic bag.

'Just a couple of playsuits that I made him and a few toys,' Angie explained. Then she crouched down to Danek. 'Remember what I said, Danny boy.' Danek nodded, his eyes wide. Tears glistened, one blink and they would flow. 'Good boy. Nikoleta, *your mummy* –' she glanced up at Nikoleta and smiled '– has my phone number. I just need to get better and then…' She didn't finish. Nikoleta knew that Angie might not get better and now she too wanted to cry.

Nikoleta spoke in the same no-nonsense tone as Angie. If she didn't, they would all start howling and then parting Danek from Angie would be impossible.

The black Audi was waiting, as Kamil promised. It was frustrating that they had been living hand to mouth and now Kamil was throwing money away on fancy transport. She and Danek could have done with a cab when they first arrived in London.

Nikoleta and Danek had barely settled themselves in the back seat of the car, when it pulled away. 'Wait, my partner's joining us,' Nikoleta said.

'I have instructions to take you and the boy. Mr Kröl had urgent business but he said to tell you he would be with you as soon as possible.'

Nikoleta was disappointed. They had both looked forward to this reunion; it was a special day. If she was disappointed, then Kamil must be more so. She was being silly, there was plenty of time for him to catch up with Danek. She had to remember that he was a successful businessman and work had to come first. Now that Danek was home, Kamil would have to make up for having so much time away from the office.

Nikoleta sat back and relaxed. It was a luxury to have London laid out before them, the different architecture of old buildings with new. Peculiarly shaped towers, one that looked like a fat rocket. At last, she could enjoy being a tourist. Nikoleta pointed things out to Danek, the Tower of London, the River Thames. Her sister, Angelika, would have loved this little tour. She wished that the driver would tell her what they were passing, but the driver, like Danek, was silent. No matter, she would absorb it all and ask Kamil later.

The car pulled up outside a semi-detached house in a tree-lined street. It wasn't 137 Lenham Avenue. Nikoleta explained to the driver that it was the wrong address, but he insisted that this was the destination that Mr Kröl had requested. 'You and the boy are to use the top floor,' he said and handed Nikoleta a door key.

She wished that Kamil would communicate better. He hadn't said anything about this house. Hopefully, it would all become clear when he caught up with them. In the meantime, Danek would need to use the toilet and have something to eat.

Nikoleta remembered that the journey from Clacton to London took over an hour.

The smell of damp and stale tobacco hit them when they opened the door. And a musty, stale smell like unwashed clothes. Nikoleta resisted the urge to hold her nose, as they mounted the stairs. It was nothing like 137 with its plush carpet and freshly painted walls. The stairwell was gloomy. A dark wood dado rail topped Anaglypta wallpaper painted brown and above that the wall was a dirty cream. At one time, before Nikoleta's lifetime, it might have been fashionable, but now it looked old and neglected.

A thin grey shadow of a boy slipped past them on the stairs. Barefoot and boney, he disappeared into one of the doors on the first landing. Something about that young man made Nikoleta shiver.

They climbed two flights of stairs to reach the second landing where there was a narrower staircase. 'Do you think we are meant to go up there?' she asked Danek.

Danek looked worried and Nikoleta remembered that she was supposed to be a brave adult who knew what she was doing and so she said, as though it were a great adventure, 'Shall we take a look?'

The top floor had been built into the attic. There were three rooms: a bedroom, living room, and a small kitchen. It wasn't much bigger than their flat at 137, despite having separate rooms. 'No bathroom or toilet,' Nikoleta said. 'Perhaps we are meant to share the toilet we passed on the second landing.'

At least the rooms smelt fresh and the bed had clean sheets. Danek relaxed a little and followed Nikoleta as she explored, opening cupboard doors to see what had been provided.

'Look at this, Danek,' Nikoleta called him to the bedroom window. The house had a tiny backyard but beyond that was a wide green open space. A couple pushed a buggy along a path. A man threw a stick to a beagle. 'A great big park for us to play in. Aren't we lucky?'

Danek nodded. His thumb still plugged in his mouth.

Kamil arrived soon after Nikoleta and Danek. His presence lit up the dismal space and Nikoleta thought maybe they could be happy here after all. They were, apparently, in a house that backed onto Hampstead Heath, in North London.

'There's a playground on the Heath. Shall we go and take a look, Danek?' This was what Nikoleta had been waiting for: Kamil's reunion with his son. Danek seemed a little shy or overwhelmed. He hadn't spent much time with his father before coming to Poland; it was going to take a while.

'Why did we move here so quickly?' Nikoleta said. 'You could have warned me.'

'You said you wanted to move, that Danek needed more space to play. I thought you would be pleased with my suprise.'

'I am. But what about our things? And my work? Will I be able to get to the Emporium from here? I know that we'll need to find day care for Danek first. I'm not trying to rush things, but I need to get a sense of where we are.'

Kamil put his arms around Nikoleta. 'You will have everything that you need, *slonka*. Don't worry about your little job at the grocery store. Now that we have Danek you can find a job worthy of your talent. And you will have all of your things by later today. Now how's my boy?' Kamil lifted Danek up. The child went rigid. 'Where's that little rabbit of yours?'

'His things are in that plastic bag,' Nikoleta said.

Kamil planted Danek back down. 'Let's see what we have in here.' Kamil dug into the plastic bag and pulled out a furry garment and another strangely shaped with stuffed spikes down the back. There was a tin that rattled but nothing else. 'Where's the fucking rabbit?'

Nikoleta recoiled. She had never heard Kamil swear. Danek looked afraid and Nikoleta frowned at Kamil. This wasn't like him.

'I'm sorry. Look, I have to go out again. Take Danek to the park or something.'

'Leave me my phone, Kamil. I have to phone Tavit to tell him I won't be in tomorrow.'

'I haven't got it on me. I'm going by 137 to collect our things. I'll drop in and let them know.'

When he had gone Danek said, 'I left Licky with Namma, so that she would get cuddles, to make her better.'

39

The train slowed and tears of rain that had been slanting across the window straightened. As did Angie; she had no business feeling sorry for herself. The last couple of weeks had been the best days of her life: loving Danny, meeting Tomasz. Was that what falling in love felt like? Thinking about someone all of the time? Catching yourself smiling like an imbecile? Angie had never been in love, didn't understand what all the fuss was about, until now. Finding love at this age was something of a miracle, but at the end of her life – it was a bloody tragedy. Someone up there was having a laugh.

Danny, Tomasz, and amazing friends. She had been loved and valued for being herself. *Not yourself*, a goblin grumbled, *for being Lorraine Jeffers.* But Danny didn't care what her name was; she was his namma.

The rain, a hazy drizzle when Angie boarded the bus, was coming down in heavy sheets when she disembarked. With nothing to shield her Angie surrendered and it seeped into her skin. Her sundress clung to her like a wet flannel. She'd packed all that she could stuff into her supersized handbag – her smalls, a few of the dresses that she'd run up, and the silky red swimsuit. She would never wear it again, but it was a reminder of a perfect day. *He said she was beautiful.* She was doing it again – smiling like a moron. She wore the bracelet that Danny made for her and tucked her other gifts, a fossil and half-eaten honeycomb, down the sides – her prized possessions.

So, with a bulging bag, feet sloshing in saturated sandals, and a now see-through dress, Angie coaxed open the front door. A pile of mail scattered across the brown linoleum hall-way. The smell of decomposing vegetable matter, or worse, turned her stomach. She'd left food rotting in the bin and a pint of milk in the fridge that would now be solid. In Jaywick, neighbours might have popped in – or, she smiled to herself, squatters. In Dagenham, she doubted if anyone even knew she'd been away. There was a time, in her parents' day, when the neighbours knew each other, but now there were lots of foreigners and they mostly kept to themselves.

Three letters from Sullivan's, the factory where she worked, two letters from the hospital and bills. Sullivan's letters started off sounding sympathetic and helpful. *Please arrange to see the occupational health doctor. We do not seem to have a doctor's certificate for you covering the period...*

Then they got more formal. *If you do not send a doctor's certificate or make arrangements to see occupational health your sick pay will be reviewed.* Couldn't a person be left to die in peace? She'd told them she was off sick. They'd soon get to hear, once she popped her clogs. Still, best leave everything straight – her bills paid and the house clean.

Angie dumped her bag at the bottom of the stairs and dragged herself into the kitchen. The stench was overpower-ing. She used a chair to prop open the back door against the driving rain and gulped in freshly laundered air. It was hard to get moving, when all she wanted to do was curl up under a duvet and never come out. Then she thought of Josie and Molly. They were strong women – facing everything life dealt them. She tried to picture them standing either side of her. Josie would fire off instructions – *get a bowl of disinfectant and rubber gloves, throw out that rubbish.* Molly would be finding things to laugh about, to keep Angie's spirits up. God, she missed them.

'Okay,' she said firmly, trying to incite a sense of purpose. 'Let's do this.'

Why hadn't she emptied her fridge and bin before leaving for Jaywick? Angie remembered the bewildered woman who had bolted up in bed and made what had seemed a rash decision – there was no planning, just instinct. Her instincts were right though – they always were. Except about Danny; she had misjudged Nikoleta. What would Danny boy be doing now? Would he remember his namma and their little holiday in Jaywick?

The housework brought on a gnawing pain, like a sharp-toothed rat tearing into her womb. Angie filled a glass with water. Maybe she had done a bit too much. Josie would tell her to sit down and take it easy. She trembled as a hot flush soaked her in sweat and lowered herself into a kitchen chair.

The pile of mail taunted her. Angie opened the bills first. All those letters and none of them good news. The first letter from the hospital said that she had to rearrange an appointment urgently. It was dated the day after her missed appointment. The next letter advised her to call them immediately – that was over a week ago.

Best get it over with let them tell her what she already

knew. Towards the end she would have to be admitted some-where to die – a hospice or the hospital. She didn't want to die alone in the house. The clutter of hospital noise would be of some comfort, when she was dying with no one at her side. The GP in Jaywick had prescribed some pills; the hospital might want to know what they were. Angie rooted around in her bag and a silky red bundle rolled across the room. Her gorgeous swimsuit and folded inside – Licky. Oh no, Danny couldn't have gone without Licky. He wouldn't sleep without his rabbit. How could she have let him leave without Licky? Then, she remembered Danny fussing about, making a bed for Licky so that he could sleep on the train journey.

Angie sank onto the stair. Licky smelt of the sea, sugar, and Danny's honeyed skin. She clutched the raggedy rabbit to her womb and rocked in pain. 'Oh, Danny my darling, I'm going to miss you so much.' She cried, giving in to the luxury of loud wailing sobs. There was nobody to hear.

Eventually, Angie wiped her eyes with Licky's floppy ears. 'Enough. What does Zoe say? *Man up.* Right –' Angie took a deep breath '– phone Nikoleta and tell her I have Licky. Maybe I can drop him off at Earl's Court.' Even as she said this to herself, Angie knew that she couldn't make the journey, not tonight. There was no reply and so Angie left a message with her address and house phone number. Maybe Danny's dad would drop in and collect the rabbit.

Angie inspected Licky. He had been in and out of the sea helping Danny build sandcastles. Pickles had slobbered over him and carried him like a pup in his drooling mouth. He had been fed candy floss and banana milkshakes.

'Let's clean you up. Make you as good as new. Then we'll get you back to Danny boy.'

Angie filled a sink with washing-up liquid and warm water. She massaged soap into Licky's matted fur and splashed him as though he were a newborn babe. The fur around his neck was rough and hard. Angie used a washing-up brush to try to soften it, to loosen the matted clumps. The brush slipped and tore the neck seam open.

'Blast. Sorry, mate.' What was the matter with her, talking to a soft toy? Angie squeezed then wrung out Licky. 'Wish someone would make me good as new,' she mused to the rabbit's vacant stare.

Angie wrapped Licky in a hand towel and attempted to roll him dry. Then she used a hairdryer, fluffing up his matted fur. He wasn't looking too bad, apart from his head hanging precariously from the torn seam. Her mum had a sewing tin somewhere – maybe in the old chest of drawers in the parlour? Ridiculous for them to have a parlour; nobody of any importance ever visited them. Her mum would dust and polish the unused room every week. After she died, Angie used it for storage. The room had always given her the creeps as a girl. There was something cold and unwelcoming in the formal furniture and sparse decoration.

'Right, this won't hurt.' Angie held a needle up to Licky. 'Let's see if we can give you a bit more stuffing.' If she packed the stuffing down, then maybe she could put in a bit extra using an old cushion or shredded nylons.

Angie poked an index finger into the gash at Licky's neck. The stuffing was loose. She pushed into the soft wadding. Then her finger found a different texture. It was slippery, like a plastic bag. Odd. She used her thumb and forefinger to probe deeper. There was a big lump in there.

'We're not so different after all.' Licky had a lump of plastic in his head. But, there was an elastic band wrapped around it. Her fingers explored the lump. She flicked the elastic. This wasn't what you would expect to find in a soft toy.

There was no reason other than idle curiosity and

boredom that made Angie pick apart the seam. She had nothing else to do and was glad of the focus to make Licky 'as good as new'. He was still damp and she reasoned that if she took the obstruction out he might dry a bit quicker.

When Angie extracted the plastic bag from Licky, she knew straight away what it was. Not because she'd ever seen drugs in anything other than TV and films, but white powder packed in a tight package and hidden in a child's toy – what else could it be?

It took a bit longer for the implications to sink in. What kind of parents used their child to smuggle drugs? Did Nikoleta know? Angie had guessed something was wrong. She should have trusted her instincts. Danny's detachment from his parents. The shy, nervous, and undernourished child she had rescued on the Underground. A couple of weeks of good food and loving care had transformed him. What had she sent Danny back to?

Angie's first instinct was to call Tomasz; he would know what to do. If she told Tomasz about finding the drugs, then she would have to tell him that she wasn't Lorraine Jeffers and that she had abducted Danny. Should she go to Lenham Avenue and confront them?

The house phone rang and Angie threw the bag of white powder across the floor. *Calm down, it's only the phone.* Was it Nikoleta or one of the gang phoning with a threat to slice her neck if she didn't give them back their merchandise? She had seen the films. The phone rang four times before Angie picked it up.

'Lorraine? I wanted to check that you had got back safely.' It was Tomasz.

Angie was both relieved and apprehensive. She could pretend everything was fine, but the temptation to share her troubles was too much and she started tentatively, 'There's something I have to tell you. Before I do, I just want to say that meeting you – these past few days – have been precious. What I'm going to say may hurt you, and that's the last thing that I want to do. You are very dear to me.'

'Okay.' Tomasz sounded calm. Angie could imagine his twinkly eyes narrowing as he concentrated on what she had to say.

'First, my name's not Lorraine. It's Angie Winkle.' Angie told Tomasz about rescuing Danny – well, not giving him back straight away. How she thought he was in danger and acted on her instincts. Tomasz did not say anything. Angie wished that she could see his face. She continued to tell her story, finishing with the discovery of the bag of white powder.

Tomasz took a deep breath and Angie held hers. 'Lorraine – I mean Angie. I want you to leave that house and go back to Jaywick. I will join you there as soon as I can. Take the package with you. Can you sew it back inside the rabbit?'

'Yes,' Angie said. He sounded so in control. It was what she needed but she didn't know how he felt about her deceit.

'I'm sorry, Tomasz,' she said, hoping to prompt a reaction that would give some clue to how he was feeling.

'We'll talk later. Promise me you'll leave straight away. They know where you are and they will come after you.'

Angie sat on the stair until it grew dark. *They know where you are and they will come after you.* She was afraid to stay but too exhausted to make the journey to Jaywick. After falling asleep and jolting awake a couple of times, Angie gave in and went to bed. Let them come looking.

40

Nikoleta wriggled to the edge of the bed and flipped her pillow. Kamil snored gently beside her. How could he sleep? Unsaid recriminations burned in her chest. Danek was upset enough, without rowing in front of him. The boy had been distraught when his father left in a temper. Nikoleta had tried to coax Danek into visiting the park but he huddled in a corner, rocking and sniffling. She was angry on Danek's behalf, as he had done nothing wrong. Anyone would think that mangy toy was a priceless antique. It was Danek's and if he wanted his namma, Angie, to have the rabbit then Nikoleta couldn't see why it should grieve Kamil. To make matters worse, Kamil had said as a parting shot that he didn't want Danek to have any more contact with Angie. No wonder the boy became hysterical. He adored the woman who he called Namma. Perhaps Kamil was jealous.

Nikoleta had settled Danek in the living room, making up a bed on the sofa. Kamil hadn't thought things through. The flat was entirely unsuitable for a small child. The toilet and bathroom were on the second floor and shared with the other occupants of the house. Nikoleta didn't know how many people lived there; she had only seen the young man who passed them on the stairs. They didn't have a door to their flat so anyone could wander in. It wasn't safe to leave Danek so exposed. She had wanted him to share her bed and suggested Kamil sleep on the sofa, until they bought a put-up bed for their room, but Kamil dismissed her concerns as though she was overreacting.

Kamil snorted in his sleep and Nikoleta dug an elbow into his side. He flung out an arm, taking more than his share of the bed, and went back to snoring. Nikoleta huffed and sighed as she got out of bed. Still he slept.

Moonlight fell across Danek's makeshift bed. In the morning, the sun would wake him, as there were no curtains. Nikoleta crouched beside him. 'Shall I take you to the toilet, Danek?'

Nikoleta pulled on a pair of jeans and fleece over her nightdress and lifted Danek from his bed. He wouldn't be able to go to the toilet on his own. What had Kamil been thinking when he rented this place? The stairs creaked underfoot and Danek rubbed his eyes. 'Namma?'

'Shh, mummy Nikki is taking you to the toilet, Danek.' He twisted to see where they were going.

Danek was a good boy, he went to the toilet as soon as Nikoleta sat him on the seat. Then she went. It was three-thirty and she had not yet had a wink of sleep.

As they came out of the toilet, the front door opened. Voices – Ukranian and Polish, maybe some Russsian. They woke Danek, who might otherwise have drifted back to sleep. Nikoleta peered over the bannister. She counted twelve men in the downstairs hallway. Several were carrying backpacks. They ambled around each other, heads bowed – uncertain, as though disorientated – then one of the men said something and they fell into a line ready to mount the stairs. Nikoleta was pleased that she had the foresight to get dressed over her nightclothes. She clutched Danek to her and disappeared up their flight of stairs, before the men reached the second-floor landing.

'Where are the whispering men?' Danek asked when Nikoleta tucked him back into bed.

'They will be going to bed just like you,' she said and kissed him goodnight.

'I don't like the whispering men. They might come upstairs.'

Nikoleta didn't like the look of them either. Danek was right; there was nothing to stop them entering their flat.

'I'll stay with you until the morning.' She stroked Danek's hair. The sun would be up in a couple of hours and sleep was now impossible. Two nights with little to no sleep; she would be exhausted in the morning.

Kamil woke up irritatingly chirpy after a good night's rest. 'I'll wash and shave and then I'm going to take you and Danek out for breakfast.' He kissed Nikoleta, caressing her bottom as he passed.

Danek seemed to have forgotten any grievance against his dad and played happily on the floor, surrounded by plastic toy figures. At least when Kamil returned yesterday he had her wheelie case. He said that he had phoned Tavit to explain that she would not be going back to work, but Nikoleta wanted to speak to Tavit herself. She wanted to have the option of returning to the Emporium once they had made plans for Daneks's day care, besides she had to return that silly pink overall and collect her wages. It was only a few days' pay but at least she would have some money of her own again.

Kamil chivvied Nikoleta and Danek to get ready, so that they could leave.

'Can I have my phone back?' Nikoleta asked.

'Use mine.'

'Why? Just let me have my phone back, Kamil.' There was a whine to her voice. She was tired and irritable. No wonder, with no sleep. Nikoleta knew that she should go carefully or risk ruining another day by starting a row. But she was so tired.

Kamil's eyes softened. 'Come here, *slonka.*' He opened his arms and Nikoleta sunk into them. She wished she could lay her head on his chest and sleep. Sleep for fourteen hours or more. 'I'm really sorry but I can't let you have your phone, at least not your SIM card. You gave that woman your phone number and now your phone can be tracked. We have to keep a low profile. I know it's hard for you to understand but you have to trust me. Immigrants are not welcome here. It's our word against theirs. If that woman claims we're neglecting our son, they will take Danek away from us. After all I went through getting him out of Poland, I couldn't go through that again.'

'Angie won't,' Nikoleta started to argue but gave up. When Kamil got something into his head he wouldn't budge. She reached out for his phone. 'Okay, but I want a new SIM card. I need a phone to keep in touch with my family. Take Danek down and I'll join you in a minute.'

Kamil passed Nikoleta his mobile and gave her a kiss before leaving, holding Danek's hand. Nikoleta watched them count the stairs as they went. Danek looked up at his dad, happy to have his attention. She was being hard on Kamil; he was just having a bad day yesterday. They had both been tired after lying awake all night in their excitement at collecting Danek.

When Nikoleta had finished talking to Liza, she had a thought. Kamil went back to 137 yesterday to collect her clothes. She trusted Kamil but couldn't help a niggling doubt. Had anything gone on between him and Mrs Lisowski? Is that why he was in a better mood this morning? She clicked on his messages. Nothing from Lenka Lisowski. Nikoleta glanced out of the window. Kamil was showing Danek how to blow through a blade of grass to make a whistle. It was a trick her dad taught her as a girl. The thought pressed a bruise in her heart and she looked away. Photographs – if something was going on between them then he would have a photograph of Lenka on his phone. Nikoleta scrolled quickly. She stopped when she found a selfie of Danek with Angie and some other people. When did Kamil receive that? There was a man in the photograph who Nikoleta recognised as an associate of Kamil's. Had Kamil always known where to find Danek? Of course not, he would have brought him home sooner. She glanced out of the window. Kamil was retying Danek's trainer. What was the matter with her, behaving like one of the old villagers – suspicious of everyone and everything? It was because she was so tired. But there were no photographs of Lenka. Nikoleta plodded down the stairs to join Kamil and Danek.

The café was called Boris's Café, after its owner, a huge lumbering man who lurked behind a grill pan. It was steamy from cooking and smelt of chip fat and wet dog. Kamil was effusive in his greeting and Boris came out from behind the grill and hugged him. He had an angry boil on his thick neck.

'Boris, this is my girl, Nikki. I want you to look after her.'

Nikoleta wondered what Boris was expected to do, in looking after her. There was nothing that she would want this greasy man to do for her, even cooking her breakfast was not very appealing. What was happening to her? She was becoming ungrateful and spiteful. *Forgive me, Mother of God.* Nikoleta forced a smile.

As they ate their breakfast a group of young men meandered in. They all wore dark clothes and looked like the whispering men who had crept into their house last night. Kamil stared at them. A few of the men dipped their heads, others looked away.

'I wonder what they're doing here,' Nikoleta said. She guessed that they worked together; they all looked as though they were Eastern European but there was a sadness about them.

'That's none of our concern. I don't want you or Danek talking to the men who share our house. I know the owner, he's a good man, but these men – they work for him and they can't all be trusted. Now, have you finished or would you like some more? Danek loves his sausage, he's eaten the lot.'

Nikoleta had barely touched her buttered toast. Boris's boils put her off eating anything that he prepared. 'I'll do a shop, buy some sausages, and then Danek can have them every day for breakfast.' Nikoleta wiped egg from Danek's chin.

'I bought you in here to meet Boris because he'll look after you and Danek whilst I'm away. There's no need for you to cook. Boris will prepare all of your meals.'

It was the first Nikoleta had heard about Kamil's plans to work away from home again. 'Surely not straight away, Kamil. What about Danek?'

'It will just be for a couple of days, *slonka*. I tried to get out of it but I have had too long away from work.'

'Not immediately?' She knew he would have to go back to work but not abroad. The thought of being left alone in that house scared her.

'I'm afraid so, *slonka*. You know what my business is like. You and Danek can see London, enjoy yourselves.'

She spoke before she thought. 'Kamil, I don't think it's safe, us having no front door.' Danek's head jerked up. *Matko Boska*, what had she said? Danek was jittery enough as it was. She tried a wan smile, but Danek was no fool. His big blue eyes were upon her.

'I've thought of that, *slonka*. I'll get a lock fitted to our bedroom door. Danek can sleep in the double bed with you until I get back.'

'What about our things? My passport? Our money?' She softened her voice so that Danek didn't pick up on her anxiety.

'I have your passport in my attaché case and I never leave money at home. But don't worry, *slonka*, I will make sure that you have everything you need. Here, take this.' Kamil handed Nikoleta a twenty-pound note. 'Boris will provide all of your meals and I'll settle up when I'm back. That way you can relax and sightsee without having to worry about cooking.'

'If you're leaving the country you must give me back my passport and I need my phone. Maybe I should look after Danek's too, just until you get back.'

Kamil tucked a strand of hair behind her ear. 'I know the flat is not ideal, *slonka*. Do you *really* want to look after the passports living in that house? I'm only going to be away a few days. As soon as I get back we will find you a phone.' He unlocked his case to find the passports. 'Do you mind if I hang on to Danek's?'

Nikoleta guessed he didn't trust her to keep Danek's passport safe and she didn't blame him. 'Maybe you should hang on to them both. It's not as if we will need them whilst you are away.'

'If you're sure?' Kamil waited and when Nikoleta nodded her agreement, snapped the case.

She was just tired, it was making her oversensitive and wary. Kamil was only going to be away for two or three days; it would give her and Danek some time to get to know each other. Maybe they would do a little sightseeing – once she had had a good night's sleep.

When Angie opened her eyes, she was surprised to see the walnut wardrobe and then she remembered where she was and the cocaine-stuffed rabbit hidden under her duvet. Ruddy Nora, what if they came looking for her? Angie scrambled out of bed as fast as her weary limbs would allow. Tomasz was right, she was a sitting duck in Dagenham. Her hands shook as she struggled with her bra fastening.

Something was wrong. She could sense it as soon as she stepped out from her bedroom. A door or window was open somewhere letting in a breeze. Downstairs a door slammed. Angie tucked Licky inside her blouse and crept down the stairs. Nothing, just the sound of traffic. At the bottom of the stairs Angie scanned the hall. The sitting room and parlour doors were wide open and she always closed them before going to bed. But she was in shock last night, had she forgotten to lock the back door too?

Someone had paid her a visit during the night. Everywhere was in disarray. The drawers in her dad's bureau were strewn across the floor, along with the sofa cushions. All of the kitchen cupboards were open and the contents scattered as Rice Krispies and pretzels spilled across the lino. The back door was ajar – damn, she hadn't locked up. But when she took a closer look Angie surmised that it had been jemmied open with a screwdriver. The intruder must have got in by cutting across the back gardens. Angie shivered. She could have been murdered in her bed.

'Is that you, luv?' Mrs Shilling called from the neighbouring garden. Her voice was a comfort and Angie joined her neighbour at the low fence between their gardens, where Mum had spent many an hour chatting. But that was when Beryl lived there, before she bought a flat closer to her daughter.

'Did you hear that hullabaloo last night? I'm getting onto the council about those foxes, something's got to be done. George got out of bed in the early hours to see them off. He said your back door was open. You need to be careful, luv, you don't want those beasts getting inside – they'll get at your food and make a right mess of the place.'

So, Mr Shilling had frightened her visitor away. Tomasz was right, she shouldn't have stayed in the Dagenham house.

Settled on a train to Clacton, Angie began to feel a bit calmer. She had tried to clear up and secure the house before leaving but was shaking too much, and so in the end she gave up and got the hell out of there. It wasn't as though she had anything worth stealing, apart from Licky, who was tucked into her bag. Oh Lord, she was carrying a shedload of cocaine. Could anyone tell she was guilty just by looking at her? *Try and relax, if you keep on shaking you will look suspicious.* Angie concentrated on the other passengers to take her mind off the drugs in her bag.

The carriage was busy; not surprising with it being the school holidays. Families spread themselves out where they could, and children squabbled with siblings or played games. Angie sat alone clutching her bag.

She hoped that Tomasz would be in Jaywick waiting for her, but what reception would she get? He hadn't given any clue on the phone, just practical advice. Was he stern because he was worried about her or angry? She had deceived him, pretending to be Lorraine, and in romantic comedies when the protagonist lied about their true identity it always ended badly. Angie felt sick. What if he hated her? Then there were her friends, she had lied to them too – betrayed their trust, and in Jaywick trust and honour were everything. But whatever they thought of her, they would want to help Danny. *Danny.* He tried to tell her that he was unhappy at home and she had ignored him, she'd pushed him away. If anything happened to that boy, she would hold herself responsible.

Distracted, Angie had slipped Licky from her bag and was stroking his ears. *I'll find you, Danny boy, as long as I'm still breathing – I will find you.* To think this little rabbit was hiding a big secret – bigger than Angie's. She wondered whether Pickles could smell the drug and that was why he wouldn't leave the rabbit alone. How could she have been so wrong about Nikoleta, when her instincts were usually spot on? She'd spent forty years learning to read the signs and listen to her intuition and it hadn't done her any bloody good.

The train had pulled into a station. A girl got on with a bicycle and a few more seats were filled with young families carrying beach balls and cool bags.

Was she doing the right thing going back to Jaywick? It was wasting time when she should be going after Danny.

Maybe she should have gone straight to Lenham Avenue and made a deal – Danny for the drugs. Tomasz was a kind man but he was a community worker, for heaven's sake – a do-gooder. What did he know about the criminal underworld? What was she thinking? There was nothing Tomasz could do to find Danny, he was just trying to keep her safe. She was a coward, running back to Tomasz when she should have gone straight to Nikoleta's flat to confront her.

A coward. She'd been a coward, hiding from her diagnosis. And hiding from her past. She had to go back to London and find Danny. But she was afraid and so yes, she was a coward.

Two men and a woman in uniform entered the carriage. 'Tickets, please.'

Angie craned her neck to see their uniforms. It was hard to tell, but it looked as though the Old Bill were doing the rounds with the ticket inspector. Her heart hammered in her chest. Were they looking for her? Angie was reminded of the time that she awoke to find Danny missing. Those wretched Polish men had taken him to the toilet. A fleeting memory of the older man, his salt-and-pepper hair and sunglasses – she remembered thinking him like George Clooney.

'Where did you get on?' They were questioning passengers.

Her heart couldn't take any more. Maybe she should just give herself in – hand the cocaine-stuffed rabbit to the police and be done with it. They were getting close. Should she get off the train?

'Ticket, please.' Too late.

Angie stuffed Licky into her bag and pushed it under her seat, before showing her ticket. One of the police officers was talking on her phone, the other caught Angie's eye and smiled. 'Another beautiful day. Where are you headed?'

Angie kicked her bag further under the seat. 'Clacton.'

The ticket inspector handed back her ticket. They had

moved on when a woman in the seat behind said, 'Give that to me. It's not yours. Where did you find it?'

'It was on the floor.' A child's voice.

Angie was almost kneeling as she reached under her seat to try and retrieve her bag. It was tricky but she caught it between her feet and scooted it forward. She pushed her hand deeper and deeper into the bag but didn't come into contact with Licky's fur. She felt hot and then cold; this was worse than when she had lost Danny on the train.

'Who's this fella?'

Angie twisted in her seat to see the policeman holding Licky.

'He's mine. If you're going to arrest me you might as well do it now.' Never mind the cancer, she would die of a heart attack if she had to take any more.

'Can I?' The policewoman indicated that she wanted to sit down next to Angie and Angie shifted her bag.

'Sorry, we didn't mean to upset you. Me and Tom are community police in training. I guess we have a lot to learn. Here.' She handed Angie Licky. 'Are you alright or would you like someone to talk to?'

42

A ngie couldn't get to Jaywick fast enough. As soon as the bus turned into the familiar streets she was on her feet, willing it to go faster. At last she was home. But in her rush to find Josie and seek her council, Angie hadn't really thought through the consequences of admitting what she had done and she was afraid. Angie slowed her pace as she approached the Seashell. *Coward. Coward.* Had she always been a coward? She hadn't been that night, when she went willingly with Pete to the pier.

She would tell Josie that she had something important to say. Josie would be surprised to see her, concerned that she wasn't in hospital. She would make a fuss and tell Angie to sit down whilst she made her a cold drink and something to eat. But Angie would say, 'No, let me tell you first,' and she would take Josie's hands in hers.

Josie glanced up from the till and Angie was stabbed by the coldness in her eyes. Something was wrong. By the time Angie pushed open the door, which jangled with the pretense of a normal day, Josie had disappeared out back and the part-timer had taken her place.

Angie's breath was tight in her chest. 'I wanted to talk to Josie.' She could feel the gaze of other customers, nobody she recognised, but there was definitely an atmosphere.

The part-timer shrugged. 'She's not on duty.'

'I'll pop up and see her then,' Angie said.

The part-timer frowned. 'Josie said to say that she was busy.' And then, when Angie was still standing there gawping at the closed door to Josie's apartment, 'Sorry.'

As Angie left the Seashell red-faced she remembered a similar feeling when she went back to school to collect her things. All of her friends were on the playground but nobody stopped to talk to her, they just watched her walk of shame – embarrassed for her. Was Josie watching from an upstairs window? Who else knew and what exactly did they know?

The walk from the Seashell to Sea Spray Avenue had always been a joyful one, but today Angie trudged the well-worn path in misery.

Sal trundled towards her pushing the supermarket trolley. As Angie approached, she wrestled the trolley over the kerb and tugged it across the street. There could be no reason for Sal to cross the road; she was avoiding her.

Keep on walking. Angie had to dig deep for the courage to continue, when all she wanted to do was collapse in a heap and howl.

How had they found out that she wasn't Lorraine Jeffers? Tomasz or Lorraine could have given her away. When she didn't have any friends, she was fine with it – what you don't have you don't miss. But now, after being immersed in the warmth and friendship of this supportive community, Angie was bereft. She was past her sell-by date and was no longer welcome. She should never have come back – not as *Angie*

Winkle. Angie Winkle was and would always be an outcast. Maybe, just maybe, Tomasz would be waiting for her at the Jeffers place. Angie quickened her step, anxious to get off the streets before being shunned by more of her friends and neighbours.

Three boys on bicycles were doing wheelies in the road when Angie turned into Sea Spray Avenue. One of them yelled to the other about a crazy old man with a gun. *Higgins.* What was he up to now?

'Get out of there. I know what you're up to. You won't find anything. I've hidden it.' Higgins was waving his pistol at Lorraine, when Angie crept up on them.

'Hey there, Higgins. What are you up to?'

Higgins lowered his pistol. 'Betsy?'

Angie remembered a photograph of his wife, Betsy, on their wedding day. Higgins was confused. Her mum had got like that sometimes, when she had a water infection. 'It's me, Lorraine.' Angie cringed but there was no point confusing Higgins any more than he was already. 'Shall we get you inside and find you some trousers?'

Dressed in a long shirt and baggy underpants, the bandages around his legs stained with yellow pus and blood, Higgins didn't look like himself. His shabby old suit had seen better days, but Higgins always tried to look like a gentleman.

Lorraine had regained her composure and lit a cigarette. 'What are you doing back here? I thought you were going to stay in Dagenham.'

Angie knew then who had given her away. 'What have you told them, Lorraine?'

Lorraine sniffed. 'Well, they were going to find out anyway, once I put this place on the market. I didn't expect you to come back. That snooty one at the café really got the hump about you pretending to be me. I wanted some help moving all of this junk into a skip but nobody would lift a finger. So, I told them who I was – but it didn't make any difference. In the end I had to hire help.'

Angie noticed for the first time a skip filled with all of her treasures: the Aztec throw, the lumpy old sofa that Liam and Darren had carried in on that wonderful morning when she felt as though she truly belonged, her sewing machine, and the dragon and mermaid sleeping bags she'd made for Danny.

'You can't stay here, I'm locking up and going back to Chelmsford. Really, Ange, you should be in hospital.'

She couldn't go back to Dagenham either. She didn't belong anywhere. 'Don't worry about me, Lorraine. I'll see to Higgins here and then I'll sort out something with the hospital.'

Angie slipped Higgins's gun into her bag and coaxed him inside. As soon as he was settled in his favourite chair, an old tartan blanket over his knees, Angie went back to find Lorraine.

'Did Tomasz come by?'

'Oh yes, he asked me to give you a message.' Lorraine fussed with stubbing out her cigarette and Angie nearly shook her. 'He seemed in a hurry and got all narky when I said you wasn't here.'

'What do you mean by narky? Was he angry?'

'No. You know, just agitated. He kept trying to peer around me as if I was hiding you or something. I told him that you were in Dagenham but he wouldn't have it. Then his mate beeped the horn and Tomasz had to go. He said to tell you to wait in Jaywick, no matter what happened.'

'Who was he with? Are you sure it was Tomasz?'

Lorraine sighed heavily. 'Yes, it was Tomasz.'

'Is he coming back?'

'How do I know? That's all he said.'

She had missed him.

'Namma,' a voice called from across the street.

Angie's heart leapt, but it wasn't Danny, just Alfie. Molly was ahead of him with Pickles. Angie raised a hand ready to greet them but Molly ducked her head and hurried past.

She had left Dagenham that morning, expecting to find comfort and support in Jaywick, but there was nothing for her here. Nothing at all. And she had missed Tomasz. If Angie had the energy she would weep, but she felt comatosed by the events of the past two days and she was in pain. All she could do was hide out at Higgins's place until she was strong enough to go after Danny.

43

Nikoleta's nightdress was soaking wet and so was the mattress. Seven o'clock, she had slept for eleven hours without waking. Danek had discovered a bookshelf of old and musty books that belonged to the owner and was pulling them out to build some kind of fortress.

'Danek, I'm sorry I didn't take you to the toilet.' Nikoleta sprung out of the sodden bed. It wasn't Danek's fault; the bedroom door was locked from the inside and she hadn't had the foresight to provide a potty.

Danek jumped as though caught out doing something naughty and tried to wriggle through the door of his construction, causing it to collapse. 'I'm sorry, Nikki. I'm sorry.'

Nikoleta stripped the bed and pulled on some clothes, then she took Danek downstairs to bathe him. A greasy scum line around the bath and a sprinkling of shaved whiskers in the basin. Nikoleta shuddered. There was no way that she would use that bath. At least hot steamy water gushed from the tap. She bathed Danek, soaping his little arms and legs.

'I don't like the whispering men,' Danek said. He meant the men who traipsed in and out of the house like shadows.

'They won't hurt us, Danek.' Nikoleta cupped a hand to rinse Danek's shoulders. 'I don't think that we will stay here long. Daddy will find us somewhere better to live.'

Danek cocked his head, as though trying to work something out. His serious expression gave him the look of an old soul. Nikoleta had lifted Danek from the bathtub and was toweling him dry when he said, 'The cross man is not my daddy.'

Nikoleta went cold. Something about Danek's words rung true. Of course, he could be disturbed by all of the disruption in his life. He was a baby when Kamil left the family home and they had spent very little time together in London. If Kamil wasn't Danek's father what was he doing with the boy? The possibilities were frightening. If she believed that Kamil wasn't Danek's father then she had to question everything else about him. It was too dreadful to contemplate and so Nikoleta buried the thought.

'We won't stay in this house long.' She tried to sound bright and positive. 'Now it's my turn to freshen up and then we'll see about the sheets.'

Danek was playing happily with the house of books and his action figures whilst Nikoleta bundled the laundry into a refuse sack. The realisation that she had no passport and very little money unsettled her. Nikoleta released a sheet and sank back on her haunches. Dad's warnings reverberated in her head. *Don't let him make a fool of you.* Was that what she was doing? She had to collect her wages; it was little more than two hundred pounds but at least then she could buy a phone. Kamil had promised her a new one and had offered the loan of his but he would have stood over her waiting and it would be awkward having a proper conversation. Six days since her last call home, the one when she had words with Dad. Mum would think that she had abandoned them all, would probably be haranguing Dad for chasing her away. There would be unanswered messages from Angelika. And Nikoleta missed them with a longing that physically hurt.

'I'm going downstairs to ask about a laundry,' Nikoleta said, when she had finished stuffing the sheets into a bag.

She dumped her washing by the front door and ventured along the hallway, 'Hello, is anyone there?'

A swarthy-looking man dressed in dirty white vest and trousers slung below his bulging belly stepped out to greet her.

'I was wondering where I could do some laundry.'

The man scratched at the white hairs on his chest and looked her up and down. 'There's a laundry in the same street as Boris's Café.' Then, he thankfully disappeared behind one of the doors. Nikoleta caught herself longing for the interfering Mrs Lisowski, instead of the thuggish-looking landlord that Kamil purported to be his friend.

'Are you ready to go, Danek?' Nikoleta called as she collected her handbag and keys. There was no reply from the bedroom. Nikoleta nudged open the door. 'Danek? Where are you hiding, *świnka?*' She peered under the bed. It was filthy and smelt damp. 'I'm not playing, Danek. We need to go out.' He wasn't there. Her heart hammered. *Keep calm, he can't have gone far.* She ran down the stairs calling his name.

Danek wasn't in the bathroom or toilet on either floor. Raised voices came from one of the rooms. Two men were shouting at each other. Other voices joined in. Should she knock? What if they had Danek? Nikoleta pressed her ear to the door. The voices stopped and then resumed in hushed tones. Nikoleta felt sick. *Where are you, Danek?*

The front door hung open; it was closed when she left her laundry. *Matko Boska*, if Danek had left the house he could be picked up by anyone. The traffic! *Sweet Mother of Jesus, don't let me lose Danek again.*

There was a road opposite; if Danek went that way he would have crossed the road. It wasn't a busy one, but the cars that did pass were driving fast for a residential street. Which way would he go? To the right was the entrance to the park, Hampstead Heath. They turned left to walk to Boris's Café. Maybe Danek was hungry and had gone to get some breakfast. Nikoleta ran in that direction. It was ten-thirty, of course he was hungry.

A mum passed by with a buggy and a little girl who skipped along holding her hand. Ahead was a man in a baseball cap walking a dog, but no Danek. Nikoleta didn't know whether to turn back and look in the other direction or continue on to the café. She decided to turn back. *Please, please let me find him.* The thought of telling Kamil that she had lost Danek *again* was too much to even contemplate. This time they might not be so lucky. How could she have felt resentment at Angie? At least Angie had cared for Danek. This was her punishment for being so uncharitable.

As Nikoleta reached the house, a man and child approached holding hands. The man stooped to listen to the little boy, who was about the same age as Danek. *It was Danek.* Nikoleta ran towards them.

'What are you doing with my child?' she snapped. It was the boy who had passed them on the stairs, the day they arrived.

He glared at Nikoleta. 'Taking better care of him than you.'

'If you hadn't left the front door open, Danek would have

been perfectly safe.' She was furious with the boy. Danek could have got run over.

Danek hung his head. 'I am sorry, Nikki. Don't send me back to the home for naughty boys.'

The boy scowled at Nikoleta and then shook his head and sneered, as though he despised her. There was no need for him to be so rude. It was partly his fault that Danek had got out. It wasn't until the boy left them that Nikoleta realised she hadn't even thanked him.

With the sheets tumbling in a washing machine, Nikoleta and Danek went to Boris's Café.

'This isn't as good as the Seashell Café,' Danek said when they sat down at a table for a late breakfast – sausage and egg for Danek and a ham roll for Nikoleta.

At last, Danek was talking to her. He had been so quiet and guarded. Nikoleta asked Danek about the Seashell. He told her about Aunty Josie and Uncle Bill. How he helped in the café, wiping ketchup bottles and wrapping cutlery with his namma. His face relaxed and he looked happy for the first time since coming home. Nikoleta cut up some of his sausage. 'It sounds as though you had a good time at the seaside with Angie.'

The familiar frown was back, furrowing Danek's brow. 'My namma.' Then he whispered, 'I love my namma.'

Maybe in time Danek would forget Angie, but Kamil had to accept that this woman had become important to his son. It wasn't fair stopping the boy from having any contact with her. 'I'll talk to Kamil. See if we can persuade him to let us go and visit Angie together in Jaywick.' She didn't want to raise Danek's hopes but Nikoleta was sure she could talk Kamil round.

Danek beamed and waved what was left of the sausage on

his fork. This was more like the behaviour of a four-year-old. Nikoleta laughed with him.

'I'm glad you had a lovely time with Angie in Jaywick but we missed you. Me and your…' She didn't like to say 'dad', not when Danek had been so firm in his statement that Kamil was not his father. It was going to take time and patience helping Danek adjust to a new life with her and Kamil. 'We missed you – me and Kamil,' she said.

Danek's face closed. His lips pursed together and the frown was back. Nikoleta tried another tact. 'Tell me about your mummy, Danek.' He must miss his mum, no matter what Kamil thought of her. The poor child had been through so much change. No wonder he was confused.

'I don't have a mummy. They said in the home for naughty boys that you would be my mummy. I was glad when you gave me away to Namma.' Danek blushed. 'I like you, but I like my namma better. She was going to teach me how to swim.'

Nikoleta had trouble swallowing her roll, her mouth was so dry. 'Is that where you were living before I took you to London?' She didn't really want to hear the answer.

Danek nodded. 'I was naughty.'

If Danek wasn't Kamil's son, if he had lied to her, what else was he capable of?

'Where were you going when I found you with the boy from our house, Danek?'

'To Namma.'

Nikoleta didn't know what to believe. She wanted to give Kamil the benefit of doubt, but she was beginning to realise that her dad was right: she didn't know Kamil at all. In London, Kamil was a different person and Nikoleta wondered whether she had fabricated an image of the man that she wanted Kamil to be, instead of seeing him as he really was.

One thing was certain, she had to collect her wages – without any money or a passport she was dependent upon him.

Danek was watching her with eyes that held too much pain for one so young. 'I won't let anyone send you away, Danek. I promised your namma that I would keep you safe and I will.'

44

The following day, Ana, Tavit, and Liza welcomed Nikoleta and Danek as though they were long-lost family.

'This is cause for celebration!' Tavit raised his arms. 'We have missed our little Nikoleta, and who is this handsome boy?'

Danek stunned them all with a dazzling smile that Nikoleta had not seen before. The convivial atmosphere and genuine warmth of Tavit and Liza had worked their magic on Danek. It must be exhausting for him, to be guarded all of the time, afraid of doing or saying the wrong thing.

'What can we open up, Ana-Maria? A bottle of pop and some snakes?'

Danek's eyes widened and he stepped closer to Nikoleta.

'Snakes! The maize and potato ones in the store room.'

Ana giggled. 'Okay. Shall I find some pastries too?'

'Yes, yes. Nikoleta likes baklava. Let's go mad and open a box. A small one, mind. Don't want to fritter away the profit.

You see, Nikoleta, I take notice of your advice.' He winked at her, flashing his broken tooth in a roguish grin.

Nikoleta left Danek helping Tavit at the till. There were no customers but Danek assured Tavit that he had shop experience from his time helping Aunty Josie at the Seashell Café and so now he was sitting on the tall stool at Tavit's side.

'Danek is adorable. You must be so happy to have him home, safe and well,' Ana gushed.

'I don't know how safe we are, Ana.' It came out before she could censor herself.

Ana's face collapsed with concern. 'Why? What's happened?'

'Oh, nothing really. It's just that Kamil doesn't seem interested in Danek now that he is home, and Danek says that Kamil is not his father. I know he's had a troubled time, Ana, but really I don't know what to believe.'

'What about you? Is Kamil treating you properly? Has he hit you, Nikoleta?' Ana's face was grave, encouraging Nikoleta to tell her the truth.

'No, no, nothing like that. I am probably making too much of it. It is bound to be difficult for Kamil and Danek. They didn't have much contact before we came to London and then his abduction. Of course, he is traumatised. It must be difficult for Kamil too.'

Ana didn't look convinced and Nikoleta regretted her indiscretion. 'Really, Ana, it will be alright but thank you for caring, you are a good friend.'

Liza joined them. 'What's taking you so long? Here, throw over a bag of snakes.'

The girls followed Liza back into the shop. They had a little tea party, mostly for Danek's benefit. When the maize and potato snacks were reduced to a few remaining crumbs and the box of baklava parcelled away, Nikoleta took Tavit to one side. 'Do you have my wages from last week?'

Tavit looked surprised. 'I gave them to Kamil.'

Did Tavit know Kamil? Kamil had never said as much.

'He came by a couple of days ago to collect them for you.'

When had he collected them? Why hadn't he told her?

'I am sorry, Nikoleta, I could not say no. Kamil set me and Liza up in business years ago. We had nothing when we met him and now we have three shops.' He shrugged. 'I am sure he thought to save you the trouble. Had you known, then we would not have been graced with your visit, so all is well that ends well, is it not?'

Ana followed Nikoleta out onto the street. 'You have my number. Call me if there is anything you need. Even if you just need to talk. I mean it, Nikoleta, anything – anytime.'

'God sent me an angel in you, dear friend.' Nikoleta kissed Ana goodbye. Just knowing she had Ana's support made her feel stronger and more positive, so it had not been a wasted journey.

Nikoleta and Danek were nearly home when a black sports car passed them honking its horn. It stopped outside their house, and Nikoleta was surprised to see Kamil jump out.

Danek shrunk into Nikoleta. 'Don't tell the man I was naughty.'

Nikoleta wanted to hug Danek, the poor child. Kamil was going to have to work hard to earn his trust. It had taken time for Danek to relax with her but their connection was as fragile as the sparkling dew-covered webs that cloaked the farm on crisp autumn mornings. This little boy needed a lot of love and reassurance if he was to recover from his ordeal.

'My two favourite people – my little *slonka* and my little fish.' Kamil opened his arms to them.

Nikoleta kissed Kamil. 'Where did you get the car? Is it ours or is it on loan?'

'I haven't decided. Are you pleased to have me home sooner than expected?'

If she was, it was to have some explanations – like why he had collected her wages without telling her. There was a lot they needed to discuss, but not in front of Danek.

'Where were you coming back from?' Kamil asked as they entered their flat.

'I'll tell you later.'

Kamil frowned and Nikoleta cocked her head at Danek, who was watching them, a thumb plugged in his mouth. A damp patch seeped through his shorts.

'Let's go and explore the playground on the Heath,' Nikoleta said, as soon as she had finished changing Danek.

'You see? This is why I love coming home to you, my little *slonka*. It is an excellent idea. You can tell me all about the adventures my two *swinkas* have been up to roaming London. At least you didn't lose our little treasure this time.' Nikoleta gave a wan smile. If only he knew.

Danek didn't need much encouragement to join the other children playing on a climbing frame with a slide.

'So, where did you go this morning?' Was there an edge to his voice? No, she was being paranoid.

'I went to the European Foods Emporium to collect my wages.'

Kamil slapped a hand to his forehead. 'I'm sorry, I forgot to tell you. Tavit gave me your wages!'

Nikoleta wanted to ask Kamil to give her the money but it

sounded churlish when he was paying for everything. 'You didn't tell me that you knew Tavit.'

'Didn't I? I thought I did.' Kamil shrugged as if it was nothing. Maybe it was nothing, after all Kamil knew everyone.

Danek was at the top of the climbing frame watching other children slide down the metal chute. Nikoleta guessed that he wanted a go and would if she helped him. 'Do you think he's alright on his own?' Danek was half the size of some of the other children.

Kamil stretched out his legs and crossed his arms behind his head. 'Of course. He's a sturdy boy. I'm glad you two are getting along so well. I worried about you when I was away.'

This was her chance to ask all of the questions that had been burning a hole in her head. Where did she start? 'Danek is a wonderful child. Already I am beginning to love him as though he were my own. I think that he must have been through a lot in Poland. You haven't told me much about his mother and I haven't asked. To get close to Danek, I need to understand what he has experienced. He's still very troubled, Kamil. I know that you are busy with work but Danek is going to need both of us to help him adjust to a new life in England.'

Kamil did not turn to look at her. It was in some ways easier talking like this, both of them watching Danek. A couple went by; the girl with her hand in her partner's back pocket, the boy with an arm slung across her shoulder. When they had passed Kamil said, 'I know. Life hasn't been easy for the boy. That's why I brought him here. He seems happy, doesn't he?'

Danek cowered at the top of the slide, letting other children pass him to take their go. Nikoleta wasn't so sure. 'He's a resilient child but we must not underestimate the effect of being separated from his mother. Did you know that Danek got sent to an orphanage? He thinks it's because he was naughty.' Kamil would have to take this news seriously. It was dreadful to imagine what was going through the poor child's mind. No wonder he was afraid of doing anything wrong.

'That is true, he did spend time in an orphanage when his drunk mother could no longer care for him. It was a dreadful place. I had to get him out of there and away from his mother's influence.' Nikoleta sighed with relief, there *was* an explanation. Poor Danek, no wonder he was so mixed up.

'While I was in Paris, I gave our situation a lot of thought. The flat we are using is not suitable for bringing up a family. It was only meant to be temporary. I can see now how impossible it is. For a start, Danek gets to share your bed while I sleep on the sofa. That will not do at all.' He put his arm around Nikoleta and she leant in to him.

'I know! It's impossible trying to look after Danek, when we don't even have a front door. I was going to say that we need to move as soon as possible. It doesn't have to be anywhere grand. Just somewhere safe, where we can go to sleep at night without worrying about Danek wandering off or being snatched.'

'Good. We are having the same thoughts.' Kamil took a deep breath. 'I was also thinking that you need to get back to work, *slonka*. You are young, clever, and ambitious. When I persuaded you to come to London with me, I told you that there would be more job opportunities. You dreamed of becoming a qualified accountant and ended up working in a dead-end grocery store. Your dreams are as important to me as my own, *slonka*. It's not fair of me to saddle you with child caring responsibilities.'

'I don't mind working part-time in a shop until Danek goes to school full-time. I enjoyed working in the European Foods Emporium. Maybe I could go back, just for a while.'

Danek slid down the slide. Nikoleta leapt to her feet and

cheered him. Danek looked up to see if she had witnessed his daring and Nikoleta waved. He ran back to climb up again and Nikoleta sunk onto the bench, exhilarated by his achievement.

'You are putting your own plans on hold, *slonka*, and that is not fair. Danek is my responsibility. I told you that I did some serious thinking when I was in Paris. And you know that when I think, I plan. Well, I have a plan that will solve everything.'

Nikoleta took Kamil's arm and wriggled in. 'Go on.' She should have guessed that Kamil would think ahead. Nobody was as resourceful as Kamil. He even had the use of a car. She was excited to hear this plan.

'I have found the perfect basement flat for us in Ealing. We will have a little courtyard garden and plenty of space. Brent has a vibrant Polish community. You will be able to join in activities, like book clubs or jam making, whatever you women do at these things.'

This was better than she had hoped for. Danek would have more freedom. He could make friends and go to school. Maybe they should find him a child psychologist or therapist. But this was all going to be expensive. 'Can we afford it?'

'I had a little cash flow problem because a business deal faltered but it looks as though things are back on track. You have been patient, *slonka*. Now, it is time for me to reward you and show you the life that I promised, when I prised you away from your family farm.'

Danek clambered up the wooden climbing frame and hurtled down the slide, again and again, taking his turn between older boys. He seemed to have made friends with them too. Good for Danek.

'Danek will love it,' Nikoleta said. She was imagining him joining clubs with other small boys. They would make friends with young Polish families, have his friends over for tea.

Maybe they would find other couples that they both liked so that they could go out to dinner or the cinema. There would be babysitters in a close community. As Nikoleta's mind raced ahead, she nearly missed Kamil's bombshell.

'I think it best that Danek goes away to boarding school. I didn't realise how much work it was caring for a boy of his age. My work takes me away so much and as I said, it's not fair asking you to care for my child.'

'I thought Danek was *our* child. I don't mind, Kamil. He's a beautiful little boy. Oh, look at him, Kamil!' Danek was tending to a little girl who had toppled off the bottom of the slide. He had squatted down and bent his head to peer up at her. 'He's so caring. And confident. Look how quickly he got the hang of the slide. Danek just needs lots of love. He needs *you*, Kamil. His father.'

'Let's be honest, there's no bond between me and Danek. I would go so far as to say he doesn't like me. No, Nikki, I have made up my mind. Danek will leave on Friday, five days' time. It will give us the weekend to settle into our new home in Ealing.'

45

Exhausted, emotionally and physically, Angie spent two nights sleeping in Higgins's spare bedroom. Sandwiched between the sleeping bags that she rescued from the skip, Angie buried her face in the nylon, hoping that the lingering the scent of Danny would diffuse the dank aroma of fungus which came from a thriving mushroom farm under the bed. The other items in the skip had disappeared during the night, probably reclaimed by the same neighbours who had generously shared what little they had.

A day of rest had helped her to regain a little energy and although she was in constant pain, Angie knew that she had to try to find Danny before it was too late. If she hadn't been such a coward then she would have gone after him straight away, instead of listening to Tomasz. Maybe she was pushing her body too hard, but saving Danny was more important than extending her life by a few weeks or months. Angie had considered going to the authorities, the police, or social services, but there would be lots of bureaucracy and she couldn't risk wasting time. Higgins started to wheeze.

'I'm coming, mate. You stay in bed and I'll get you a cuppa.'

As she made their tea, Angie kept a lookout hoping to see Tomasz. She had left a note on the Jefferses' door but was afraid that Tomasz wouldn't see it. When she had settled Higgins with tea and toast in bed, Angie popped next door to check that Tomasz hadn't returned.

The note was where she had taped it to the door. Angie paced around the backyard hoping desperately that there would be a sign, something that would reassure her that Tomasz would be back. Why hadn't he waited for her?

Angie's heart was heavy when she pushed open Higgins's back door. But then she heard voices – Higgins had company. For one second Angie thought it might be Tomasz and rushed across the kitchen but she stopped in the hallway when she heard Josie's voice coming from Higgins's bedroom.

She was about to skulk away when Higgins called out, 'Is that you, girl? Come on in. Come in!'

Angie's feet were leaden; she couldn't face Josie. To be rejected by her dearest friend was more than she could bear. 'I'll put the kettle on,' she said as she retreated. If Josie wanted to avoid her she could slip out now.

But Josie followed Angie into the kitchen. Angie could feel her eyes boring into her back as she concentrated on the boiling kettle.

'Do you want a coffee?'

'Yes, please. Here, let me.' Josie sidled alongside Angie and spooned coffee into two mugs. 'Are you making one for Higgins?'

Angie daren't turn and face her. 'He's just had a cup of tea so I'll make him one later.'

'I heard that he caused a bit of a commotion.'

How did news travel so fast in this place?

'He was a bit confused, waving a gun at...' Oh no, she had

to say *Lorraine*. Why had she started that sentence? 'At his neighbour,' Angie finished. A blush crept up her neck.

'*Lorraine?*' Josie said.

Angie turned to face Josie and they spoke at the same time.

'I shouldn't have lied –'

'You could have trusted me –'

Josie paused. 'You first.'

Angie took a deep breath. 'I shouldn't have lied about being Lorraine Jeffers. It was wrong and I'm sorry. It is just that you were so kind. I thought that if I was Lorraine then I would... belong. I know that sounds silly, but I never felt like I belonged anywhere until I came here.'

Josie lifted the kettle and poured. Angie stole a glance. Josie bit her lower lip, a slight frown. She was thinking before she spoke. It was going to be bad. Angie prepared herself for the worst.

Josie put the kettle down, her face set in disappointment, and Angie crumpled inside. Eventually she said, 'You know that we don't ask any questions round here. When your friend told me that you weren't Lorraine, Si filled us in. He said that you're on the run, that a Polish woman came looking for you. I don't care what you've done. I thought you could trust me, but lying like that? You took me for an idiot.' Josie's face was a mask, giving nothing away.

All Angie could say was 'sorry.' She wished she could disappear.

'You didn't look anything like the miserable old cow anyhow,' Josie muttered. And then she laughed, her face mobile and relaxed.

Thank God, she had forgiven her. Josie's approval and friendship meant more to Angie than anyone else's. It was such a relief to have her friend back.

'Josie, I'm not Danny's real grandma. I'll be straight with

you.' Angie told Josie all that had happened from the day that she rescued Danny on the Tube. About the welts on his back and how he told her that the girl, Nikoleta, wasn't his mum. 'I knew something was wrong, Josie. I never should have given him back.'

'So where's the rabbit now?'

Angie pointed to her bag on a kitchen chair.

'What, in there?' Josie peered into Angie's bottomless bag. 'Where?'

Angie fished out a spanner, Alfie's half-eaten honeycomb, a pebble or two, spare knickers, Higgins's gun, a sanitary towel, painkillers, and the letter from the hospital before reaching Licky at the bottom of her bag, a deceiving image of innocence.

'Shit. Is that safe?'

Her reaction unnerved Angie, although the bag of powder was hidden tightly inside his head and the seam was now double-stitched. 'Tomasz told me to take him with me, and where else could I stash it?

'When's Tomasz getting here?'

Angie wished she knew. 'I'm praying that he will get here soon. I have to find Danny, Josie. If anything happens to him, I'll never forgive myself.'

Josie covered Angie's hand with hers. 'You're not alone, babe. We'll find him together: you, me, Bill, Tomasz, Slippery Si. We'll find a way. Now, what about you? What did the doctor say? I was worried about you travelling to London in your condition.'

Oh dear, she had to admit to another lie. Best be completely honest from now on.

Josie tapped the hospital letter where it lay amongst the other contents spilled from Angie's bag. 'Is this the letter?'

Angie nodded.

'May I?' Josie read the letter. 'Lorraine – I mean Angie, you have to contact the consultant. They said it was urgent. You're as important to me as Danny is to you. If you don't care enough about yourself to do it, then do it for me and for Danny. You'll be no use to him in your grave.'

Angie was scared. She didn't want to know the truth. But Josie was right, she had to do this for Danny.

Josie kept her eyes on Angie as she pulled a mobile from her overall pocket. Then she took the letter and made the call, before handing her phone to Angie.

As soon as the receptionist knew who was calling, she insisted on finding the consultant. Angie bit her lip and tried to take comfort in Josie's steady gaze. Josie put her hand over Angie's and nodded encouragement.

'Miss Winkle.' It was the consultant. Here goes. 'We have been trying to contact you urgently, since your missed appointment. I didn't want to have this conversation with you over the telephone, but if that is the only way I can get the message through then we must.'

There was a pause, the consultant preparing herself. Angie almost felt sorry for her; it couldn't be easy delivering bad news. Angie was about to say, *It's okay, I know*, when the consultant continued.

'You have uterine cancer. It's not uncommon for women after menopause. And you do have a family history.' She paused and Angie wondered whether she should have done something to reduce the risk, but it was too late now.

'The cancer you have attacks the lining of the uterus, that's your womb. It's called endometrial cancer.'

Why couldn't she just get on with it and tell Angie how long she had left to live?

'So how long have I got?'

The consultant sighed. 'If you had asked me that two

weeks ago, Miss Winkle, I would have told you that you had a very good chance of survival. Diagnosis at an early stage can lead to a favourable outcome.'

Angie let out her breath and Josie gave her the thumbs up. She'd had all of the tests, and guessing that she had cancer assumed the letter summoning her to the hospital had been to prepare her for her demise. But now the consultant was telling her that she had a chance to live. *To live!* To really live. Not the excuse for living she had endured the past forty years. If Danny was with her now, Angie would have whooped with joy. Without Danny, knowing that she had sent him back to drug dealers, Angie didn't know whether she deserved to live.

The consultant continued, 'However, Miss Winkle, a good outcome is dependent upon timely surgery: the removal of your uterus, fallopian tubes, and ovaries. We've been trying to contact you for the past two weeks. Every day that you delay having surgery, your risk of dying from the disease increases.' The consultant waited for this to sink in.

Angie didn't know what to say. Of course she wanted the surgery as soon as possible. It wasn't until she thought that she was going to die that Angie realised just how much she had to live for – finding Danny for a start.

'When were you thinking of?'

The consultant kept her waiting while she checked with her secretary and Angie gave Josie a quick summary. Josie grinned. 'I told you!'

'We could find a space for you on Friday's list, as this is an urgent case. You would have to come in the night before.'

Would she be able to find Danny in five days? Angie said, 'What if we delayed surgery by, say a fortnight? Would it make a lot of difference to the um…to the outcome?'

Josie glared at her.

"I don't think you understand the urgency, Miss Winkle.

I'm not being dramatic when I say it's a matter of life and death. Surely, nothing could be more important to you than saving your life? I am sorry to put it so crudely but that is what we are talking about.'

Danny's life was more important than her own, but there was little she could do before Thursday.

The consultant took a deep breath. 'Miss Winkle – Angie, endometrial cancer is easily treated when diagnosed at an early stage. If we'd arranged for you to have an abdominal hysterectomy two weeks ago, then you could have been recovering now with a healthy life expectancy. Every single day that the operation is delayed increases the risk of the cancer spreading. Of course, you can refuse treatment or ask for it to be delayed, but I want to be sure you understand the risks. Even with surgery on Friday, we might need a course of radiation and chemotherapy. If you're worried about the procedure you can come in and talk to a specialist nurse. We will book surgery for you on Friday and arrange for your admission on Thursday. Please keep your appointment, Miss Winkle.'

Josie seemed to have heard part of the conversation and Angie filled her in on what she had missed.

'You could have been recovering from surgery now – tucked up in bed. Angie, you have to do what the doctor says. I just wish I'd known sooner.'

But then Angie would not have met Danny, or her friends in Jaywick. She would still be living in the shadows, a black-and-white version of life. Instead, she was living in colour. Maybe carrying a handgun and cocaine in her handbag was going a bit far. But she had tasted the sweetness of life and didn't want to give it up just yet. If only Danny was safe then she would be euphoric – she really did have another chance.

'I have to go and find Danny. Don't you see, Josie, I only have four days.'

Josie tried to dissuade her but Angie was determined. She had been a coward avoiding the consultant's diagnosis and it had nearly cost her her life. It was time to be brave. When Angie refused to reconsider, Josie persuaded her to wait until the next day whilst they helped her to prepare.

Josie called a powwow at the Seashell, summoning Bill and Slippery Si from the Queen's Head where they were discussing important business – how much they could get for imitation handbags from a supplier in Hackney. Josie had given them the three-line whip and she wasn't a woman to be ignored. With Zoe holding the fort, Angie, Josie, Bill, and Slippery Si sat upstairs in Josie's living room.

'You sure there's coke in here?' Slippery poked at a seam that barely supported Licky's floppy head.

'Go ahead and cut him open. Just keep to the seam so that I can repair him for Danny.'

Slippery drew a penknife from his jacket pocket. The blade flicked open with a chilling efficiency. He slit Licky's throat and then probed with his fingers. For a moment Angie was afraid it had gone – that it had just been her imagination. The last few days felt unreal. Then Slippery yanked out the bag.

'Shit!' He had struck gold.

Angie glared at him. 'If these people used Danny to smuggle drugs what are they doing to him now?'

'Don't worry, Angie love. Bill and Si will help you find Danny. Won't you?' Josie fixed Bill with her grey eyes.

Bill snapped to attention. 'Of course we'll help, won't we, Si?'

Slippery was dipping a damp fingertip into the white powder. 'It's genuine. This'll be worth hundreds – no, thousands. Bloody hell.' He looked up when Josie's stare bore into him. 'Yeah, of course we'll help you. How?'

Angie refused Bill and Si's tentative offers of accompanying her to Danny's parents and they looked relieved when she assured them that the loan of a mobile phone, and a lift to and from the station the next day, was all she needed from them for now.

'Promise to keep in touch, babe. I'll worry myself sick until you get back here safely.'

46

'Why are you sending me back?' Danek sat like a hunched gnome, his knees drawn up to his chest.

Nikoleta stroked his back. 'Danek, you should be asleep. It's gone ten o'clock. We are not sending you back to Poland. You are going to a new school in France, isn't that exciting?'

'I don't want to go to France. I want to go to Jaywick.'

'You don't know anything about the school. How do you know that you won't like it more than living in Jaywick? There will be other boys the same age as you. Lots of children to play with and you will have lessons. You may learn to speak French as well as English and Polish.'

Danek unfurled his limbs and scrambled into Nikoleta. He buried his face in her nightdress. Hot tears seeped through the cotton, dampening her breast. 'Will you come with me?'

Nikoleta's heart ached. 'I can't, *swinka*. I have to find a new job but your father, Kamil, will fly to Paris with you and make sure that you are settled. The weeks will rush by and then we'll be seeing you again.'

Danek sighed. 'I don't understand. That man, Kamil, said that he wanted me. Then he changed his mind and he won't let you keep me, so why can't I just go back to Jaywick? Namma wants a little boy.'

There was nothing Nikoleta could say. Everything was black and white to Danek. Kamil was right when he said there was no father/son bond. Instead of trying to justify Kamil's decision, she tried to convince Danek that everything would be alright. The repetitive motion of stroking Danek's hair lulled Nikoleta and she continued for some time after he had fallen asleep. Kamil was giving her everything that she wanted: a home, his financial support, and encouragement as she worked her way to the position of a qualified accountant. He even talked about them getting married one day and starting a family of their own. Danek snuffled and burrowed under the sheet, like a small animal making a nest. Angie's words came back to Nikoleta: *Promise me that you'll make a home for Danny where he feels safe and secure. It's important to feel that you belong and matter.* She made that promise, God was her witness. The truth was, Nikoleta would give up everything that Kamil offered her to give Danek a happy home. The kind of upbringing that she had taken for granted. Then it occurred to her that her parents had put her and Angelika before themselves. Maybe they did have dreams and ambitions after all. They had just put them to one side to raise a family. Maybe there was no greater achievement.

The next morning, Nikoleta was determined to find a way to change Kamil's mind about sending Danek away to boarding school. But it wasn't going to be easy; he wouldn't listen to reason and had made it very clear that Danek was his concern and not Nikoleta's, which was unfair, given the responsibility he had delegated to her in escorting his son to London. It was true, she had let Kamil down by losing Danek but surely, he could forgive her, now that she had found him. It wasn't just a matter of forgiveness, it felt as though Kamil had given up on trying to be a father to Danek and it was all her fault for messing things up. If only Kamil would spend a bit of time with his son then he would learn to be a father. It was impossible not to love Danek, he was adorable.

'Let's take Danek to a museum – somewhere that has dinosaur exhibits,' Nikoleta said, as Kamil rifled through his attaché case. 'I promised him an American-style milkshake too.'

'Here, I got this for you.' Kamil handed Nikoleta a mobile phone. At last, she could call home – things were taking a turn for the better. If only Kamil would change his mind, they could all have a fresh start in Ealing.

'So, shall we do something as a family before Danek goes to boarding school?' Nikoleta said.

'Sorry, *slonka*, I have to go to work.'

Nikoleta checked out her phone. 'Thank you for the phone, Kamil. Have you got my passport in there too?'

Kamil passed it to her without hesitation. 'Where will you keep it?'

'In my handbag,' Nikoleta said, as she went looking for her bag, her passport tight in her grasp. She always kept it beside their bed, away from the door.

'Is this what you're looking for?' Kamil held up her hand-bag. Nikoleta frowned. 'You left it on the landing where anyone could steal it.'

Nikoleta was sure that she had not, although there was nothing valuable in it and she had been preoccupied when they got home from the Heath.

'Why don't you let me look after your passport until we

move to Ealing? I am sorry to say that there are some undesir-
ables sharing this house with us. You can't risk losing it,
slonka.'

Nikoleta hesitated. It felt good to have her passport back
but Kamil was right, it would be safer locked away. They
would be moving in just four days and her priority now was
to get Kamil to change his mind about Danek. She acquiesced
and handed back her passport. 'Can't you spend a little time
with us, Kamil? I've missed you.'

Kamil agreed to have breakfast with them at Boris's and
they arranged to meet outside whilst Nikoleta took Danek to
the toilet.

She was following Danek out of the toilet, when he ran
headlong into the boy who had found him, the day he tried to
run away, and hammered his fists against the boy's thighs.
'Why did you stop me? I could have got away.'

The boy held Danek's fists away from him. 'Hey, hey, I'm
not your enemy.'

'Sorry,' Nikoleta said. 'Danek is being sent away to
boarding school, so he is a little upset. His father thought it
best.'

'His father?' The boy raised his eyebrows.

'I don't have a daddy or a mummy,' Danek said. The boy let
go of Danek's wrists.

'Boarding school, eh? Bullshit.'

Nikoleta screwed up her face. What was this word
'bullshit'?

'Button-truth,' the boy said. 'He's as much Kröl's son as I
am. Boarding school? So that's what they call it now.' He
pushed past Nikoleta. 'Sorry I couldn't help you, brother,' he
called over his shoulder to Danek.

Nikoleta's arms prickled with goose bumps. 'Go outside
and meet Kamil, Danek. I just need to make a phone call.'

Danek whined and clung to her. 'Tell Kamil that Nikki had to pop back up for something. I promise I won't be long, *swinka*.'

Nikoleta's knees trembled as she climbed the stairs. It was eight-thirty, Ana wouldn't have left for work yet.

'Ana,' Nikoleta whispered. Kamil was outside but she had a creepy feeling that she was always being watched. 'Danek and I have to get away from Kamil.' It sounded wrong; she didn't want to believe it but they only had four days. She paused for what must have been a second, but it felt longer. 'He's going to send Danek away somewhere and I am afraid for him.' Nikoleta heard a sharp intake of breath. 'I hate to ask but could you lend me some money? Just enough for us to get to Jaywick?'

'Of course. I told you *anything*. I'll phone in sick and meet you – where?'

'I don't know. Our nearest Tube is Belsize Park. Is there somewhere between us?'

They arranged to meet at one o'clock by the ticket office in King's Cross Station. They had a plan, she would make sure Danek was safe and then worry about herself. Why hadn't she taken her passport when she had the chance? If only her face was not so easy to read. Nikoleta took a deep breath and with, what she hoped was a serene smile, bounced down the stairs.

Everything felt wrong – the shadowy men who wouldn't make eye contact with Kamil or Nikoleta when they entered the café, Danek's misery as he scuffed his shoes and pulled on her arm, Kamil's jollity as he talked about his plans for their future. What was she doing here? How had she deceived herself for so long? *Smile, pretend to be happy. Stop checking your watch.* Three hours until she could meet Ana.

'So, how are you going to spend your day, *slonka?*'

Nikoleta blushed. 'Maybe find a milkshake bar.'

'Have you googled it?'

'Not yet.'

'Well, do it now. Do you like your new phone?'

Nikoleta googled milkshake bars in central London. There were too many to choose from, even one in Hampstead, which would have been her choice had she not needed to travel to King's Cross. 'There's one in Covent Garden.' It was only three stops from King's Cross. They could meet Ana and have a milkshake and then they wouldn't have to lie.

'Let me see.' Kamil took her phone and it beeped, just as she let go.

'You have a message,' he said. 'Shall I look?'

What if it was Ana? 'No, thank you.' Did she sound too curt? Suspicious?

Kamil scrolled through the list of milkshake bars and then handed Nikoleta's phone back with a shrug of his shoulders. When Kamil went to the counter to have a word with Boris, Nikoleta checked her messages. It *was* Ana. She asked whether one hundred pounds would be enough. Nikoleta was texting her reply when Kamil returned.

'Who was it?' he asked.

'Just Angelika.' But Nikoleta had hesitated.

'Maybe I should come with you. I've never had an American milkshake. What do you think, Danek?' Danek stared at his uneaten sausage.

The outing was a miserable event. Kamil spent all of his time on the phone, making calls and looking things up. Whatever he was doing, he didn't involve Nikoleta, and apart from ruining their day, he served no useful purpose. He didn't even have a milkshake, just an espresso coffee. It was twelve forty-five; they could still get away to meet Ana if they left now.

'That was a treat,' Nikoleta said with a broad smile and happy voice. 'It was lovely to have your company darling but you are busy. I would like to look around the shops. Why don't I meet you back at the house?' Her voice had faltered, she was sure of it.

Kamil glanced up from his phone. 'What did you want to buy?'

'Nothing, really. I just wanted to look around.' Nikoleta smiled but she could tell from Kamil's eyes that he wasn't fooled.

'No, we will go back together. Danek will need an afternoon nap and you should start looking for a job. Isn't that why you came to London to get your accountancy exams? Just think, in four days' time we will be moving into our new house. Aren't you excited, *slonka*?'

In four days, Danek would be shipped God knows where. Nikoleta checked her watch – it had gone one. They were too late.

47

Of course she was scared, she was carrying a gun – Higgins's air pistol, but it looked like the real thing – and a bunny's head of cocaine. Angie imagined herself as a dealer. 'I can give you a bunny's head but it doesn't come cheap.' What was she thinking? This was serious business and she'd got herself in deep. It was easier to be brave, with Josie's support. Knowing that she had been forgiven, that her friends in Jaywick would do anything to help her and Danny, Angie had grown in stature – her heart expanded and with it her courage.

Standing outside 137 Lenham Avenue, Angie's heart was thumping so hard it bounced against her ribs. Just for a few seconds she considered turning back, but then she thought of Danny. He could be in there right now. She had to save him. Before she could change her mind, Angie pressed the bell. Hopefully, she wouldn't have to use the gun, just wave it around a bit, like they did in the films. As before, the door was opened by Nikoleta's landlady.

'Oh, it's you,' the landlady said.

Angie barged in. This time the woman stepped to one side and made no attempt to stop her entry. 'I hope you're not going to tread more sand into my carpets.'

'I've no business with you. It's them upstairs I've come to see.' Angie didn't wait for an invitation to climb the stairs. The landlady followed.

When she reached the flat that Nikoleta had shown her into just three days ago, Angie hammered both fists on the door. 'Open up!'

The landlady smiled, as though suppressing great mirth, the condescending bitch. Then she took a key from her pocket and unlocked the door. She opened it wide and stood back as Angie pushed past. There was nobody home. Angie checked the bathroom and toilet, she looked under the bed and opened the wardrobe door.

'You haven't looked in the drawers.' The landlady smirked.

Angie opened the drawers of a dresser, in case there was a clue to Danny's whereabouts. All empty.

'You're too late. They've gone back to Poland.'

Angie sank onto the bed. 'Did they take the boy, Danny?'

'The whole family. Having their son kidnapped on their first day in London did not enchant them to our city. Was there anything else you wanted?'

'Did they leave a forwarding address?'

The woman's hollow laughter mocked Angie as she traipsed back down the stairs.

When they reached the front door the landlady prodded Angie in the chest. 'I don't want to see you here ever again. Do you understand?'

Shaking with adrenaline, Angie hurried away from the house, afraid that someone might be watching her. Was that it? Danny had left with his family for Poland and there was nothing that she could do? She had failed him.

Angie stumbled back the way that she had come; there was a café near the station. On a mission to finish what they had started, the cancer rats were back gnawing ruddy great holes in her womb. It took a while for Angie to recover from her ordeal, but a glass of cool lemonade helped and eventually the pain subsided and her pulse righted itself. If Nikoleta had taken Danny back to Poland, Angie might not be able to reach him before her operation but maybe Tomasz could go after him. She took out the mobile and after checking her note keyed in Tomasz's number. He'd told her to stay in Jaywick. Hopefully he would understand.

'I'm sorry but I'm unable to take your call…'

Angie hung up. She had Tomasz's address in Colchester; she would ask Slippery to pick her up from Colchester Station and then they could visit him together. Even if she had to sit on his doorstep until he came home, Angie was determined to find Tomasz. He was their only hope.

Slippery drove Angie to Colchester in his cranky transit. 'If he knows about the coke and they know he knows, maybe they've done him in,' Slippery said helpfully.

Angie shuddered. She imagined Tomasz being held prisoner by beefy Mexicans with thick moustaches and machine guns. The baron of a drugs cartel demanding his minions find Angie and bring her to him. Tomasz would say, 'No amount of torture will persuade me to tell you of her whereabouts.'

They pulled up outside what looked like an ex-council house.

'Perhaps we should've brought backup,' Slippery said.

Angie didn't think Bill or a few of Si's mates from the Queen's Head would intimidate a drugs gang, if that was what Si was suggesting.

It was a sixties-style terraced house, identical to all the others on that estate. Slippery rang the doorbell, and when there was no reply, he rapped hard on the door.

Angie slunk behind him, her heart racing. Apart from her desperation to enlist Tomasz's help, she was anxious to see him to get some reassurance that he still cared for her. What if he hated her? Slippery stepped back and trod on her foot.

'What now?' he asked, after a bit of a tussle.

'I'm not leaving until I speak to him,' Angie said.

'Perhaps we should break in. Just in case he's bound and gagged. What if he's in there, hears our voices, thinks he's going to be rescued, and we just walk away?' Si said.

It was ridiculous. Deep down, Angie knew that Si just wanted to show off his breaking and entering skills. She should have known better, but Si had stirred her imagination and now all she could think of was Tomasz tied to a chair, a rag in his mouth. 'Can you get in without smashing anything up? Maybe through an open window or something?'

Si didn't need to be asked twice. He went straight to the back of his van and returned with an untwisted coat hanger. 'I'll have the door open in a couple of seconds.' And he did.

Oh well, she might as well add breaking and entering to her list of crimes.

There was nobody home. Angie checked out the kitchen, while Slippery had a snoop in the living room. The kitchen looked as though it was rarely used. No dirty plates or crumbs on the work surfaces – a bitter tang of cockroach, the only scent. No trace of garlic or beef stew, a ghost of meals past. She opened the fridge. It was bare. She opened each of the cupboards. Empty. Empty. A couple of mugs with logos – freebies. Some polystyrene cups in a plastic sleeve. No packets of food or cans. If Tomasz hadn't given Angie this address she would have guessed that nobody lived there.

'Nothing here,' she called to Slippery.

Angie waited in the hallway for Slippery. She didn't like trespassing in Tomasz's home. What if he came home and caught them? 'Hurry up, Si.'

Angie heard Slippery opening and closing drawers. Then it went quiet.

'Si?'

There was no reply. Angie crept closer, afraid now that there really were gangsters holding Tomasz for ransom. If they had Slippery, she was next. A splintering sound and then a rustling of papers. Angie peered into the front room. Slippery was on his knees at a desk; the front of a drawer had been prised open with a screwdriver.

'It was locked,' Slippery said. He tugged out a laptop and with it came a manila file. It fell to the floor scattering its contents.

'You shouldn't have broken the lock. It's bad enough breaking into Tomasz's house.' Angie fell to her knees to rescue the paper and photographs that had spilled from the file. It took a few seconds for Angie to recognise the woman in the photograph. She was wading into the sea in big knickers, a shirt tucked into her bra. There were more, black-and-white images of Angie and Danny the day they arrived in Clacton. Angie asleep on the train, Danny looking up at the camera with a lost, dazed look. She had almost forgotten how Danny looked when they first met. Angie and Danny sitting on the beach. Her hand shook as she passed them to Si.

'He must have used a zoom lens. Why would he take these photos, Si? What's going on?'

'Let's have a look at this.' Slippery opened Tomasz's laptop 'Shit – too secure. Zoe's boyfriend, Spider, could get in. He can hack into anything.'

'Do you think it would help us find Danny?' She couldn't be sentimental – not now.

'Worth a try.'

Angie nodded. 'Okay.'

She was numb, as though she wasn't really there. The photographs sickened her. Then she had a terrible thought and a bubble of dread crept coldly up her chest until it lodged in her throat. The two Polish men on the train. The young one took Danny to the toilet. She didn't get a good look at his father. He wore dark glasses, she remembered, was unshaven and had grey hair. That's where she had seen him. How could she have been so gullible? All that talk about his stillborn child. It must have been calculated to win her trust and he had; she'd been an utter fool. To think that she was suffering for telling him a lie when all along he knew exactly who she was. He was a lie. The whole, embarrassing charade a lie.

'Let's get out of here,' she said to Slippery.

Tomasz could be dangerous. Dear, sweet Tomasz was a cold-hearted villain. He had used her. Tomasz was no different to Pete, the pier pervert – of course he wasn't interested in her. Angie pushed away the photographs. Pete knew what he wanted and so did Tomasz. Angie was the fool for believing he saw something in her. How could she have been so stupid? However long her life, she would *never* trust a man again – *never*.

'Look at this.' Slippery threw some ID cards at Angie. The headshots were Tomasz, but he had other names. Angie didn't want to know any more.

48

Three days to get Danek away from Kamil. Nikoleta had no doubts about Kamil's intentions, Danek was being sent somewhere and it wasn't boarding school. *He could get anything for anyone.* A shiver down her spine. *So that's what they call it* – the boy's words. And then there was the conversation between Lenka and Kamil that she had overheard. *Were they interested in the boy?* How could she have been so blind? Dad was right, Kamil lacked integrity – *He would sell his mother for the right price.* The rural life in Poland had provided a cloak for Kamil, his difference setting him apart as distinguished, and in Nikoleta's eyes glamorous. Here in London, he was exposed for who he really was and Nikoleta felt betrayed. The anguish at losing his precious son, the guilt and torment that she had suffered – how could he?

Danek sat in a corner throwing his action figures against the wall. If she hadn't gone looking for him, Danek could have been in Jaywick now with his namma. Kamil hammered away at his laptop. *Whack*, from the wall, *thump*, from the keyboard.

'Can I have my passport in case I need to refer to it when

making job applications?' Nikoleta said. Kamil carried on thumping. 'Kamil?'

'Not now, *slonka*. Can't you keep that child quiet?'

'I'll take him to the Heath,' Nikoleta said. Now was their chance to get away. They would have to leave without their passports and it didn't feel right. Maybe she could go to the Polish embassy and say that she had lost them. 'Come on, Danek.' Nikoleta scooped up his action figures and stowed them in her handbag. There was nothing else she could take without raising suspicion. Kamil didn't even look up as they left the flat.

Outside, Nikoleta sighed with relief. It had been easier than she thought. It was a fifteen-minute walk to the Tube station. 'Keep close to me, Danek. I have to make a couple of phone calls but we need to walk fast. Is that okay?' Danek nodded, his thumb was back in his mouth.

The first call was to Ana. She picked up straight away. 'Sweet Jesus, you are safe. When you didn't turn up I was worried.'

Nikoleta caught her breath. 'I'm sorry, Ana. I would have sent a text but I was afraid that Kamil would read it. Are you at work and do you have the money with you?' They walked past the Heath.

'Yes, can you get here to pick it up?'

'Nikki, you missed it,' Danek said.

'Hold on, Ana.' Nikoleta turned to Danek. 'We are going to visit Tavit instead.' They continued to walk, a little skip now in Danek's step.

'Oh, thank you, Ana. You have no idea what this means to me and Danek. We should be there in…' A car slowed down behind them and crawled to a stop alongside. It was Kamil.

'*Matko Boska*, it's Kamil.'

'He's tracking your phone! Get rid of it, Nikoleta. I'll hold on to your money until you collect it. You know where to find me. I'll be praying for you.'

Kamil wound down his window. 'Great, I caught you, jump in.'

Danek hung back. Nikoleta wondered how Kamil expected Danek to travel in the sports car; he didn't even have a child seat. She opened the passenger door. 'Where are you going?'

'I thought we could go and have a look at our new home. I finished my work and you had gone. Sorry if I was a bit preoccupied this morning, we are trying to close a deal.'

'Where's Danek going to sit?'

'In the back, there's enough space. It's not as though he needs much leg room. I thought you were going to the Heath.'

'I changed my mind. We thought we would go to the Science Museum instead.' Nikoleta threw a look at Danek, hoping that he wouldn't tell Kamil that they were going to visit the Emporium.

Nikoleta tried to sound excited as Kamil weaved in and out of traffic. They were going to view their new home, but all she could think about was Danek being tossed around in the back seat and how time was running out.

'Here we are.' They pulled up in front of a white semi-detached house. It was not unlike 137: three floors, the top one a loft extension. It was a pretty house in a residential street and two weeks ago, Nikoleta would have been over-joyed. 'We have the ground floor and the back garden. What do you think, *slonka*?' Kamil puffed out his chest. A cat who had dropped a dead bird at his mistress's feet.

Nikoleta smiled and nodded in what she hoped looked like approval. Kamil leapt out of the car and rattled his keys leaving Nikoleta to release Danek. He wrapped his legs around Nikoleta and buried his face in her chest.

'Put the boy down. He's going to boarding school on

Friday, and they won't fuss him there. He needs to get tougher.' Nikoleta ignored Kamil and hugged Danek close.

The flat was light and spacious: an open plan kitchen/diner, doors out onto a little courtyard, a bedroom and bathroom. It would have been perfect, if things had been different.

'I know the family upstairs. I'll see if they are in. Stefan's wife can tell you what goes on. I think that the Polish church has classes and things.' Kamil made a call and a few minutes later Stefan knocked on the door.

Kamil was trying so hard, Nikoleta almost felt sorry for him, but then she remembered his deceit and she hardened her heart. Stefan was affable. If his wife was as easy-going then they might become friends. What was she thinking? She wasn't going to live here. They had to get away.

'Tell Nikki what Mary gets up to with the Polish church,' Kamil said. His phone rang. 'Forgive me, Stefan, I have to take this call.' Kamil took his phone into the bedroom.

'Mary goes to yoga and arranges social outings. We have been happy living here. I hope you will be too. Who is this young man?' Stefan tickled Danek and he sneaked a peek at their would-be neighbour.

'Can you look after Nikki while I pop out for a few minutes, Stefan? I won't be long.'

When Kamil had left in his car, they stood around making stilted conversation. 'How far away is the station?' Nikoleta asked.

'Ealing Broadway is a four-minute walk in that direction.' Stefan pointed.

Nikoleta's heart beat a little faster. How could she lose Stefan? He seemed to be a perfectly decent man, but she was learning that Kamil used his contacts to keep him informed at all times. *Think. Think.*

She opened a cupboard in the kitchen, but of course they were bare. 'What a shame there is no tea and coffee. I would love a coffee – maybe there is a coffee bar close by?'

'Only up near Brent Cross Station. I don't expect Kamil will be long.' He avoided her eyes.

'When you need coffee, five minutes is too long. I don't suppose you could make me one?' If Stefan had known Nikoleta longer than ten minutes he would have known that it was out of character for her to make such a request. Thirty seconds passed but it felt like thirty minutes.

'How do you like your coffee?'

'Strong and white, please.' Just in case Stefan found coffee in a cupboard she hadn't checked. There definitely wasn't any milk.

'Do you want to come upstairs with me? You can see our flat.'

She was right, he was reluctant to leave her alone. 'No, thank you. I need to take Danek to the toilet.'

'Kamil should be back in just a few minutes,' Stefan said, hovering near the door.

'You are very kind, Stefan. I will return the favour, once we are neighbours. I can't wait to meet Mary.'

Stefan left the door of the flat open and went upstairs. As soon as Nikoleta heard his footsteps overhead she grabbed Danek and charged out of the front door. He might be looking out of his window. She ran, carrying Danek. He might be phoning Kamil now. *Matko Boska*, her phone! Nikoleta put Danek down and fumbled in her bag for her mobile. She threw it into a front garden. 'Come on, Danek. This time we *are* going to see Tavit. Hold on tight!' And she ran all the way to Brent Cross Tube.

It didn't take long to get to Earl's Court. Kamil would guess where she had gone; he may have seen Ana's text offering the hundred pounds. He would contact Tavit, maybe Mrs Lisowski, they all worked for Kamil in some way. Nikoleta had not thought beyond getting Danek to Jaywick Sands. She didn't know what Angie could do to keep Danek safe but it would stop Kamil sending him away. Neither of them had passports and she couldn't afford the airfare to Poland.

'We can't stay long in the shop, Danek.' Nikoleta pushed open the door and was greeted by the smell of warm spices, disinfectant, and cardboard.

Tavit gave her a long look and then ducked his head. 'Ana-Maria,' he called.

Ana came out of the back as soon as she saw Nikoleta she dived back into the store room and returned. 'I won't be a minute, Tavit.'

Tavit kept his head down as though he hadn't heard.

Anna ushered Nikoleta and Danek out of the shop. 'Tavit knows I am helping you, but he won't give you away. Best not to involve him more than we have to. Are you sure that this is enough?' She counted five twenties into Nikoleta's palm.

'I just need enough to get us to Jaywick,' Nikoleta whispered.

'Jaywick!' Danek whooped.

'Shush,' they both said. Nikoleta lifted Danek up and Ana gave him a kiss.

'Is there anything else you need?'

Nikoleta hated to ask; Ana had already done so much for them. 'Could I phone my parents? I had to throw my phone away before I got the chance.'

'Of course.' Ana gave Nikoleta her phone and took Danek from her.

The phone rang unanswered. *Please, please, Angelika, pick up.* It went to message. 'Mum, Dad, I'm sorry.' Nikoleta started to cry and Ana looked concerned. Nikoleta turned her back and tried to compose herself. 'I am using my friend Ana's phone.' What could she say? It was hard leaving a message, maybe the last time that she would talk to them for a long while. 'I'm sorry. Dad was right. I may not be able to talk for a while because I don't have a phone. As soon as I have a passport and the airfare, I'll come home. I hope it won't be too long. I love you. I'm sorry. Sorry…' There was nothing else she could say and so she hung up.

Ana transferred Danek to Nikoleta's arms and hugged them both. 'God be with you.'

Nikoleta made haste; Kamil was probably on his way to the Emporium right now. She hoped that he would not be harsh with Stefan or Tavit for letting them get away.

Please Mother of God let Angie still be in Jaywick. If they couldn't find Angie, Nikoleta didn't know what they would do.

49

A ngie probed gently, exploring the cushion of fungi, as she tested for some give in the floorboards beneath Higgins's spare bed. Afraid of crossing Josie, Slippery had been reluctant to drop Angie off at Higgins's place the day before. His instructions were to collect Angie from the station and take her straight back to the Seashell and Josie's loving care. But Angie needed to be alone. Tomasz's deceit and her foolhardiness in trusting him – after all she had been through – hit hard. She unspooled and replayed the day he visited her to collect his jacket. His sadness at losing Lydia, his stillborn child, had seemed genuine. She had *felt* it. Was she just looking for comfort by imagining that they had experienced a similar pain at the loss of a child? How could he lie about something like that? And how did he know that this would strike a chord with Angie? Nobody knew about Todd.

The floorboard gave way beneath Angie's touch, as soft as soggy cardboard. Lying on her belly she wriggled closer and carefully eased it up.

DEBORAH KLÉE

'You'll be safe enough in there, Licky,' Angie said, as she peeked inside the rabbit's newspaper swaddling. Then she stretched her arm in as far as she could reach and tossed the bundle out of sight. 'Danny will be missing you. And I him.'

It felt as though she was saying goodbye to Danny. There was no chance of finding him before her operation and there was a possibility that she wouldn't survive. What would happen to Danny boy then? Angie was beyond sad – she was utterly heartbroken. First Danny and then Tomasz. She replaced the floorboard, gently arranging the mushrooms so that they covered the rotting edges.

A car drew up outside; it would be Zoe. Angie checked that she had everything. Maybe it was unwise going back to the Dagenham house, but Angie wanted to get it ready for when she was discharged from hospital. She had left everything as it was following the break-in. Nowhere was safe. Tomasz had told her to wait in Jaywick and she thought it was because he wanted to protect her. Now she understood, it was so he could get his hands on the drugs. The gang were probably double-crossing one another, like they did in the Westerns. All of them hunting her down – her and Licky. Well, they would be disappointed.

Why hadn't she read the signs? There was a single magpie on the dustbin, the day she went to the beach with Tomasz. If she had paid attention to this sign then she might have... missed one of the best days of her life.

When Tomasz had said, 'You're beautiful,' she had felt beautiful. That day she was brimming over with love and happiness. She could recall with amazing clarity the feel of the sea as it tingled her skin, the pull of the sand beneath her toes, even the collection of shells that Danny spread before her: the tiny cone-shaped one, another like mother-of-pearl, a smooth shard of blue sea glass.

310

No, she had been given a second chance and she was grateful. From this day on, she would take everything life threw at her – the good and the bad. And she would find Danny, however long it took.

'Ready?' Zoe called from the hallway.

Angie pulled back her shoulders and held her head high. 'I am ready.'

Higgins and Zoe were waiting for her at the front door. 'Spider has found something on Tomasz's laptop but he said not to get your hopes up. We'll visit him first in Colchester but I'll get you to the station by eleven at the latest. By leaving from Colchester you'll cut out thirty minutes of your journey and should get there within an hour. But I still think that you should stay with us tonight and go tomorrow.'

Angie hugged her. 'I need to go back. But it's good of Spider to look at the laptop.' There was still a flicker of hope and despite Spider's caution Angie hung on to this.

'You've got ham and potato salad in the fridge,' she said to Higgins. 'And don't forget to keep drinking lots of water, especially on hot days.'

'Come on.' Zoe nudged Angie towards the door. 'Me and Mum will keep an eye on him.'

Spider's den was a shared student house on an estate. An all-male house going by the boat-sized trainers and boots that littered the hallway. Spider was so called because of a spiderweb tattoo on his elbow. Zoe had met him at the pub where she worked in St Osyth.

'Come in, ladies.' He was surprisingly well spoken.

Spider cleared a couple of kitchen chairs of discarded jackets, a crash helmet, and a propped-up guitar. 'Take a seat.'

He flipped open Tomasz's laptop. 'There's not much to tell

you,' he said. 'The computer is property of the council and as far as I can see it's only been used for council business.'

Angie held her breath. Zoe said that he had found *something*. However small it might seem, she was anxious to know.

'So, it's all above board?' Zoe said.

'I didn't say that. There's some dodgy stuff going on but nothing about the boy or drug trafficking.'

'Nothing?' Hope sank, a heavy stone in Angie's heart.

'Not about the boy. But look at this.' He was talking to Zoe, who leant in to peer at the screen. 'First, I read this email – nothing much, just an announcement about a new property development and a newsletter.' They bent their heads together over the laptop and Angie tried to stir up the positive resolve she had felt earlier. 'It says here that Stephenson Construction have been awarded a contract for a housing development in Jaywick.'

'That can't be right.'

But whatever optimism Angie might have felt, it had deserted her now. It was like losing Todd all over again – but worse, because Danny wasn't being looked after properly. Todd had gone to decent parents; at least that's what her mum had said. Danny hadn't wanted to go back. She had handed him over, congratulating herself on being noble and self-sacrificing. She had betrayed him.

'I knew that you wouldn't like it and so I hacked into the council. And found this.'

Once she was admitted to hospital she would have no chance of finding Danny. By the time she was well enough to be of any use, anything could have happened to him. The worst thing would be the not knowing.

'How can he say that these houses in Clacton are some of the most deprived in Tendring? What about the old shacks in Jaywick?'

'That's what I thought, so I did some research. All of the properties that are going to be improved as part of this development deal belong to private landlords and surprise, surprise, there's a connection to Councillor Radford.'

Maybe she should postpone her admission to hospital. 'Is there anything else we can do?' Angie asked Spider.

'We could change the list of properties for renovation,' he said.

'Wow! Could we, Spider?' Zoe seemed excited. They weren't talking about Danny.

Spider and Zoe bent over the laptop while Spider's fingers did a tap dance on the keys. 'Done!'

Angie was tired. She had been running on empty for days, and even though she hadn't expected a miracle, she felt flattened by the hopelessness of it all. She tuned back in to Zoe and Spider's conversation. Something about ripping out old floorboards, reroofing, and modernising some of the chalets in Seaspray Avenue.

'Be a love and run me to the station, Zoe.' Angie heaved herself out of the chair.

Standing on the platform, waiting for her train to London, Angie was a zombie – going through the motions. She would never find Danny; it was impossible. He was lost to her, forever. The train from Clacton pulled in. Zoe was right, the journey would be quicker from Colchester, but silly and sentimental though it was, she was disappointed that she couldn't wave goodbye to the sea. It had been part of their holiday ritual and there was no certainty that she would return.

50

'I think it's this stop,' Danek said when the train stopped, just as he had at every station since they got on the train to Clacton.

'Here, play with your little men.' Nikoleta tipped the action figures from her bag.

'Mario!' Danek seemed interested in only one of the little men. 'Will Dexter and Alfie be at school?'

'Let's see when we get there.' Nikoleta prayed that Angie would still be in Jaywick. There was no money for a hotel. They would have to go back to Kamil, unless she went to the police or the Polish embassy.

Danek was wriggling in his seat. 'Put your toys away. I'll take you to the toilet.'

They swayed through two carriages before they reached the toilet. It wasn't easy as the train was busy. They negotiated their way around a bike propped in a doorway and then a pushchair in an aisle.

Danek pulled on her arm. 'That's my namma. There she is, Nikki!'

He had been like that the whole of the journey. Every stop was Jaywick, every lady over forty was Namma. He was going to be so disappointed if Angie wasn't there. So was she.

A little girl, smaller than Danek, dived across the aisle to reach her brother, nearly knocking them over. Nikoleta picked Danek up and they swayed through the carriage. He twisted in her arms looking for his namma.

They had just settled back down in seats near the toilet when Danek asked for his Mario. It wasn't in Nikoleta's bag, or in Danek's pockets.

'I have to find him,' he wailed. 'My namma bought him for me. I want my Mario.'

Nikoleta couldn't face fighting their way back through the carriages. 'I'll buy you another one,' she said. 'Look out of the window and tell me when you think that we're in Clacton.'

They were the first passengers off the train. Danek tugged Nikoleta's arm. 'This way. This way.'

Behind them, a group of teenagers laughed together, a mum passed by loaded up with buckets and spades, her two children ran ahead, impatient to find the sea. Nikoleta had butterflies in her belly. How would they find Angie when they got to Jaywick? If it was as big as Clacton they didn't have a hope. Maybe it was a foolish idea.

Outside the station there were a few cars waiting to collect friends. One young woman, about the same age as Nikoleta, jumped into a car and kissed the driver, her boyfriend or husband. But there were no taxis.

'We can walk. I'll show you the way. You will love Jaywick, Nikki.'

Nikoleta kept a tight hold of Danek's hand. If she wasn't careful he would take off on his own. 'No, we will wait here for a cab, Danek. Do you remember where you lived with your namma?'

'Next door to Old Man Higgins.' Danek said.

'Can you remember the name of the street?'

'Aunty Molly lived across the road a few houses along,' he added helpfully.

A man with a case waited behind them, which reassured Nikoleta that cabs did stop outside the station. Then, a woman with a big bag. She wiped her forehead with what looked like a pair of knickers.

Just as Nikoleta's eyes met the woman's Danek broke free. He flew at the woman, 'Namma! Namma! I saw you on the train.'

Angie dropped her enormous bag and lifted Danek into her arms. 'My boy, my precious boy.' The knickers came out again, as the woman howled, a mixture of joy and grief.

Nikoleta was flooded with relief and then shyness.

It was a few minutes before Angie acknowledged Nikoleta. She planted Danek on the pavement and then wiped away her tears. 'I didn't think I would see him again.'

Before Nikoleta had a chance to speak, Danek did the explaining for her.

'They don't really want me, Namma, and so I am going to live with you and make you better. Where's Licky?'

'You've already made me better, Danny boy. Licky's in Jaywick waiting for us. I found this little chap on the train.' Mario had left an imprint in Angie's left palm where she had been squeezing him. 'I was about to get on the train for London but then I remembered something I had to do – something urgent. It was like I was meant to come back. If I hadn't then I would never have found you. Oh, my darling boy! What if we had missed each other? Always listen to your instincts, that's what I say. Then, I found this little fella on the carriage floor and I thought maybe it was a sign. And here you are!' She hugged him

317

again, so tight Nikoleta wondered that she hadn't crushed him.

'Except I didn't follow my instincts when I gave you back Danny. I'm sorry I let you go, my darling. I should have known better.' Angie glared at Nikoleta. 'I thought I could trust you to give Danny a good home. To think I handed him back. You are *evil*.'

Danek clung to Angie. Both of them stared at her, as though she were the devil himself. It was unfair, unkind. Nikoleta had taken a risk running away with Danek. She had put his needs before her own. Tears gathered behind her eyes, pressing against her temples, clogging her nose. Nikoleta had been looking forward to seeing Angie again, imagining her motherly support and kindness. It was too much. She had kept everything in for so long: her loneliness, fear, guilt. A dam broke and it all came pouring out.

'Now, now, what's all this about?' Angie handed Nikoleta her knickers.

Nikoleta wiped her eyes on the big knickers; between sobs she laughed and then hiccupped. 'I brought him back to you, to keep him safe. I don't know what to do, Angie. Oh, I am so pleased we found you.'

'Look, here's a cab. We'll go back and have a nice cuppa tea and you can tell Namma everything.' Angie put an arm around Nikoleta, who was still holding the knickers and didn't know what to do with them. Danny told the cab driver that they wanted to go to the Seashell Café.

'That's right, Danny boy. We'll go and see Aunty Josie. She always knows what to do.'

The Seashell Café was as different to Boris's Café, as the warm and chirpy owner, Josie, was to surly Boris. It was as though she had been swept into an exuberant, raucous family, as everyone clamoured for her attention or Angie's. Between questions, people would exclaim at finding Danek, kissing him or lifting him up. Danek was completely at home, accepting the affection poured upon him as though he had grown up with these people.

'Aunty Molly,' Danek cried, as he rushed to embrace a woman with dark skin and freckles who had just come in. She was followed by two boys and then a girl with a dog. 'Dexter, Alfie.' Danek was like a child at a birthday party. 'Pickles.' He threw himself on the dog and smothered it in kisses.

Nikoleta was a bit overwhelmed. Everyone spoke so quickly, talking over each other and raising their voices to be heard. Josie broke away every now and again to serve a customer or give an order to a woman with an asymmetrical haircut, who was working behind the counter.

Gradually the level of noise simmered down. The woman, Molly, left with her dog and children. Two of the men, Bill and Si, left, after hugging Angie and giving Danek high-fives. Josie deposited a tray of tea things and sandwiches on the table and slid onto the bench alongside Nikoleta. Angie poured the tea and Danek reached for a sandwich.

'You can all stay with us tonight. Zoe will sleep at her boyfriend Spider's place, so you can have her bed, Angie; Nikoleta and Danny can use the front room. Only tonight, mind – tomorrow we have to get you back to London for your operation.'

'I want to sleep with Namma,' Danek said.

'Your Namma isn't well, Danny boy. You sleep downstairs with Nikoleta. I think that she deserves some of your hugs too, after bringing you home.'

Danek ducked under the table and reappeared between Nikoleta and Josie. He wriggled between them and put his arms around Nikoleta's neck. It was almost as good as being at home with her own family.

'That's tonight sorted but we need to make plans. Your Camel, or whatever his name is, will come looking for you and the rabbit,' Josie said.

Nikoleta thought she had misheard. 'Camel? Rabbit?' she said.

'Kamil,' Angie said. 'Licky, Danny's cuddly rabbit.'

Nikoleta screwed up her face. Why would Kamil come looking for Danek's toy rabbit?'

'You don't know, do you?' Angie said. Nikoleta's stomach plummeted.

'He used the rabbit to smuggle cocaine into the country.'

She felt sick. 'I carried drugs through customs?' Nikoleta's cup rattled as she tried to find the saucer.

'Hey, Liam, go and get a shot of brandy from the Queen's Head. Tell them Josie needs it for medicinal purposes.'

If she had been arrested, her parents would have died of shame. It was unthinkable. Kamil couldn't have loved her at all.

'Alright, love?' Angie reached across the table to touch Nikoleta's arm. She nodded, unable to speak.

'So, we need a plan because your old man isn't going to sit at home waiting for you to come back.' Josie pushed aside the tea things. 'When do you think he'll get here?'

Liam arrived with a shot of brandy. Nikoleta didn't think she liked brandy but slugged it back in one gulp, under Josie's instruction. It burned her throat and then flooded her chest with a pleasant glow. 'Thank you. Kamil will guess where I am. He will have one or two of his men keeping a watch on Angie, making sure the cocaine doesn't exchange hands.'

Josie flashed her eyes at Angie and Angie sighed, as though deeply troubled. She hadn't meant to worry them more than they were already. 'I really didn't know about the drugs,' she said. 'No wonder you said I was evil. It *was* evil to use Danek and me like that. Tell me what to do to help. I brought this trouble upon you and so I must put things right.' Nikoleta meant every word, even though it seemed an impossible task.

'I know you will, babe,' Josie said. 'Angie and Danny have a lot of friends in Jaywick. We won't let anyone bully us. So, you think Camel will be here today or tomorrow?'

'Kamil will guess and by tomorrow he will come looking for the cocaine and Danek. He knows we won't be able to go anywhere tonight and with his men everywhere he will know exactly where we are. I don't think he will be interested in finding me.' Now that she had served her purpose. How could she have been so naive?

'Right, we need to get word out. Liam, over here.' The same boy who went on an errand to get Nikoleta a brandy reported to Josie. 'You and Darren go to all of the publicans and tell them to be on the lookout for a Polish man. Any distinguishing features, Nikoleta?'

'He might be driving a black sports car.' Nikoleta described Kamil as best she could.

'Here.' The girl with the asymmetrical hair joined them from behind the counter. 'I've got a photo on my phone – sorry, Nikoleta, I found it on your Facebook page. I'll send it to you, Liam.'

'They'd better keep an eye out for Tomasz too,' Angie said.

'I saw a selfie of you and Danek with a business contact of Kamil's on his phone,' Nikoleta said. 'Maybe this is Tomasz?'

Angie sighed. Her face clouded over and Nikoleta worried that she was in pain. Angie was so kind and generous with her love, it was easy to forget the poor woman was terminally ill.

'I should keep a bottle of brandy under the counter,' Josie

said. 'Do you want to go upstairs and lie down, babe?' This was said to Angie.

'No. I have to go and get Licky.'

'Where is Licky?' Danek said.

'Old Man Higgins is keeping him safe. That's why I had to come back, Zoe. It didn't sink in what you said about Higgins's place being renovated, until I was about to get on the train to London. Licky's hidden under his floorboards.'

'You're not going lifting floorboards tonight, babe. You've done too much already. You get to bed, and Bill and Si will fetch Licky.

'Zoe, you go to Molly and ask her to get all the dog owners together. Ask Spider too. He can talk to Sid, the one with a Rottweiler, and Mental Micky with the pit bull. Make sure they can be contacted to respond, any time in the next forty-eight hours. We need the kids' help too. Ask Dexter to round up his friends. They can circle Jaywick on their bikes and get word back if they see Camel, Tomasz, or any other suspicious strangers. Bill can get a message to the Harley Hell Raisers in St Osyth.

'I think that has it covered. Ice-cream sundaes all round and then I want you to go and have a lie-down, Angie. You too, Nikoleta love, you look done in. Danny can help me down here. I've missed my little helper.'

51

Angie, Nikoleta, Danny, and Licky sat in Josie's front room as though waiting for a party to begin. Everything was ready, now all they had to do was wait.

'Does Licky know what to do?' Danny asked.

'He does. How about you, Danny boy?'

'I must hide in the eaves in Zoe's room until it is safe to come out. How will I know when to hide or when it is safe?'

Angie hated asking Danny to hide in the dark space under the eaves. It was spacious enough and hidden by a door. They had given him a torch and a few toys provided by Molly's boys. Liam and Dexter wanted to hide with him, thinking it a great game but they would have made too much noise. 'You may not have to hide at all. If you do, Nikoleta or I will help you hide and will come and get you when it's safe to come out. It's so cosy in there, I bet you'll want to stay. Your own little hide out. Dexter and Alfie are jealous of your camp.'

Danny didn't look convinced. He knew it wasn't a game. The boy had seen too much in his short life.

The three of them had little sleep the night before. Angie

was already awake when Danny slipped into her room at three in the morning and climbed into her bed. She hugged him tight, drinking in the scent of biscuits, cotton, and baby shampoo. Yesterday, she thought that he was lost to her forever. Miracles really did happen: first, the news that she might live a few more years after all, and now Danny boy snuggled up with his namma, as though he had never been away.

The hallway light slanted across the bed. 'Is he in with you?' It was Nikoleta. 'I thought I had lost him again.'

Angie patted the duvet. Nikoleta crept in and settled herself at the foot of the king-sized bed. 'He keeps on disappearing. I wish I could put a little bell on him.'

Danny struggled up to see what was going on. Angie stroked his hair. 'Go back to sleep.' She sang to him, 'Rings on his fingers and bells on his toes, he shall have music wherever he goes.'

'My dad used to sing me to sleep,' Nikoleta whispered. 'Sometimes I think I will never see him again.' She sounded as though tears may not be far off. They were all overwrought.

'Here, climb in. There's enough room for a little one.' Nikoleta edged in the other side of Danny, who had gone back to sleep. 'Why do you think that you won't see your dad again, sweetheart?'

Nikoleta sighed. 'I have no income and very little money. I cannot afford the plane fare. I let them down badly. My dad is angry with me because I went against his advice when I left Poland for London. Dad knew what Kamil was like but I wouldn't listen to him, thinking I knew better. I've made a mess of everything and I don't know what to do. I can't stay here and I can't go back. It's like I am lost and can't see a way out.'

Danny murmured in his sleep as though he was having a

bad dream. Nikoleta stroked his forehead. She would make a good mum, one day. 'You'll find your way. It's funny how things have a way of sorting themselves out. Sometimes, when you think that you are at the end of a road and have no place to go, a new way opens up to you. We can't see everything standing in one place.' Angie was thinking of the day she found Danny. How different her world looked then.

'Like being small and hiding in a field of rye,' Nikoleta said, her voice almost a whisper.

Angie left her to her thoughts, hoping that she would find sleep. There was little chance of Angie sleeping. Tomasz's betrayal was a knife twisting her heart. Every single word he said, everything he did, was a lie. Was it vanity that had deceived her? Her instincts were usually sound – even her trust in Nikoleta had turned out to be right. Whatever happened tomorrow, she would have to go back to London for the operation.

Josie popped up to check that they were all okay. 'It's quiet downstairs, just a few regulars having morning coffee. Everyone is on standby. Anything I can get you? Some pastries? Do you want a Pop-Tart, Danny?'

None of them could eat anything, even Danny. 'How long do we have to wait?' he asked.

They exchanged a look. Angie and Nikoleta had tried their best to distract Danny by playing games and singing songs but the air was heavy with anticipation and dread. Josie walked over to the window, her arms crossed. After a couple of minutes, she said, 'This might be a message. A couple of kids have dropped their bicycles outside the café. Wait here.'

Angie followed Josie downstairs. She recognised the two boys as the ones who had been doing wheelies in Sea Spray.

The taller of the two was spokesperson; his friend hung back. 'The do-gooder guy might be on his way here. Peggy-Sue stopped him to ask what they were doing about the chalets.'

'Good lad. Here, have a donut and one for your friend.'

'Tomasz,' Angie said. Her heart did a little skip, ignoring all of the evidence that Tomasz was a liar and a cheat. 'I have to talk to him.'

'No, Angie. I've sent Liam and Darren. Stay here with Licky until it's time.'

Angie ignored Josie; she had to see Tomasz. There would still be time for her to get back and play her part in their plan.

The street looked like it did on any normal day. Nobody would guess that behind curtains neighbours were watching, kids on scooters and bikes were circling, and dog walkers were waiting for a signal. Angie headed for the road that curved around the avenues, marking the boundary to the holiday village, like a protective arm.

As soon as she turned into the road, Angie saw them fighting. Liam was on Tomasz's back, his arms around Tomasz's neck, legs flailing like a daddy-long-legs. Darren was squaring up to Tomasz with a broken bottle. Angie ran a few paces before stopping to gasp. She hadn't tried to run anywhere in years, now was not the time to start.

Tomasz punched Darren in his solar plexus and he crumpled, dropping the bottle. Angie took a few big strides before stopping, the pain in her pelvis was now full on, a power tool boring into her centre. Angie clasped her side and sank onto an old sink that was lying in a front yard. With a bit of luck, she could crawl back to the Seashell, before Tomasz noticed her.

Tomasz threw Liam off his back as though he were a pesky child, then he picked up the broken bottle. Liam cowered behind Darren, who was still holding his stomach. Angie thought Tomasz was going to slice up the boys' faces but he found a takeaway box and lay the bottle inside, adding the broken shards from the pavement. As Tomasz turned he caught Angie squatting on the old sink. He was walking towards her. The humiliation. Why did she care? This man was a criminal, a drug smuggler. He had stolen Danny – used them both. Nikoleta recognised him from his visits to Kamil in Poland. He was dangerous. Angie scrambled up. Where were Liam and Darren? Fine help they turned out to be. She hobbled back the way she had come, desperately clinging to a shred of dignity.

'Angie. Stay right there,' he commanded and Angie froze.

ngie had been gone for forty-five minutes and Nikoleta was getting worried. She made Danek promise that he wouldn't leave the living room before nipping downstairs to find out what was going on.

Josie turned a sign on the door to closed. Customers were leaving. 'Sorry, our electrics aren't working. No need to pay, but I must ask you to leave. Please come back another time.'

As the last one left, she bolted the door. 'Good. I was going to come up to see you. Tomasz knocked out Liam and Darren. He's got Angie. Bill, Si, Zoe, Spider, and me are going after him. You stay here with Danny. I'll come back with Angie, don't you worry.'

Nikoleta saw Josie out and locked the door behind her. Danek was waiting at the bottom of the stairs. 'Where's Aunty Josie? Where's my namma?'

'Remember our plan, Danek? We are going to trick the bad men.'

'I don't want to play any more. I want Namma.' Danek started to cry.

It was a bit creepy being in the café on their own. Josie's presence downstairs and the bustle of activity had been a comfort, but now it was eerily quiet. 'They'll soon be back. Let's go and look at the toys that Molly brought over.' Nikoleta didn't think she had fooled Danek. Her voice was too thin and reedy.

'There! There!' Danek cried. He pointed at the window.

Nikoleta turned to see Kamil's face pressed against the glass between cupped hands. She couldn't tell if he had seen them. 'Quick, upstairs.'

Nikoleta scooped Danek up and then carried him on wobbly legs up to the top floor.

'We are both going to hide in your camp. Shall we hide Licky too?' Danek nodded. She could tell he was as terrified as her. They crawled in and sat, hunched up waiting.

Angie wanted to shout at Tomasz and pummel her fists into his chest. But all she could do was clutch her belly and groan.

'It's alright. I've got you.' Tomasz said.

One minute, Angie was perched on the upturned sink, the next, she was upside down as an arm pinned her legs in a fireman lift. He carried her as though she were a lightweight and Angie gave in, allowing her hands to brush against his jeans as she swayed in the rhythm of his stride. He *did* care about her.

Angie must have passed out because she opened her eyes to see a yellow stain on the ceiling. There was a familiar smell of fungus. She struggled against a scratchy army blanket that had been tucked tightly around her, like swaddling. Higgins was standing over her.

'Alright, girl. You stay here with Higgins. I'll see you right.'

Angie eased her legs off the bed. Her head was woozy. 'I have to get back to Danny.'

Higgins disappeared and returned with his air pistol. 'Nobody will get past me.' He waved it in a way that made Angie nervous.

'You did a good job, Higgins. Why don't I look after that for you?' She took the gun and stuffed it in her bra. 'Don't open the door to anyone, Higgins.'

'I told your man that I would look after you and keep you safe here,' Higgins said.

Your man – if only. Angie found some painkillers that she had left in one of Higgins's drawers. 'If you could just get me some water, I'll be alright. Really, I've got to go, Higgins.'

But when Angie tried to stand she fell back onto the bed. 'Maybe I should just rest a few minutes and wait for the pills to do their work.'

'I'll be guarding you, girl, don't you worry. Nobody will get past Higgins.'

Angie shut her eyes. It was no good tearing off if she just collapsed again. Tomasz had carried her on his back, like an old-fashioned hero. He might be in his fifties but Tomasz had fought off Liam and Darren, who were half his age, as though he were play-fighting children. Then, he had lifted her with the strength of Hercules. And she remembered the beauty of his muscular thighs as he marched her away to safety. He was a regular heart-throb. *Fool Angie Winkle. A man like that would never be interested in the likes of you.* He was a good'un though. That was one thing Angie Winkle always got right – she had sound instincts. Her instincts were telling her now that Danny and Nikoleta were in danger and it was no time to lie about daydreaming.

. . .

Nikoleta and Danek had been in the eaves for fifty minutes. It was hot and stuffy and the toy cars and building bricks were having little effect in distracting Danek. Downstairs, a door slammed and then a clatter. Nikoleta pressed a finger to her lips before easing the door open a fraction. The slight gap in the door freshened the air a little. Nikoleta strained her ears. There were voices downstairs. Bill and Si must have returned to the café.

'Stay here, Danek, whilst I take a look to see if Josie or Bill are back. I'll leave the door open a crack.' Danek stared out at her from their hiding place, a thumb in his mouth. 'I promise I will only be a couple of minutes. If it's safe, I'll come back and get you.'

Nikoleta crept down the stairs. There was nobody in Josie's flat, so the voices must be coming from the café. She peered out of the living room window. Just a couple with a Labrador strolling past. A man with an Alsatian dog across the street. There were definitely voices in the café – maybe Josie had opened up again. Kamil couldn't have got in, the café was locked. She needed to let the others know that he was prowling around, if they didn't know already.

Nikoleta took the stairs down to the café two at a time. She was anxious to release Danek from the stuffy confines of the attic. The back door to the café hung open; a metal pail and mop had been knocked over and lay across her path.

'Hello, Josie? Bill?' She went through to the café.

'Hello, *slonka*. You had me worried, disappearing like that. I've been up all night fretting about you.' He was the same Kamil that she had once admired and adored but now he turned her stomach.

'Where is it?' A man's voice, as he twisted Nikoleta's arm up behind her back.

'Christos, be gentle. Nikki will cooperate. This is all a

misunderstanding.'

Nikoleta saw both men's eyes light up and she turned to see Danek in the doorway clutching his toy rabbit.

'Danek, my golden-haired angel. Come to Dadda.'

Danek looked to Nikoleta, unsure what to do, a wet patch on his shorts. She nodded, encouraging him to humour Kamil, so that it would buy them some time. Danek edged towards Kamil, thumb in mouth.

Kamil's associate, Christos, snatched the rabbit from Danek and pulled out a knife. Danek flung himself at Nikoleta.

'It's alright, *swinka*.' She put an arm around him.

'Don't do that here in front of the boy. Go and get the car. Pick me up at the front – quick!'

Christos removed the bolt from the front door and ran.

'Why did you disappear like that, *slonka*? Didn't you like the flat? Was Stefan rude?' Kamil had the nerve to sound wounded. 'Why would you run away from me like that? I was willing to give you everything. Everything that you wanted. I don't understand.'

'You used me and Danek to smuggle drugs into this country. How could you, Kamil? What if I had been caught?'

He didn't even look ashamed, just smiled. 'Who would suspect you, *slonka*? You are so clean and pure, it would be like searching Mother Teresa. I knew that you would get away with it.'

'And Danek? He's not your son?' Nikoleta knew the answer but the betrayal felt worse than using her to smuggle drugs. The pain she had felt at losing Kamil's only son, the guilt. Rage throbbed in her throat.

'I rescued Danek from a godawful orphanage. I paid to get him out of there. His mum probably was a drunk.'

The metal pail clattered from the back room of the café

and Angie strode in, aiming a pistol at Kamil. 'Take the rabbit and get out of here. I am warning you, if you harm so much as a hair on Danny boy's head or Nikoleta's, I will put a bullet through you. Maybe I should anyway, after what you've done to my precious boy.' Angie pointed the gun at his head and then lowered it to his genitals.

Kamil put both hands over his groin, the rabbit dangling between his legs. 'Okay, okay. Put the fucking gun down, grandma.'

He shouldn't have said that. It made Angie mad and she pulled the trigger. A mug exploded in a burst of shards, then a plate on another table. Nikoleta shielded Danek, backing away from the bullet's path. Kamil went white and then realising he wasn't hurt charged out through the back of the café.

'Rud...' Angie glanced at Danek. 'Rubber duck. DUCK, I didn't think it was loaded!'

'Super Namma!' Danek cheered.

'Come here, Danny boy.' Angie hugged Danek tight.

Bill and Si came through the front door. 'Come on, you're missing the fun.'

As they left the café, dogs bounded past – a greyhound, black Labrador, golden setter, a bulldog. Bill and Si chased after them.

'Where's Kamil?' Nikoleta couldn't see him.

'He's just legged it over the sea wall,' Si shouted back at them.

Molly came up an avenue with Pickles tugging on the lead. 'Come on, Angie. The show's on the beach.' Unable to hold Pickles back, Molly broke into a trot.

There was quite a crowd on the beach. The main attraction was Kamil, who unable to outrun the pack of dogs, was now trying to stop them from tearing the toy rabbit from his grasp.

'Is Licky doing it right?' Danek asked Angie.

Three men arrived with two vicious-looking dogs. They growled and snarled, baring their teeth and slobbering.

Josie's daughter, Zoe, the girl with the asymmetrical hair, joined them. 'Hi, Spider. Thanks, boys. I think it's time to let these bad boys off their leads. I hope they're hungry.'

Spider, a man dressed in what looked like a Halloween outfit, led the way across the sand to Kamil, who was doing a surprisingly good job fighting off the dogs. They yapped and jumped, trying to get hold of Licky.

'Okay, mate. This is your last chance to let go of the rabbit before we set these two on you.'

'No. No,' Kamil said. The boys took that to mean no, he would not let go, and they unfastened the leads.

Nikoleta almost felt sorry for Kamil. His greed for money had warped his brain; those dogs would chew him up. He kept hold of the rabbit's head as the Rottweiler sunk its teeth into the body. Danek buried his head in Angie's skirt. 'Poor Licky.'

'It's okay, sweetheart. Licky knows what to do.'

Kamil pulled a lump of meat out of the rabbit's head and flung it towards the sea. The greyhound and a spaniel chased after it. The other dogs were competing for the sausages that had been stuffed into Licky's body. All except the two vicious dogs, a pit bull and a Rottweiler; they snarled at Kamil, waiting for an order to maim him.

'Want more of this?' Spider said.

Kamil shook his head.

'Then fuck off where you came from.'

Kamil didn't need to be told twice. He left the dismembered rabbit to the dogs and ran.

Liam and Darren joined them on the beach, each lugging a couple of hubcaps. 'We syphoned off his petrol. Took these for our trouble. They won't get far.'

Josie joined them. 'Angie, I've been worried sick about you.

They got Tomasz but we couldn't find you. Are you alright, babe? He didn't hurt you?'

Angie hugged Josie. What had she done to deserve these wonderful friends? 'I don't think he's a wrong'un, Josie. He tucked me up in Higgins's spare bed. I hope the boys didn't rough him up.'

'Peggy-Sue is keeping an eye on him.'

Angie screwed up her face. Peggy-Sue was a tough old boot but surely there was nothing she could do to restrain Tomasz, not when he floored Liam and Darren without breaking a sweat.

Nikoleta joined them holding Danny's hand. 'Danek wants us to rescue Licky.'

'Of course, sweetheart.' Angie cuddled Danny. She called to Molly, who was rounding up the dogs with the other dog owners. 'I'll make him good as new, Danny boy. He may have a few war wounds, mind.'

'We should make him an award for bravery,' Nikoleta said.

'Yes. A gold medal to wear around his neck.' Danny cheered up.

'Come on, let's go back to the Seashell and I'll find a soda float for Danny and a reward for Licky.'

It was a happy band that meandered their way back to the Seashell. Bill, Si, Liam, and Darren congratulating each other as they strode ahead. Danny skipped between them, impatient to get to the café for a soda float.

The red Clio came out of nowhere. The roar of its engine tore open the still day. It swerved up onto the pavement between the women and the men who were now a few metres ahead. The passenger door swung open. The car accelerated. 'What the fuck?' Darren or Si shouted. Then it took off, the passenger door hanging open like a partially severed limb.

'Danny? Where's Danny?' Angie screamed.

53

Josie wasted no time in whipping out her phone from her apron pocket. She speed-dialled the Three-Legged Donkey, a pub on the road out of Jaywick. 'Tell the Harleys it's time to raise hell. A red Clio, registration number...'

Bill and the boys joined them. 'The bikers are ready and waiting. They won't let them get away.' He put an arm awkwardly around Angie. 'Danny will be dandy; don't you worry, doll.'

Angie hoped Bill was right. 'What about Tomasz? Where is he?' If Tomasz was a good guy, they could do with his help. Her mind boggled as she tried to imagine what Peggy-Sue was doing to restrain him.

Bill and the boys headed for the Seashell to be on standby until needed. Josie was the commander in this operation. Zoe had left with Spider and his friends.

'Why don't you go up to the flat, Nikoleta love? You've had quite a scare. Bill will find you a shot of something for your nerves. Have a little lie-down. I'm going to take Angie to

Tomasz, see what he's got to say for himself. We'll soon have word about Danny. Reckon he'll be back in a few minutes, with a twenty-bike escort.'

Angie didn't doubt Josie. Outsiders didn't stand a chance when Jaywick came together to protect their own. Angie swelled with love and gratitude that she was one *of their own.*

Peggy-Sue lived in a ramshackle chalet not far from the Club House. An old bath in the front yard had been planted up with geraniums and marigolds, their blaze of colour a rebellion to the grey decaying woodwork beneath the splintered paint and hardboard where there had once been windows.

The side of the house was free of junk, unlike the neighbouring chalets, and Josie and Angie found their way in through the back door.

'And that's another thing,' Peggy-Sue was ranting at someone. 'What are you doing about the drainage? There's a right old stink when folks tip their doodas down the drain.'

Tomasz was gagged and bound to a kitchen chair. Peggy-Sue must have been talking him to death. Angie couldn't help smiling at the scene. The old woman sat opposite Tomasz, a ball of crimson wool in her lap as she crocheted a square. 'I know you all say that you're going to do something but we don't see nothing. I've lived here thirty years and things have gone from bad to worse.'

'Peggy-Sue, do you mind if we have a word with Tomasz?' Josie asked.

'Be my guest. He doesn't say much.' Peggy-Sue abandoned her crocheting. 'Want a cuppa?'

Josie removed a floral scarf from Tomasz mouth. 'What's going on, Tomasz?'

Tomasz gave Angie a concerned look. 'Shouldn't you be resting?'

'We're looking after Angie. You've got some explaining to do.'

Tomasz nodded at his bound arms. 'Could you cut me loose?'

Angie wanted to untie him, make him comfortable, but Josie would not compromise until she heard what Tomasz had to say.

'I'm an undercover cop. We've had Kamil Król under surveillance for some time.

Now untie me, I'm on police business.' He was like a different man. The gentle, sensitive Tomasz replaced by a commanding alpha male. Angie's tummy did a flip.

When Josie had cut through the rope and gaffer tape, Tomasz shook out his arms and rubbed the blood back into them. 'Where's Danek?' He said this to Angie. His eyes hard and determined. No twinkle or loving gaze. Had she imagined it all?

'They snatched him again,' she croaked.

Tomasz pulled out his phone and strode into the backyard.

Josie arched her eyebrows. 'He's a dark horse. A proper Bruce Willis on the quiet.'

Angie just hoped that he would rescue Danny.

Tomasz returned. 'It's alright, he's safe. A load of bikers surrounded the car and forced the driver to pull over. The police are there now. A car's coming to get me.'

'Don't go yet, I've made a pot of tea.' Peggy-Sue gathered balls of wool from the table and slipped them into a cloth knitting bag.

It was a relief that Danny was safe but Angie couldn't look at Tomasz to thank him. She was afraid that she would make a fool of herself again. He did something to her. The gentle, loving Tomasz and this strong, confident version who had carried her over his shoulder.

Tomasz paced up and down, obviously in a hurry to get away. Angie wished he would, so that she could try to forget him. Within a few minutes, two plainclothes officers arrived with a sniffer dog. As soon as they were in the door, the dog went for Peggy-Sue. It jumped up and tore the knitting bag from her grasp. Balls of orange, crimson, and lime rolled across the floor and another – a tightly packaged ball of white powder.

'Oh dear. Am I under arrest?'

'What for? Imprisoning a police officer, perverting the course of justice, possessing illegal drugs, or nagging me to death about the state of housing?' Tomasz said.

'Um, would you like a biscuit with your tea?' Peggy-Sue rattled a tin of custard creams.

Tomasz retrieved the cocaine, gathering an armful of the knitting balls whilst he was on his haunches.

The policemen exchanged a look of dismay. 'If you're ready, sir, we should go and get the boy.'

When Tomasz stood up, Angie made herself meet his eyes. They were still the colour of burnt toffee. 'What will you do with Danny? He'll be frightened. Can't we keep him here with us until you've sorted things out for him? What will happen to my boy?'

'I don't know, Angie. I'll see what I can do.' There was a warmth to his voice. Why did he have to do that when she was trying to rein herself in? Then he left with his colleagues and the dog.

As soon as they were alone, Josie said, 'We have to get you back to London right away, so that you can check in at the hospital tomorrow. Bill, Si, or Zoe will drive you.'

Angie didn't want to inconvenience anyone; London was a

fair old trek and she knew that Bill wouldn't drive willingly up to *the smoke.* Zoe had already given up her bed to Angie, she wasn't going to ask her to drive her back to London. Si would have sunk a few beers in the Queen's Head by now. 'No, it's alright, Josie, I'll be fine. What about Danny boy? Shouldn't I wait to see him before I go? Find out what's going to happen to him?'

Bill came in looking for Josie. 'Where's Tomasz?'

'Turns out he was the Old Bill,' Josie said. 'We need to get Ange back to London for her operation.'

'I'll take you, girl,' he said. Angie was amazed, Bill hated driving more than five miles out of Jaywick. It was a day for heroes. 'I'll fix your back door while I'm there, so that your house is secure.'

'*Now* can we get you on your bloody way?'

'What about Danny? Tomasz said he might bring him back here. Who's going to mind him?'

'We are. Me, Bill, Zoe, and Nikoleta, if she's sticking around. Now, get going. Everything here is covered.'

'I haven't said goodbye to anyone – Nikoleta, Danny, Molly…'

'You'll be seeing them all again soon. Now GO.'

Nikoleta stood at the window in Josie's flat. The community here had made her feel welcome, but she didn't belong. Bill had stuck his head around the living room door to tell her that Danny was safe and being looked after by the authorities.

'What about Kamil?' she asked.

'Police have been after him for some time. Looks like he'll be going down.'

Nikoleta screwed up her face. What did that mean, *going* down?

'Going to prison,' Bill said.

Nikoleta didn't know how she felt about that. Kamil deserved to be locked away for what he had done; using her and Danek to smuggle drugs was a terrible thing to do. She was sad, but it was for the Kamil she thought she had loved. Was it possible to love a person that never existed, the idea of a person? It was a loss that she felt in her heart, even if she couldn't make sense of the emotion.

Danek was safe and she was free of Kamil, but what now? She had less than fifty pounds in her purse, not enough to keep her, until she had the fare home. There was no choice but to ring her parents and ask them to bail her out. The cost of her airfare would make a dent in their savings. She had let them down badly. Nikoleta considered the other options: finding work and then saving until she had the airfare, but with the cost of living in England that wasn't realistic. Could she go home after all of this? Her dad was already disappointed in her. What would he say when he found out she had carried drugs through customs? Nikoleta shivered. No, she would have to keep up a pretence, tell Mum and Dad that everything was fine. The truth would hurt them and she had already caused enough stress. Maybe she would never save enough money to go home. Angelika would be a young woman next time she saw her. Now she was crying – tears of self-pity. That wouldn't do, she had to put up a good face for a bad game, that's all there was to it.

Under the window a brawl was simmering, growly voices, threats. What was it with men? They got as overexcited as children, all riled up with testosterone and ready for a fight, no matter whether there was a cause or not. The young lads, Liam and Darren, were squaring up to a man in a khaki hat. One of them, she didn't know which one was Liam and which one was Darren, shoved the man in the chest and his hat fell off. When the man bent down to pick it up, the other boy restrained his overzealous friend. At least one of them had some sense. Si joined them, hopefully to calm things down.

Nikoleta had half turned from the window when her heart did something funny. It stuttered but she didn't know why. What had she seen? Nikoleta turned back to the window and there it was: a sprinkling of freckles, like a bird's egg, no longer covered by wisps of fair hair. He settled his hat back on his head. It couldn't be, could it? Nikoleta opened the window and leaned out.

'He's Polish. He's not from around here. I reckon he's in with the other lot.'

He's Polish. He's Polish! Nikoleta flew down the stairs and out of the café. 'Dad?'

It was her wonderful, darling dad. Here in Jaywick. It made no sense, but she didn't care. It was a miracle.

When the men found out the Polish man they were threatening was Nikoleta's father, they wanted to buy him a drink. It was hard for her to steal him away from them and for a while she thought he might disappear into the Queen's Head with Si, Liam, and Darren. Now they were treating him like a brother and she could tell her dad was tempted to go with the flow and embrace these new friends.

She clung to his arm. It was solid, real. Her dad. She was safe. Like the little girl he lifted out of the rye field, Nikoleta saw the world differently. Dad looked down at her. 'Hello, kitten. So, this is where you were hiding.'

54

I t felt as though her stomach had been sawn in two and stapled back together. It hurt like hell, but so long as they had exterminated that nest of sharp-toothed rats, Angie didn't care. She moved her arm and felt the sting of a needle. Best go carefully in surveying the damage. There was someone sitting by her bed. Angie struggled up to get a closer look. He was wearing glasses and peering at a book, like a cosy grandpa. She watched him turn a page, not wanting to disturb him.

Tomasz looked up. 'You're awake. Ooh careful, you have a drip.' He rescued her flailing arm as she tried to reach for him and gently folded it across her chest. 'How are you feeling?'

'Like shit, but I'm still alive. Are you here to arrest me?' That was why he was there. The crimes that she had been chalking up were of no consequence when she thought that she had days left to live. But now she would have to do the time: child abduction – although she was rescuing Danny; carrying illegal drugs – but she didn't know that she was, not until Licky split open; breaking and entering – only because they thought Tomasz was being held captive by drug barons; stealing council property – well, borrowing, they would give it back; using firearms – how was she to know it was a real gun? Higgins said it was an air pistol. 'How long will I get?'

'You'll have to stand trial but that's not why I'm here.'

'Then why?' Angie croaked; her mouth just dry. Tomasz removed his glasses and tucked them in the top pocket of his shirt. He smelt good, aftershave and soap. 'Why are you here?'

They were interrupted by a nurse in navy blue. She adjusted the drip. 'Your man's been here since you went in for surgery. You can stop worrying now, she's doing fine. Can you manage some tea and toast, Angie?'

'Have you really been here all morning?'

Tomasz nodded and Angie stroked a finger across his face, tracing the laughter lines and grazing his stubble.

He caught her hand and kissed her fingers, one at a time. 'Sorry I didn't get a chance to shave.'

'Ouch!' The stitches pulled as Angie's stomach contracted with longing.

Tomasz dropped her hand. 'I'm sorry. Should I get a nurse?'

'No, don't stop. I'll try not to get so excited.'

Tomasz perched on the edge of the bed, moving slowly so as not to hurt Angie. 'You don't mind that I'm a cop?'

'No. You don't mind that I'm Angie Winkle?'

Tomasz smoothed the frizz of hair around her face and leant in. Then he kissed her. A long, warm kiss – soft, sensual lips and the scratch of stubble. 'I *love* that you are Angie Winkle. I've never met a woman like you. A woman who keeps a spare toothbrush in her hair and wears mad princess gowns. A woman with a huge heart and free spirit. And I love your crazy recklessness – nothing and nobody can intimidate you.'

Who was this woman Tomasz spoke about with such passion?

'A free spirit?' Reckless, maybe – although she would call it foolhardy – but a free spirit? The woman who had been tethered to the past for forty years?

'You don't care what anyone thinks. You are your own person.'

'Oh, I get it *weird.*'

'No.' Tomasz kissed her, a fleeting brush of his lips on hers and Angie melted. 'Unique. There's only one Angie Winkle.'

Wow, he really meant it. But they knew so little about each other. She had to ask.

'What you said about your baby, Lydia, and your wife?'

'All true. I shouldn't have divulged anything of my personal history but right from the start I kind of recognised something in you. A kindred spirit.' He dipped his head and Angie detected a blush.

'I wanted to tell you about Danny, that he wasn't my grandson. That day on the beach...'

'I guessed you were, because I already knew and I loved you for that.'

'Do you know why I took him?'

'Because you could tell that he was being mistreated?'

'That and another reason. I too lost a child.' Angie told him about Todd. The telling exhausted her, but if Tomasz was disgusted by her behaviour, then let him walk away now. She couldn't cope with any more heartbreak.

'Shh,' he whispered, as he stroked Angie's hair. And she slept, her pillow damp with tears.

· · ·

Nikoleta's dad got on with Bill, as though they had been best friends for years. Her dad was quick to get the measure of people. It was frustrating at times, like when he took a dislike to Kamil, but his judgement was sound. Bill and Josie were good people.

It was Monday, two days after Angie's surgery. The three of them, Dad, Danek and Nikoleta, were going back to Poland. The authorities agreed that it was best for Danek to stay with Nikoleta, supported by her parents for the time being. There was a lot of paperwork to complete but it seemed straight-forward.

'Are you sure about this?' her dad had said. They were sitting on the beach as the sun dropped and the evening cooled with a sea breeze. 'What about your career ambitions? Your mum and I can't take care of him on our own; we have to work and we're getting older. It's a big responsibility.'

'I promised Angie that I would give Danek the same sense of belonging that I experienced as a child. It was a precious gift that I did not truly appreciate until now. The farm, our family, friends – neighbours, the community – I took it for granted. When you have that, those roots, it makes you strong. You and Mum did that for me. I know that I can have a successful career, because I will work for it. I have everything that I need here.' She thumped her heart.

They watched the waves coming in. Gulls circled over-head, their cries like laughter. Tomorrow, they would leave for Poland, but next summer Nikoleta and Danek would return to spend the summer in Jaywick. She had a feeling that Jaywick would become as important to her soul as their farm in Poland.

'Ana was a good friend, telling you where to find me when you tried to return my call. I just wish you didn't have to use the money for your tractor. I'll pay you back, Dad, I promise. And Ana, she lent me the money for my fare to Jaywick.'

Dad chose a smooth pebble. He stood up and skimmed it out to sea where it skipped on a wave. 'I never trusted the man. There was talk at the club. I should have stopped you from leaving with him.'

'You tried, Dad, but I wouldn't listen.' Nikoleta tried to skim a stone, but it didn't reach the sea.

'Try this one.' Dad handed her a slither of white, shaped by the turning tides, and she stroked her finger across its smooth surface. 'I can get another tractor any day.'

'I'm sorry, Dad.'

'Don't be. We don't always understand why things happen, but they do, and they change us. I'm proud of the woman you have become, Nikoleta.'

'Namma! Namma!' Danny would have crashed onto Angie's abdomen where the stitches still stung like crazy had Tomasz not caught him.

He dangled Danny upside down, so that his face met Angie's. 'Give Namma a kiss.'

Danny giggled. 'I'm upsy down.'

Nikoleta joined them in the side ward, accompanied by a man in his fifties. He had a ruddy skin and broad chest, a farmer through and through. Nikoleta introduced her father to Angie and Tomasz, who greeted him in Polish.

Angie cuddled Danny the best that she could. It was hard saying goodbye, but she was happy that he was going to live with Nikoleta's family, at least for the foreseeable future.

'We're coming back to Jaywick next summer,' Danny said.

'It would be wonderful if that were true.'

'It is, Angie. Danek and I would like to spend next summer with you in Jaywick Sands, if that is okay.'

'It is more than okay. I'd better find us somewhere to live in Jaywick, or we'll all be sleeping on the beach.'

Danny threaded his fingers into Angie's hair. 'You can come and visit us in Poland too.' He extracted a pencil and held it up as though a prize.

'Hey, that's for my crossword.' Angie smiled apologetically at Nikoleta's father.

'You're very welcome in our home, whenever you would like to stay. There's plenty of room,' he said.

Two months ago, she had no one. Now she had what felt like, a partner, grandson, daughter-in-law, and her father. Angie couldn't help thinking about Todd, her son. His presence would have made her world complete.

EPILOGUE

Ten months later

Angie sat at the table in their new home, the Jeffers Place. She would have to stop calling it that, it was *their* home now – hers and Tomasz's. Her first proper boyfriend, and in less than ten months they had jointly bought the chalet at auction. But they both knew that life was short and you had to grab all the happiness that came your way. And she *was* happy. Although the letter that arrived that morning – forwarded from Dagenham – had unsettled her. She read it for what must have been the hundredth time and then folded it tightly, as though the words might escape and leak out. Of course she would tell Tomasz, but not until after Danny and Nikoleta's visit. In fact, she ought to get a move on. Tomasz would be arriving with them in a couple of hours and she had promised Josie that she would help prepare the buffet for their welcome home party at the Seashell.

In packing up the Dagenham house Angie had ripped the sealing tape from an old Sullivan's box, expecting to find more unwanted Christmas presents – embroidered hankies and novelty salt cellars – but this box was a treasure trove. Her mum had kept *everything*: drawings Angie had done as a kid, her first shoes, and photographs. Photographs Angie didn't know existed, including one of her and Lorraine on a four-wheeled cycle at Jaywick. It was in a grey plastic keyring, visible through a peek-hole. She must have bought it as a present for Mum. There were other photos of their holiday of the four of them – her, Lorraine, Grammy, and Gramps outside the chalet.

Then the most wonderful discovery of all, wrapped in tissue paper, was a tiny Babygro. Angie held it to her face and was back in the maternity ward, full of wonder and sorrow at the miracle in her arms. There was more. Beneath the tissue she found an ankle band – *Boy one of A.Winkle dob 16.05.1975* – and a photograph of Todd, swaddled in a blanket, in the hospital cot. Her poor mum, she had lost a grandson and then Dad.

Angie squeezed the letter, trying to still the pulse in her palm. And then with a heavy sigh, set off for the Seashell. Danny boy was coming home today and that was a miracle that she would never have believed possible all those months ago.

As she strolled to the Seashell, Angie admired the gardens which had been cleared of discarded furniture and now displayed flowers in old sinks, boots, or anything else Peggy-Sue had found. Peggy-Sue had embraced her community service as a community gardener and continued long after she had served her time. Si and Spider, for their community service, had helped to tidy away what the council called junk, by finding homes for the things in people's front yards. Angie had only just started her sentence – painting the exterior of houses. A job she loved. Jaywick had transformed. On the surface anyway, but Angie knew that the heart and soul of Jaywick had always been there. Hard times had only made it stronger.

'What the...?' Wally the window cleaner bit back the word that almost fell from his lips. Outside the Queen's Head, Peggy-Sue was flattening the soil around a newly planted geranium in the window cleaner's bucket. 'I only nipped in for a swift one. You'll have to take it out, Peggs, I need my bleedin' bucket.'

Angie chuckled to herself as she swung open the door to the Seashell. Josie had already baked a couple of trays of sausage rolls and was tipping them onto foil trays. 'I see Peggy-Sue's still planting up anything in sight. She'll have the day trippers' discarded trainers planted with petunias when they go in for a paddle.'

It was a wonderful party. Danny had grown so much in the past year, but he was a confident, happy boy and obviously loved life on the family farm. Angie knew from Nikoleta's frequent letters that her family had fallen in love with Danny and were making an application to adopt him.

It didn't take much for Angie's thoughts to gravitate back to the letter in her bag. The contents were like a burr beneath her skin. Focus on the present. She was surrounded by treasured friends and across the room Tomasz gave her a wink. He still made her tummy flip.

Josie put her arm around Angie and they quietly watched the party. Peggy-Sue and Albert were teaching Delila and Brewer how to rock and roll. The Harley Hell Raisers had turned up in force, proud of their part in helping to rescue Danny. After allowing all of his admirers to hug and kiss him Danny had disappeared upstairs with Liam and Dexter. When they got back home, Angie would have him to herself – two whole weeks. Nikoleta sat patiently, whilst Molly's girls tried to braid cornrows in her hair.

'It didn't take long for the buffet to disappear,' Angie said. Molly was helping Higgins to some profiteroles and Sal was smuggling sandwiches into her handbag. They would probably be sold later that day at her own café.

'Thank you, Josie, for everything.'

'There's a lot to celebrate. I couldn't imagine Jaywick without you, Ange.'

There was indeed. Inside Angie's bag was a letter. A letter that said Todd wanted to make contact with his biological mother. It was scary, but she knew that Tomasz and her friends would support her whatever the outcome.

'So, you've got the all clear?' Josie said.

Angie smiled. 'I have to go back for regular checks but it looks as though they caught it in time. And I got early retirement from the factory – so lots to celebrate.'

'Then let's crack open the Lambrusco!'

AUTHOR'S NOTE

Although this is fiction, Jaywick Sands is a real seaside village in Essex, England. It is two miles along the coast from the better-known resort of Clacton-on-Sea. Jaywick has been named the most deprived neighbourhood in England on the UK Government index, three times since 2010. But it has not always been so, in the 1960s and 1970s Jaywick Sands was still a popular holiday resort.

In 1928 Jaywick was developed as part of the Plotlands craze which was popular in South East England. Cheap agricultural land was sold off to Londoners so that they could build a holiday home. There were no building regulations and councils were not required to provide sanitation, electricity or drainage.

Land in Jaywick was bought up by employees of Fords, as it was relatively close to the Dagenham based factory. Chalets were typically constructed from Fords's packing cases and the streets were named after cars.

During the second world war, London's East-enders moved out of their bombed homes to live permanently in Jaywick. Whereas other plotland sites in England were developed into new towns, Jaywick residents refused to budge.

Over the year's residents petitioned the council for funding towards sanitation and electricity and this common purpose created a strong sense of community.

The closure of Butlins Holiday Camp in 1983 led to a further decline in the holiday village, although many Londoners today still treasure childhood memories of holidays spent on Jaywick's sandy beach.

In recent years Tendring District Council has resurfaced many of the roads and improved living conditions for residents. However, it remains a unique place full of interesting and quirky characters.

In telling this story, I have created a fictitious neighbourhood within Jaywick Sands. The Seashell Café and Queen's Head pub do not exist in Jaywick, neither do the streets I have named.

Although I drew inspiration from Jaywick Sands, any resemblance to actual persons living or dead is purely coincidental.

MORE INFORMATION

If you enjoyed reading The Borrowed Boy a review would be much appreciated as it will help other readers discover this story.

If you would like to find out more about me and my books you can find me at www.abrakdeborah.wordpress.com

If you sign up to my readers list, you will receive a quarterly newsletter with additional stories about the characters in my books, behind the scenes information, book release dates and more.

You can also follow me on:
Twitter @DeborahKlee
Instagram Deborah Klee Author

ACKNOWLEDGMENTS

This book would never have been published, if not for the help and support of so many people: family, friends, experts, professionals, and other creatives. In an attempt to remember everyone's contribution, I will start at the beginning of this book's journey and finish with the publication.

A special thank you to Judith and Sally of Caxton Books, a wonderful independent bookshop in Frinton. Not only did they provide a home for our Frinton novel writers group, but they encouraged me at every turn. When I said I wanted to interview some young Polish people, Judith popped out of the shop and returned with, Gracjam Chamula, from a neighbouring restaurant, who spent his lunch hour answering questions, whilst people around us browsed for books. I am extremely grateful to Gracjam and his friends, for sharing stories of life in Poland and their first impressions of London with me. Julia Tutko-Balena host of @HowYouSayfm, also came to my rescue when I needed help with a couple of Polish expressions.

Thank you to the Frinton Writers Group, your critiques,

and support over the years is invaluable, I am incredibly lucky to be part of this talented group of writers. Thank you to my beta-readers: Paula, Lesley, Catherine, Janet, Josephine, Mel, and Sue. Extra special thanks to Paula and Lesley, my gratitude to you both is immense.

My sincere thanks to Madeline Milburn, literary agent for believing in me and helping me to become a better writer and Anna Hogarty for her editorial genius– I learnt so much from you.

Thank you to Asya Blue for the fabulous cover design, and Beth Attwood for her meticulous copy edit.

I could not have achieved all that I have, without the love and support of my amazing husband, Sherman, and my wonderful daughter, Laura-Jade. Thank you both for everything.